# Enid Blyton

# THE
# NAUGHTIEST
# GIRL
## COLLECTION 3

**Other Enid Blyton School Stories Collections**

The St Clare's Collection 1:
*The Twins • The O'Sullivan Twins • Summer Term*

The St Clare's Collection 2:
*Second Form • Third Form • Kitty*

The St Clare's Collection 3:
*Claudine • Fifth Formers • Sixth Form*

The Malory Towers Collection 1:
*First Term • Second Form • Third Year*

The Malory Towers Collection 2:
*Upper Fourth • In the Fifth • Last Term*

The Malory Towers Collection 3:
*New Term • Summer Term • Winter Term*

The Malory Towers Collection 4:
*Fun and Games • Secrets • Goodbye*

The Naughtiest Girl Collection 1:
*In the School • Again • Is a Monitor*

The Naughtiest Girl Collection 2:
*Here's … • Keeps a Secret • Helps a Friend • Saves the Day*

The Naughtiest Girl Collection 3:
*Well Done • Wants to Win • Marches On*

*Enid Blyton*

# THE NAUGHTIEST GIRL

## GIRL
### COLLECTION 3

*Written by Anne Digby:*
Well Done, the Naughtiest Girl
The Naughtiest Girl Wants to Win
The Naughtiest Girl Marches on

Illustrated by Kate Hindley

Hodder
Children's
Books

## HODDER CHILDREN'S BOOKS

*Well Done, The Naughtiest Girl* first published in Great Britain in 1999
by Hodder & Stoughton
*The Naughtiest Girl Wants to Win* first published in Great Britain in 2000
by Hodder & Stoughton
*The Naughtiest Girl Marches On* first published in Great Britain in 2000
by Hodder & Stoughton
*The Naughtiest Girl Collection 3* first published in 2016
This reissue edition published in 2018

5 7 9 10 8 6

Enid Blyton® and Enid Blyton's signature are registered trade marks of
Hodder & Stoughton Limited
Text written by Anne Digby. Text © 1999, 2000 Hodder & Stoughton Limited
Illustrations by Kate Hindley. Illustrations © 2014 Hodder & Stoughton Limited

A Catalogue record for this book is available from the British Library.

ISBN 978 1 444 92984 3

Printed and bound in Great Britain by Clays Ltd, Elcograf S.p.A.

The paper and board used in this book are made from
wood from responsible sources.

Hodder Children's Books
An imprint of Hachette Children's Group
Part of Hodder & Stoughton
Carmelite House
50 Victoria Embankment
London EC4Y 0DZ

An Hachette UK Company
www.hachette.co.uk
www.hachettechildrens.co.uk

# CONTENTS

# Well Done,
# THE NAUGHTIEST GIRL

WHYTELEAFE

CHAO · ET · PERTINACIA

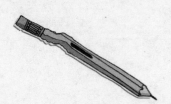

# CONTENTS

CHAPTER ONE

# A NASTY SURPRISE FOR ELIZABETH

'THE LEAVERS' Concert is going to be something very special this year, Elizabeth,' said the music master. 'Very special indeed.'

Mr Lewis was in charge of music at Whyteleafe School and also taught piano, violin and flute. Elizabeth took piano lessons with him but had been excused them for the past few weeks as she had been very busy with the Summer Play. The play had been performed now, so she was free to resume them, but she had almost forgotten her first lesson back. She had had to run all the way to the music room.

'Even more special than last year?' asked the Naughtiest Girl, puffing as she recovered her breath. 'I thought it was such a lovely concert last summer. I really enjoyed myself.'

She undid the straps of her regulation brown leather music case. Then she scrabbled inside to find her sheet music. Which piece had they been working on? She couldn't recall.

'Yes, Elizabeth, I seem to remember you were

excellent,' replied Mr Lewis. The elderly music master fingered his beard and looked thoughtful. 'You worked very hard for it.'

Elizabeth felt pleased. She was still basking in the warm afterglow of the first form play. Her interest quickened. How exciting it would be to take centre stage again so soon. The school concert – of course! It was held right at the end of the summer term and parents were invited. Her mother and father would be coming, just as they had last year. Her one tiny regret about the play was that Mummy and Daddy had not been there to see her!

How well she remembered last year's concert, at the end of her very first term at Whyteleafe School. She had started the term as the Naughtiest Girl in the School, hating the idea of boarding-school and doing everything bad she could think of – with the intention of getting herself sent home. But she had ended the term as a proud member of the school, playing two duets on the platform with a brilliant boy called Richard, as well as a little sea piece on her own. She remembered the applause ringing in her ears and the happy looks on her parents' faces . . .

'Why will this year's concert be so special, Mr Lewis?' she asked, as she found a piece of music and sat down at the piano.

# A NASTY SURPRISE FOR ELIZABETH

'Because we have some very special Leavers this time,' he reminded her. 'Last year, only two or three boys and girls were old enough to leave Whyteleafe but this year there's a whole batch. And what a fine batch they have been. Not just Roger, who's won his scholarship, but Charles and Colin and Lynette and – most important of all – our head boy and head girl. They have been the finest heads we have had at Whyteleafe for a long time.'

'William and Rita!' exclaimed Elizabeth. 'Of course. Oh dear. I just can't imagine Whyteleafe without them. I *do* wish I could make time stand still.'

'But then you would have to stay in the first form for ever, Elizabeth,' chided Mr Lewis. 'And you wouldn't like that, would you?'

She shook her head so hard that her brown curls flew back and forth across her face.

'No, I would NOT!' she exclaimed.

If there was one thing she was looking forward to with all her heart, it was the prospect of moving up in September. It would be brilliant to go up into the second form with Julian and Kathleen and Belinda and all the other boys and girls in the first form who were old enough and clever enough to go up. How grown-up they would feel then! Her friend Julian would have to stop playing so many jokes in class and start behaving like a responsible second former. And it would be lovely to be reunited with her best friend, Joan, who was already in the second form and a monitor. It was all going to be such fun! And if losing William and Rita was the price that had to be paid for time not standing still, then Elizabeth had to be willing to accept it!

'I expect excellent replacements will be found for William and Rita, when the time comes to elect a new head boy and girl,' Mr Lewis was pointing out. 'But, in the meantime, it's been decided to give them a very special send-off. To make the Leavers' Concert one of the best we've ever had. Something for them to remember for ever.'

'How wonderful!' exclaimed Elizabeth. She suddenly felt very excited. What a privilege it would be to play at William and Rita's Leavers' Concert. She thought back to the duets she had taken part in last year. To play with Richard again, some beautiful duets, to be part of William and Rita's last memories of Whyteleafe . . . How thrilling that would be.

'Richard won't be one of the Leavers, will he?' she asked suddenly.

'No! We've got Richard for another year or two yet,' replied Mr Lewis. 'I'm pleased to say. But even Richard won't be the star performer this year. You see, to make the concert extra special, Miss Belle and Miss Best have invited Courtney Wood to come and play, the well-known concert pianist. And he has accepted!' The music master could barely conceal his pleasure. 'Isn't that exciting news, Elizabeth?'

'Oh,' said Elizabeth, dully. 'Won't any of the boys and girls be playing at the concert then?'

'Of course, of course,' replied Mr Lewis, a trifle impatiently. He was glancing at his watch now and turning over the sheet of music that Elizabeth had propped up in front of her. It was time for the lesson to begin. 'But we won't be able to have half as many children as usual. Just one musician from each form. That's all we'll be able to fit into the programme. There won't be any duets this year. The very best child from each form will play, that's all. Richard will represent his, of course . . .'

Elizabeth's hopes immediately rose again. So she still had a chance of being picked, then. And as a solo performer!

She thought about it. In the first form, Harry was keen but not very good – his hands were like a bunch of bananas, Richard often said. Arabella had been learning the piano for a long time but it was well known that she was always in trouble with Mr Lewis for never doing her piano practice. Belinda and Edward were both learning the violin but they had only started last term . . .

'Tut! Tut!' exclaimed Mr Lewis, breaking into her calculations. He was removing the sheet of music from the piano. 'This won't do, Elizabeth. You've put the music on its stand upside-down! And . . . what's this?' He turned the sheet the right way up. 'We finished *Serenade* before half-term. We're on that difficult arrangement of *Greensleeves* now, don't you remember?'

Flustered, Elizabeth groped in her brown music case and found the correct sheet. It was right at the bottom.

'What's it doing buried down there?' scolded Mr Lewis, as he opened it up at the first page and placed it on the stand for her. 'Now, let's see if you've been doing your piano practice.'

It was soon very obvious that she had not.

'Really, Elizabeth,' winced the music master, as she got all tangled up on the opening bars, 'what's happened to you? You were playing that opening beautifully not long ago. And look at the little finger of your right hand, all scrunched up! You'll never reach the high notes like that. Stretch it out wide, S-T-R-E-T-C-H.'

The lesson went badly.

'Elizabeth, you are a very naughty girl,' Mr Lewis said to her afterwards. 'I don't believe you've done any piano practice at all, lately. I don't believe you once went near the piano while you were mixed up in that play of yours. Am I right?'

'Yes, you *are* right,' confessed Elizabeth, looking upset. 'I'm sorry.'

The little girl was too proud to make excuses. She was too proud to explain that going to all the rehearsals for the play, and learning such a big part until she was word perfect in every line, had been a difficult task. There had been other things to worry about, too, which had taken up all her spare time and energy. Though they were all now sorted out, they had loomed large at the time.

In the meantime, not only Elizabeth's piano practice but a lot of her school work, too, had been pushed to one side. She would not have dreamed of explaining this to anyone, for fear of looking feeble.

In any case, Mr Lewis was smiling at her now. He had spoken more in sorrow than in anger.

'Cheer up,' he said. 'I can see you really are sorry and will turn over a new leaf. If you do your practice every day, you will soon make up your lost ground. Practice makes perfect. That's what I'm always saying to Arabella.' He chuckled. 'Yes, that's what I've been telling her for a long, long time.'

Elizabeth mildly wondered what there was to chuckle about, as far as Arabella was concerned. But she was so

11

relieved that Mr Lewis was not being cross any more, she cared not.

'I *will* do my practice every day, I promise!' she said happily, as she packed her music case and prepared to leave. 'When I come for my lesson next week, you will see such a difference!'

'I shall look forward to that, Elizabeth.'

She longed to ask more questions about the Leavers' Concert. In particular, she longed to hear Mr Lewis say that she stood a good chance of being picked to represent the first form. But her good sense told her that this was hardly the right moment. She would ask him next week, when she had had a chance to catch up on her piano practice. He would see how well she was progressing with the difficult new piece. Then, surely, she would be chosen to play it at the concert? It would be such an honour to play it for William and Rita and the other Leavers, in front of the whole school, in front of all the parents! In front of her *own* parents. It was a thrilling thought.

'You're looking cheerful, Elizabeth,' said Julian Holland, as she came into the common room. 'Where've you been?'

The boy with the dark, untidy hair and humorous green eyes pushed his chessboard to one side. He had been working out a few interesting chess moves. But nothing was ever more interesting than talking to the bold, bad Elizabeth. They were great friends.

'Piano lesson,' she replied. 'Here, Julian, have a chocolate biscuit. As a matter of fact, I *am* feeling cheerful.'

'Must have been a good lesson,' grinned Julian.

'Not especially,' replied Elizabeth, airily. She was not going to admit, even to Julian, that she had been unable to cope with her piano practice recently and how disappointed Mr Lewis had been in her. 'It's just that Mr Lewis had some interesting news.'

She told him all about Courtney Wood coming to play at the end of term. And then, even though the common room was empty, she dropped her voice low and confided in Julian her secret hopes.

'I do believe you're getting quite stage-struck, Elizabeth Allen!' teased Julian. 'Not content with being the star of the Summer Play, you've now decided you'd like to appear on the same platform as Courtney Wood!'

There had been a time when the Naughtiest Girl would have flared up at that. But now she just took the joke against herself in good part.

'It's not that, and you know it,' she smiled. 'I'll tell you what it is, it's because of William and Rita. Oh, Julian, I can hardly bear to think that this is their last

13

term at Whyteleafe. I want to practise and practise until I can play my piece really *beautifully*. It's just the right music somehow and says everything I'm feeling and how sad I am at saying goodbye. They've given me so much and helped me to be a better person and . . .'

Julian gazed at his friend in admiration. He could see how sincere she was being. She was struggling to find the right words. He finished the sentence for her.

'. . . so this would be your way of saying thank you? Of giving them something back?'

'Yes, that's it exactly,' said Elizabeth, gratefully.

'Well, I expect you'll be chosen,' said Julian, airily. 'Nobody else in the first form is much good except you, Elizabeth. Least, that's what I've always heard. Blow it, I think I'd like to give William and Rita something myself. I think I'll carve them a little wooden animal each. A Mother Bear and a Father Bear. How about that, Elizabeth?'

'Oh, Julian, that's a brilliant idea.'

'I must start looking out for just the right bits of wood. I say, we *are* going to miss them, aren't we, Elizabeth?'

The two friends fell silent for a few moments.

Elizabeth swallowed hard.

'But it's got to be, hasn't it?' she said at last. 'Mr Lewis reminded me of what would happen if you made time stand still. If William and Rita were just to stay as head boy and head girl for ever and ever and never move on—'

'What?' asked Julian.

'We'd all have to stay in the first form for ever and ever, too,' said Elizabeth, wryly. 'We wouldn't be able to go up to the second form in September!'

'What a nightmare!' said Julian. He laughed. 'Oh, we couldn't stand for that. I don't know about you, Elizabeth, but I can't wait!'

'Me neither!' agreed the Naughtiest Girl.

It was such a happy thought that they both felt cheerful again.

But Elizabeth's happiness was to be very short-lived.

The next morning Miss Ranger, their form teacher, told the class the result of this month's tests. She read out the new positions in class.

Julian had come top, as usual. His cousin, Patrick, had worked hard and come second. Elizabeth, who usually came very high, waited in vain to hear her name read out.

She was in for a nasty surprise.

She had come third from bottom.

Even Arabella, the oldest in the class but usually near the bottom, was two whole places above her. Since

15

half-term she had been working frantically hard and had made her very best effort.

'You will have to do better than this in the end-of-term exams, Elizabeth,' said Miss Ranger. 'Or we may have to keep you in the first form a little longer.'

Elizabeth could hardly take it in. She had been beaten in class by Arabella!

However the sight of Arabella's gloating face made her determined not to show her true feelings.

She spoke airily, almost defiantly. She repeated what Mr Lewis had said to her the previous day, the first words to come into her head.

'I shall soon make up any lost ground, I dare say, Miss Ranger.'

But inwardly Elizabeth was shaking. She had been given a dreadful fright.

CHAPTER TWO

# TWO LITTLE PUZZLES

AFTER THAT, Elizabeth decided that she must start revising very hard indeed for the exams. But she didn't want any of her classmates to know what a fright she had been given, not even Julian. She lost no time in finding herself a secret den, somewhere that she could study in peace.

She found the perfect place high up in an oak tree. She was there now.

Above her head came little rustling sounds as two doves moved along a branch. A pair of collared turtle doves, with black half collars round the back of their pale dusty brown necks – they were permanent residents of the old oak, along with all manner of other creatures. The doves were getting quite used to Elizabeth's presence. This was the third day running that she'd been here.

As she began to recite her French verbs, they began to croon, as though to keep her company.

'Je suis . . .

'Tu es . . .'

*Coo-cooo, coo*

'Il est . . .

'Nous sommes . . .'

*Coo-coooo!*

Elizabeth's little 'tree house' had been a wonderful find. She was delighted with it.

'I'm quite near the school buildings,' she thought with a smile, 'yet nobody knows I'm here. Nobody can see me or hear me up here. It's my own secret place. Nobody can make fun of me now!'

The way that Arabella had gloated over her plunge down the form order had been almost too much to bear. The two girls disliked each other intensely. Elizabeth hated Arabella's pretty little face and perfect manners, her high opinion of herself and the airs and graces she put on. Arabella despised Elizabeth for her untidiness, her noisy, boisterous ways and the fact that she seemed to get away with things just because people seemed to like her! It puzzled her why they should.

Nor had Elizabeth taken kindly to the teasing from her classmates, even from Julian. The truth was that, unlike Elizabeth, none of them took Miss Ranger's words seriously, about her being kept down in the first form. And Elizabeth had taken such care to hide her true feelings, they had no idea how scared she was feeling.

'What would you like for your next birthday, Naughtiest Girl?' Julian had joked. 'Remind me to buy you a rattle.'

Elizabeth had pretended to laugh. But it was soon after *that* that she noticed the oak tree and decided to explore it.

From the school grounds, only the upper part of the tree was visible, for it stood on the other side of the school wall, somewhere in the outside world. But its heavy boughs brushed the top of the wall in places and some of the branches overhung the grounds.

Elizabeth had peered up into the dense green foliage. How mysterious and cool and inviting it looked up in that oak tree. Its boughs seemed to reach down like great arms, inviting her to come up into the tree's embrace. With a feeling of excitement she realized that, if she climbed to the top of the school wall, it would be extremely easy to crawl along the nearest bough and into the heart of the tree.

As soon as she did so, she knew that she had found the perfect hideaway. Where the boughs met the trunk in the midst of the tree, it was possible to sit, or even lie down, in comfort. Enclosed in a lattice-work of foliage, it was like being in a secret little house – her own tree house. Wonderful!

On her first proper visit, she took her maths book and learnt her eleven times table off by heart.

The next day she took her spelling book and carefully copied out several difficult words until she was sure that she knew how to spell them correctly.

Today, Julian had asked her to help him look for pieces of wood, as he wanted to start on his bear carvings. But Elizabeth had made an excuse and headed straight for her hideout again, this time bringing her French verb book with her.

'Vous êtes . . .'

She cheated and peeked into the book.

'Ils sont!'

She put the book back in her pocket. Then, straddling a bough, her back pressed comfortably into the curve of the tree trunk, she closed her eyes and recited the verb 'to be' all the way through, slowly and carefully. Then again, but faster. By the third time, she was able to rattle through it without stopping.

'There! I know it now!' she thought, with deep satisfaction.

It was so grand to be able to recite things out loud, as many times as she wanted to, with nobody to overhear. It was so peaceful here, with only the natural world for company.

'Hello, robin,' she said, as she opened her eyes.

The bird had hopped along the bough to within a metre. It was full grown but had not yet got its red breast, so Elizabeth knew it must be very young. 'Aren't you the lucky one, then? You don't have to learn your verbs yet, do you?'

The young robin cocked its head on one side and gave her an enquiring look, followed by a friendly chirp.

'I love it here,' thought Elizabeth. 'There's a whole busy life going on in this oak tree and, it's funny, I'm beginning to feel part of it. I'm even beginning to like the big brown moths that live here. And I think the creatures are starting to get used to me.'

She stared up into some higher branches, where a family of squirrels had their drey. On her first visit they had chattered shrilly in great alarm and refused to come out. On the second day they had made their way up and down the tree very secretively, by a back route, hoping not to be seen. But today they had twice scampered down the tree quite close to her, taking no notice of her at all.

She settled further back and rested for a while, gazing up at the chinks of blue sky through the tree's top canopy. From the road below, to her left, came the drone of an occasional car. The mighty oak stood on a grass verge beside a narrow road that led to the village.

And across the school grounds to her right, from the

school buildings, came the sound of a piano being played in one of the practice rooms.

'Oh, that's a nice piece!' thought Elizabeth. 'All ripply and sweet like a journey through the English countryside. That must be Richard playing.'

Piano practice! She had forgotten to do it today!

Elizabeth roused herself and began to edge backwards along the bough, towards the top of the school wall.

As she did so, looking down, she spotted a knobbly little chunk of oak that the tree had shed. It was lying in the grass, close to its roots, not far from the road.

'That's just the sort of wood Julian likes when he's carving things,' she thought. 'It's got an interesting shape. I wonder if I dare get it for him?'

She could see that it was an easy climb down to the ground. The trunk had several low, stubby branches sticking out. They would make perfect footholds and handholds. But, of course, it was strictly against school rules for children to venture outside the grounds on their own.

'Only, I'm not really going anywhere, am I?' Elizabeth told herself. 'Just straight down the tree to pick up the wood for Julian, then straight back up again.'

It took Elizabeth less than a minute to climb down the tree and land on the grass verge on the other side of the school wall. She scooped up the piece of wood, triumphantly. She examined it carefully. Yes, it was a really good piece. Julian should be pleased.

As she turned back towards the tree, she stared in surprise at its trunk.

'How stupid!' she thought.

On its handsome pale brown and mossy green bark, someone had painted an ugly white cross.

At that moment, from beyond the bend in the road, she heard the distant sound of a car approaching. Supposing it were one of her teachers? Help!

Elizabeth shinned back up the oak tree at speed, dived into its leafy branches, bumped along the bough atop the school wall, then down into the grounds of Whyteleafe. Phew! That was risky.

She must not do *that* again.

But as she wandered back towards the school buildings, past the end of the cricket pitch, her thoughts returned to the strange marking on the oak tree's trunk. She wondered why it made her feel uncomfortable. Then she remembered that they had once been told in a history lesson about the time of the Great Plague. How homes were similarly marked with a cross if the disease had struck.

'Could the oak tree have some sort of disease?' she wondered, in dismay. 'Oh, surely not. It looks hale and hearty to *me*.'

She wondered if she could ask one of the teachers about it. In a roundabout way, perhaps. It would be difficult, though, without giving away where she had seen it . . . Oh, surely, somebody had just been fooling about . . . ?

'Elizabeth! Whoops! Look where you're going!'

She had almost crashed into someone! He was a tall boy, carrying a cricket bat.

'Richard! Oh, I'm sorry. I was in such a dream.' She looked at the bat under his arm. 'Going off to play cricket?'

'No! Just coming *back*!' said the senior boy, smiling at her. 'I've had an hour's practice in the nets and that's long enough for me. I must get back to my piano.'

'Oh, I thought I heard you playing a few minutes ago,' said Elizabeth, in surprise. 'A lovely, ripply piece. Perhaps it was Mr Lewis, then?'

'Not him. He's gone to town to buy the piece I shall be playing at the Leavers' Concert. And it doesn't ripple, Elizabeth, I can assure you.'

Elizabeth continued on her way, frowning slightly. Who had been playing that piece so well, then, if it had not been Richard, or Mr Lewis himself?

With something new to puzzle about, she forgot all about the white cross on the oak tree.

## CHAPTER THREE

# ELIZABETH HEARS THE MUSIC AGAIN

'WHAT AN excellent piece of wood, Elizabeth!' exclaimed Julian, with pleasure. 'Why, it's the very thing.' He rolled it between his palms. 'A solid little lump of oak. I shall cut it in half and make two. Those knobbly bits at each end already look rather like bears' heads, don't they?'

'That's just what I thought, Julian,' said Elizabeth eagerly. 'And one end's fatter than the other – that can be Father Bear.'

'And the other end can be Mother Bear. Excellent! I'm going to enjoy my wood carving! Oak's good to work with, you know.'

After a good wash and tidy-up, Elizabeth had rushed through some piano practice and then come looking for Julian. She had found him in the common room. He was not bothering to revise for exams. He was reading a book about famous medical discoveries.

She had presented him with the piece of wood.

'Wherever did you find it?' he asked now.

'Oh, just lying on the ground,' replied Elizabeth, truthfully.

'You've been gone for ages!' said Julian. 'I wondered where you were.'

'Well, for one thing, I've been doing my piano practice,' smiled Elizabeth.

'Ah, yes.' Julian gave a quick nod.

Some of the other boys and girls were coming into the first form common room.

Julian quickly stuffed the piece of wood into his trouser pocket. He wanted to be quite sure that his bear carvings were successful before letting anyone know about them!

Belinda came and threw herself into a chair.

'If I have to revise another single French verb, I shall die!' she exclaimed.

'Only two weeks to go till the exams now,' said Julian cheerfully.

Jenny came and joined them. She was holding a tin.

'Have some of my birthday cake!' she said.

She cut them each a fat slice. It was a gooey chocolate cream sponge with thick chocolate icing on the top.

'It's delicious, Jenny!' exclaimed Elizabeth, as the cake melted in her mouth.

'I was trying to find you after tea, Elizabeth. Where

do you keep disappearing off to?'

'I can't bear to be indoors at this time of year,' replied Elizabeth, truthfully. 'I've been getting lots of fresh air.'

'I expect she's been helping John over in the vegetable garden,' put in Kathleen. 'That's where she usually disappears to!'

Elizabeth had no need to reply for Belinda at once jumped in with a teasing remark.

'I'm sure I'd be revising for exams if I'd come third from bottom! But there again, I'm not Elizabeth. I'm not the Naughtiest Girl!'

'Blow the silly old exams,' said Elizabeth, keeping up her brave front.

But it was very satisfying in the maths lesson next day. Miss Ranger gave them some mental arithmetic problems. Twice Elizabeth was the first to call out the correct answer.

'Eleven boys have to share out eighty eight sweets equally. What does each of them get—?'

'Eight, Miss Ranger!' cried Elizabeth.

'Tummy ache!' cried Julian.

Everybody laughed.

'That will do, Julian. Well done, Elizabeth. And if twelve rabbits have to share out one hundred and thirty two lettuce leaves equally, what do they get—?'

'Into a fight!' exclaimed Patrick Holland, determined

28

not to be outdone by his smart cousin, Julian.

The laughter was more subdued this time, as Miss Ranger was beginning to look cross.

'Please, Miss Ranger, eleven lettuce leaves,' said Elizabeth, putting her hand up.

'Yes. Good.'

Belinda sighed to herself. Elizabeth was so lucky. Without appearing to do any work, she was getting back into top form again. It was all right for some!

However it was Arabella, not Elizabeth, who got the next question right.

'Twelve men walk twelve miles each, how many miles do they walk altogether?'

'One hundred and forty four!' exclaimed Arabella eagerly.

'Very *good* Arabella,' said Miss Ranger. 'My, that was quick.'

Then Patrick, as usual, had to overdo things and show off, spoiling what had been a fun session.

'Perhaps they didn't walk all together but in single file, Miss Ranger. In that case the answer should be none!'

After that they were all made to do sums in their books and had to remain silent for the rest of the lesson.

However, as she pored over her sums, Elizabeth felt well pleased. The hard swotting sessions in her secret hideout were already bearing fruit. Of course, it was annoying to find out that Arabella was ahead of her. Arabella had revised her *twelve* times table! Elizabeth resolved to make that her very next task.

But not today. It was the day of the weekly Meeting and no pupil at Whyteleafe was allowed to miss them. Not that Elizabeth minded. On the whole she very much enjoyed Meetings.

After tea, the whole school trooped into the big hall, which doubled as a gymnasium. There were the twelve school monitors, up on the platform, with the head boy and girl seated at their own special table.

Elizabeth thought how grown up and dignified William and Rita looked, as she took her own place on the first form benches. They had a large book in front of them, known simply as the Book, in which anything important that happened at Meetings was always written down. Elizabeth had read the Book once. It contained many fascinating case histories of pupils who had misbehaved and showed the reasons for it and how their bad behaviour had been cured. She featured in the Book herself, from the days when she had been the Naughtiest Girl in the School!

For the remarkable thing about Whyteleafe School was that the children governed themselves in many respects. The Meeting was like a school parliament, where problems were discussed and solutions found.

# ELIZABETH HEARS THE MUSIC AGAIN

But it was also a kind of court, with William and Rita the Judges and the monitors their Jury. Pupils who behaved badly were forced to face up to their wrongdoing in front of the whole school and the Meeting would work out how best the problem could be dealt with and cured. And cured it invariably was, for no child was ever considered worthless, or beyond reform. No one was ever abandoned by Whyteleafe School.

The joint heads, Miss Belle and Miss Best, whom the children nicknamed the Beauty and the Beast, attended the Meetings. So did Mr Johns, the senior master. They were there simply as observers and never took part unless, in very difficult cases, their advice was sought.

Today's Meeting was not an eventful one.

All children who had received money during the week had to give it in. A monitor always brought round the school box. This week it was Joan's turn. As Elizabeth placed some money that her grandmother had sent her into the box, she exchanged smiles with her best friend. She was so proud that Joan, who had not been in the second form very long, was already a monitor.

Elizabeth had herself had a stint as a first form monitor. She had enjoyed being a leader. She looked forward to the day when she might be elected as a monitor again, as William and Rita had once hinted might happen. For the moment, though, she was thinking only of her more modest ambition – to be allowed to go up into the second form!

She would die with shame if she were made to stay down. She would never be able to look Joan in the eye again!

Once the money had been collected up, each pupil in the school was issued with two pounds for the week's spending money. 'Share and share alike' was the school motto.

Then, one by one, special requests for extra money were considered and judged on their merits.

'No, Chloe, we cannot give you extra money for your mother's birthday present. You should have saved up for it, out of your weekly allowance, as all the other children do,' said Rita.

The junior class pupil looked disappointed and sat down cross-legged on the floor again, with the rest of her class.

John, the head of the school garden, was granted some extra money for a trowel, as one had broken. Harriet was given extra stamp money because her large family was in Australia for a year. It was expensive sending all her little brothers and sisters birthday cards and airmail letters.

Colin asked for money for a new tennis racket, as

had been granted to Eileen on a previous occasion.

'That's a difficult one,' said William. 'Rita and I will have to confer with the monitors.'

It took them a while to come to a decision.

William banged a gavel on the table for silence.

'We hope you don't think it unfair, Colin, because we know you have played tennis for the school a few times. But Eileen is a regular member of the team and truly wore her racket out because she practises so hard every day. She has some years to go here and I'm sure will be playing for us much more. You will be leaving Whyteleafe in less than three weeks, as will we. When we go to our upper schools, there will be a different system. For the first time, you'll be allowed to keep any money your parents send you, Colin. If you need a new racket badly by then, we're sure they will help you out!'

'Fair enough,' agreed Colin.

There were no complaints or grumbles this week and the two head pupils began to wind up the Meeting.

Elizabeth's mind was already moving on to other things. Talk of Colin and William and Rita leaving so soon had given her a fresh jolt! It reminded her that there was very little time left before the Leavers' Concert. She longed with all her heart to be a part of that concert, to pay her special tribute to William and Rita from the concert platform. The sweet sad piece she was learning expressed her emotions far better than words.

But swotting for exams every day had not left her all the time she needed for her piano! And Mr Lewis would be expecting to see a big improvement at the next lesson. She had promised him! And, besides, her hopes depended on it.

'It's too late to go to my secret den and do my times tables *today*!' Elizabeth decided. 'I'll do extra piano practice instead. I'll do a whole hour!'

She collected her music case after the Meeting and set off for her usual practice room. But Sophie had got there ahead of her. She was practising the flute. Elizabeth reflected that Sophie would surely be chosen to represent the junior class at the Leavers' Concert. She was a remarkable little player.

'I think I'll be here till bedtime now, Elizabeth,' the younger girl said wryly. 'This is a Grade V piece and I'm only on Grade IV but Mr Lewis says he thinks I can master it.'

'Don't worry, Sophie! I'll go upstairs.'

There was a piano on the top floor, right at the end of a long corridor. It was rather out of the way. Nobody bothered to use that one much.

But when Elizabeth reached the top landing and walked down the corridor, she heard the distant rippling

of the piano being played.

'It's that lovely piece again!' she realized. 'The one I heard yesterday. It must be the same person. Now I can find out who it is.'

The piano was tucked away in an alcove, around a corner at the far end of the corridor. Anxious not to disturb the player, who was in the middle of a delicate diminuendo, she tiptoed the last distance. Then she peeped round the corner . . .

She stared in amazement.

It was Arabella! The fair-haired girl was seated at the piano, playing with the deepest concentration. Her friend, Rosemary, stood alongside her and was turning over the pages for her.

Elizabeth hurriedly drew back. Her heart was pounding. That Arabella should be playing like that!

Her mind could hardly take it in. The conceited Arabella was always showing off. If ever she had something to boast about, she liked the whole world to know.

Why had she never let anyone know she could play the piano so well? Why was she keeping it secret?

Elizabeth stood there, quietly, her body pressed to the wall.

And very soon there came the answer to her question.

CHAPTER FOUR

# JOAN STATES HER OPINION

THE MUSIC stopped. Arabella had come to the end of her piece. Then Elizabeth heard Rosemary speak.

'It's perfect now, Arabella. It really is! Shall we go down to our dormy now and I'll test you on your spelling? You know Miss Ranger's said everybody has to pass the English exam before they can go into the second form—'

Out of sight, Elizabeth held her breath in alarm and shrank back harder against the wall. She would creep away, quickly. She didn't want the pair to see her. It would look like spying!

About to turn and tiptoe back down the corridor, she heard Arabella's voice next . . .

'We're not going anywhere, Rosemary. We're staying right here! *You* may think the piece is perfect but I do not. It *is* improving though. Oh, yes, it's definitely getting better all the time!'

She sounded strangely elated. Gleeful.

Elizabeth's attention was riveted.

'But what about the exams?' asked Rosemary, timidly. 'You know I'll die if we can't go up into the second form together.'

'One thing at a time, please. Do stop bleating about the exams, Rosemary,' said Arabella, impatiently. 'Do you really think I've been wearing my fingers to the bone for nothing? Just to throw it all away? Elizabeth's started practising again! I've heard her. Now the play's over I expect she's decided to be in the school concert! Well, she's got such a surprise coming!'

'I bet Mr Lewis can't get over how much practice you've done,' giggled Rosemary. 'All the months you've complained to him about it being boring. He must be amazed.'

'I'm his pet now,' said Arabella, conceitedly. 'Silly old man. He thinks I'm doing all this to please *him*.'

Rosemary knew the real reason.

'It's going to teach Elizabeth a lesson if you're chosen this year instead of her!' She was rather a weak character. She always said what her friend wanted to hear. 'Oh, won't that be fun, Arabella?'

'It's about time she was cut down to size,' said the other girl, fiercely. 'After that, I won't do a stroke of this boring old stuff again, I can tell you. Now, come on, let me play this through again. After that I shall do my scales . . .'

Elizabeth crept away down the corridor. She had heard enough.

All kinds of thoughts and emotions were tumbling through her.

*Envy.* That Arabella could play the piano so beautifully, when she really tried. She must have a real gift. How could someone so horrid create such a lovely delicate sound?

*Realization.* Now she knew why Mr Lewis had chuckled to himself about Arabella. He had been chuckling with pleasure. He would have recognized Arabella's gifts as soon as she arrived at Whyteleafe School. For months he had nagged at her to do her piano practice, to no avail. And suddenly she had turned over a new leaf! She seemed to want to please him, after all. How delighted the elderly music master must be at her dramatic improvement. He lived for his pupils and loved to nurture their gifts.

*Scorn.* How could Arabella be so unkind about Mr Lewis? A silly old man, she had called him. What a horrid thing to say. How mean that she was not really trying to please him! Nor was she working hard for the love of music, or for the honour of playing at the Leavers' Concert. It was all being done simply to spite Elizabeth.

Elizabeth could feel a temper coming on. What a

sneaky person Arabella was. While she had been busy with the school play, Arabella had been swotting away to beat her in class and plotting to steal her piano place as well. Just to get her own back on Elizabeth for being in the play!

It didn't occur to the Naughtiest Girl that Arabella's desire for secrecy was to be expected. She was learning from past mistakes. Encouraged by the feeble Rosemary, she had been cocksure about being chosen for the play. When Elizabeth had been chosen in her place, she had been made to look a fool. She had decided to be much more careful this time.

None of this crossed Elizabeth's mind as, feeling surprised and angry, she walked downstairs, her unopened music case bumping by her side. She didn't feel like doing her piano practice now. She didn't feel like doing anything!

She would go and find Joan. Joan would understand how she was feeling!

She met her best friend coming out of the second form common room with Susan. Gentle Joan could see at once that something was wrong. Making an excuse to Susan, she linked arms with Elizabeth.

'Let's go and sit outside,' she said. 'It's a lovely evening.'

They sat on the school terrace. Elizabeth blurted

out her secret ambition to Joan. Then she told her everything that she had overheard upstairs.

'What a trial Arabella is!' said Joan, sympathetically.

'I don't know what to do now,' confessed Elizabeth. 'The worst thing is that I think she's playing better than I do. I don't know whether I should go on trying.'

Joan frowned and thought about it.

'I don't think it would be very nice if Arabella *were* chosen,' she ventured. 'I wouldn't feel happy knowing that someone was playing at the Leavers' Concert in such a mean spirit. They should want to do it for the honour! And to give the people who are going a happy last memory of Whyteleafe.'

'That's exactly how I feel,' said Elizabeth, eagerly. 'Do you think I should go on trying, then?'

'Of course,' smiled Joan, wanting to make her friend happy again. 'Arabella may be talented but so are you, Elizabeth. She has got a head start at the moment, because you've been so busy since half-term. Given that you're both talented, it's all about who can get the most practice! You must practise and practise, Elizabeth, every spare minute of the day. You must at least give it your best!'

'I will!' promised Elizabeth, her eyes shining. 'I'll practise till my fingers are worn out, Joan. You just see!'

In stating her opinion, Joan knew nothing of the

fright Elizabeth had been given about dropping behind with her school work. She never dreamt that her friend had a secret fear of the coming exams.

As with Julian and all Elizabeth's younger friends, Joan Townsend never imagined that the Naughtiest Girl could have any serious worries about her school work. And Elizabeth was certainly not going to tell her. Her pride wouldn't let her.

'Oh, Elizabeth, I *am* looking forward to your being in the second form,' were her friend's last words to her that evening.

'Yes. It's going to be really good!' replied Elizabeth, stoutly.

That weekend, however, she blanked all thought of school work out of her mind. It was easier that way. She did not once return to her secret hideout in the oak tree.

Her next piano lesson was looming up and the weekend was her last chance of making it a different story from the last one.

She practised non-stop on Saturday and again on Sunday, only taking breaks for meals and other essential activities.

She went back to basics, with Grade I piano scales. Then she worked her way up through the Grades, playing the more difficult scales and finger exercises over and over again. Only then would she tackle her latest piece, the difficult arrangement of *Greensleeves*. She knew that she must achieve technical mastery before she could make it truly expressive.

Julian did not mind at that stage. He was pleased to see that the bold, bad girl had got the bit between her teeth! He was very busy with hobbies himself and also spent a lot of time in the craft room on his wood carvings.

Nor did Kathleen or Jenny or Belinda mind. They were busy, too, revising for the exams, and only felt envious that Elizabeth could afford to be so casual about them.

The only person who minded was Arabella.

She quickly noticed what a huge effort Elizabeth was making.

Arabella had planned to revise for exams this weekend. She was going to try to learn her French verbs and read her English set book. There would be questions about the book in the English exam!

But as soon as she realized what Elizabeth was up to, she abandoned her studies and returned to the piano herself.

'She must have found out! Have you said something to her, Rosemary?' asked Arabella, pouting sulkily. '*Have* you?'

'No, of course I haven't!' said Rosemary, indignantly.

'People must have noticed you coming up here to practise! You can hear it outside when this window's open. Elizabeth must have noticed. You can't expect to keep it secret for ever.'

The new week dawned.

All too soon, in Elizabeth's opinion, it was time for her next piano lesson.

'Hello, Elizabeth!' said Mr Lewis, as she appeared in the doorway, music case in hand. He gave her a warm smile. He had noticed how much practice the first former had been putting in! 'Come and sit down. Let's see how we get on this week, shall we?'

The Naughtiest Girl sat down at the piano. Her fingers trembled slightly as she undid the case and found her music.

This was a lesson in which she must do her very best. She knew she had made great progress since last week but would it be enough? She was longing to ask Mr Lewis about the Leavers' Concert.

'A marked improvement, Elizabeth,' the music master told her, when the lesson was over. 'I can see you have worked very hard this week, to make up for lost time. I'm very pleased with you.'

Elizabeth rose from the piano. As she packed her music away, her throat had suddenly gone dry. This, surely, was the right moment to find out what she wanted to know?

'Please, Mr Lewis—' she began, nervously.

'Yes, Elizabeth?'

'I just wondered if . . . if you'd decided yet . . . about the Leavers' Concert. I mean, who's going to play for the first form? It's not very long now, is it—'

'It certainly isn't!' he chuckled.

He stroked his beard thoughtfully before replying.

Elizabeth held her breath.

## CHAPTER FIVE

# THE RIVALS

'I CAN quite see that you would like to know, Elizabeth,' the music master said kindly. 'But the fact is, I seem to have a difficult decision on my hands this year. I expect young Arabella has told you that she would like to be picked for the concert, too?'

Of course, Arabella had told her no such thing. Fearing that her expression might give her feelings away, Elizabeth just mumbled and stared at the floor.

She waited to hear what Mr Lewis would say next.

'I want to leave it as long as possible before I make up my mind, Elizabeth,' he went on. 'Apart from anything else, it seems only fair to give you more time to make up lost ground . . .'

Elizabeth's hopes rose. Only to be partly dashed again.

'I must warn you though that I can't make any promises. Arabella has made remarkable progress lately. Quite remarkable. Our lessons together are becoming a real pleasure. One of the great satisfactions of teaching, Elizabeth, is when a pupil at last starts to respond. I must say I am very much looking forward to taking Arabella forward from here . . .' He quickly cleared his throat, suddenly aware that he had been speaking his innermost thoughts out loud. 'As well as you yourself, Elizabeth, of course. And all the other boys and girls I teach.'

In spite of the pain she was suffering herself, Elizabeth's warm heart went out to the music master. Poor Mr Lewis! After this term, Arabella would lose all interest in the piano as suddenly as she had found it! It would be so sad for him.

'So what I am proposing to do is to leave it until the last moment,' he explained. 'I shall have both of you in together, some time towards the end of next week. By then you will both have had your final piano lessons of the term. You will each play your new piece and then we will decide. We can't leave it any later than that!' He chuckled. 'The programmes will need to be run off that weekend, so I will have to make my mind up, won't I?'

Elizabeth nodded eagerly. Her hopes were rising again.

Mr Lewis walked across, opened the door and showed her out. His next pupil was waiting patiently in the corridor.

'I'll see you for your final lesson next week, then. Keep it up, Elizabeth!'

'I shall, Mr Lewis,' she responded firmly.

Elizabeth went on her way, her heart pattering.

All was not lost. Time was on her side. Arabella had been so cocksure, so certain that she was teacher's pet and that she had everything in the bag. But it wasn't like that, at all. Mr Lewis was very fair. He obviously thought that they were evenly matched. He said it was going to be a difficult decision. He was leaving the decision as long as he possibly could – until the week before the concert, in fact. Until just one week before the last day of term!

In the meantime, she had been given another week and a half to improve her playing of *Greensleeves*. In today's lesson, Mr Lewis had helped her to iron out some problems with the tricky part in the middle. There would be one more lesson, next week, to sort out any last-minute difficulties. To add the finishing touches. After that, Arabella had better watch out!

The following day, Arabella had her own weekly lesson. Mr Lewis explained the position to her. After the lesson, she came straight into tea. Elizabeth noticed she looked distinctly bad-tempered. This made her feel cheerful. She remembered the fable of the tortoise and the hare. Well, Arabella had hared ahead of her but now she, the tortoise, had every chance to overtake her.

And that she was determined to do.

In the days that followed, Arabella's hopes of keeping her ambition a secret were quickly dashed. Some of the first form soon began to notice that both Arabella and Elizabeth vanished away to play the piano in every spare moment. Patrick heard them on the upstairs landing one evening, fighting over the piano. He spread the news around the common room.

'The stupid way girls behave!' he said. 'I knew I shouldn't have come to a school with girls in it.'

Privately he was very put out that he had twice asked Elizabeth to give him a game of tennis. Twice she had made up some feeble excuse.

'If you *must* know,' said Rosemary, unable to hold her tongue any longer, 'it's all because Elizabeth knows that Arabella's going to be picked for the Leavers' Concert this year and she's jealous.'

'You *wish*,' said Julian sarcastically.

Before long, the whole class knew that the two girls were engaged in bitter rivalry for the place on the concert platform. They seemed to have swept all else aside!

It was true that the teachers were no longer giving out prep. But they were leaving it to the children's good sense to revise for the summer exams. These always took place in the last week of term. And neither Arabella nor Elizabeth were ever seen doing private study.

They just seemed to be in the grips of their 'piano craze', as Belinda called it.

'It's all right for Elizabeth,' she said to Jenny one day. 'But Arabella's going to come badly unstuck at this rate. You know how hard she has to work, just to stand still!'

'And she's already the oldest in the form, as it is,' agreed Jenny. 'She should have gone into the second form ages ago. What would happen if she didn't pass her exams? Would they have to keep her down again?'

'Miss Ranger says there's no point in anyone going into the second form if they can't do the work when they get there,' replied Belinda.

'They're both going crazy, if you ask me,' said Jenny. 'Even Elizabeth. I don't think she liked us teasing her about slipping down the form order but it could be a bit more serious if she doesn't watch out!'

In Elizabeth's own mind, of course, it was already serious. Over the next ten days, she woke up each morning fully intending to find time to go to her secret hideout in the oak tree. 'I must do some work for the exams today,' she would tell herself.

But, apart from a session on the Sunday afternoon, she never *did* find time.

The end of summer term was always hectic. There was compulsory strawberry picking to do in the school gardens. There were the knockout tennis tournaments, with all children expected to play in their different age groups. Of course, Elizabeth loved these activities. She loved it when she got to the semi-final of the first form tournament. But it only left time for her vital piano practice and nothing else.

'I'm sorry I haven't been to see you lately,' she told the friendly little robin, on the Sunday. 'You'll see more of me next weekend, when I've got this piano business out of the way. You will see me then, *I* can tell you!'

In her heart, Elizabeth knew that by then it might be much too late. The exams began on the Monday! But she could no longer bear to think about them. Lately, she had begun to console herself with a new thought.

'I can't possibly be made to stay down in the first form, like a baby, if I'm chosen to play at the Leavers' Concert. It's going to be such a grown-up occasion this year, with a real concert pianist coming. Even if I don't do very well in the exams, surely Miss Ranger won't mind?'

So, even on the Sunday, it only needed the distant notes of Arabella's piece starting up to bring Elizabeth scooting down from the oak tree and back indoors to the piano.

By the time both girls had taken their last piano

lessons of term with Mr Lewis, interest in the first form had reached fever pitch.

'How did you get on in your lesson, Elizabeth?' asked Daniel Carter, who had been helping her to practise by turning the pages. Unfortunately Julian had refused. He claimed not to be able to read music. He felt she was now overdoing things.

'Fine,' she replied, confidently. 'I've sorted out that end bit now.'

Martin asked Arabella the same question the next day. He had been taking it in turns with Rosemary to be Arabella's page-turner.

'Mr Lewis seemed very pleased with me,' replied Arabella.

Julian started a sweepstake on the result of the contest, with the children putting in sweets for money.

'Five sweets for four if Arabella Buckley wins,' he announced. 'Three sweets for two if the Naughtiest Girl does.'

Their classmates were all finding it very exciting.

But when the summons from Mr Lewis finally came, the two girls themselves were pale with tension.

It was after tea on the Wednesday.

'Put your music case on the table there, Elizabeth, next to Arabella's,' he said, as she came into the music room. 'I must decide which order you will play in.'

He let both girls run through a few scales, to loosen up. Then he looked at his watch.

'Would you like to play in alphabetical order?' he asked, with a smile. 'You first, Elizabeth.' He meant alphabetically by surname of course. Allan first, then Buckley.

With Mr Lewis turning the pages for her and Arabella seated quietly near the door, Elizabeth solemnly played her piece.

She made no mistakes and put fine expression into it.

'Well done,' nodded Mr Lewis. 'Now you, Arabella, please.'

Looking neat and tidy, as usual, her fair hair brushed and gleaming, Elizabeth's rival took over at the piano. Mr Lewis straightened her music for her.

Now it was the Naughtiest Girl's turn to sit very still and listen.

During the past two weeks, she had heard snatches of Arabella's piece a great many times. She had heard some of the more difficult passages being played over and over again. She knew it was a lovely melody but only now, as she heard it through from beginning to end, did she realize just *how* lovely. It was a pastoral piece, longer and more difficult than Elizabeth's own, and played with deep expression.

For a brief time, listening to the music, Elizabeth quite forgot it was Arabella playing and their intense rivalry. She found herself, instead, feeling dreamy, with visions of fields and hedgerows and little wooded hills floating through her mind . . .

Even so, it was still a crushing disappointment when the decision came—

With a brief *Well done* to Arabella, Mr Lewis walked straight over to Elizabeth and placed a gentle hand on her shoulder. In that moment, she knew that she had lost the contest.

'You played beautifully, Elizabeth. But I have made up my mind now. I think we should give Arabella the chance to perform that in public. It distresses me that we cannot have more than one person from each form this year. You deserve to be in the concert after all your hard work. But there it is.'

Arabella was still seated at the piano. She seemed transfixed, radiant. She had surpassed herself. Her own performance had surprised even her.

Elizabeth at once walked across and shook her hand.

'Congratulations,' she said. To hide her disappointment, she gave a wobbly little smile.

For once Arabella did not gloat. She seemed to be in a happy daze.

'Thank you,' she said, politely.

54

'Thank you, Elizabeth,' echoed Mr Lewis. 'You may leave now if you wish.'

As the music master started to discuss with the other girl the arrangements for the concert, Elizabeth turned her face away and hurried to the door.

She wanted to flee now!

She grabbed the nearer of the two brown leather music cases, not realizing that it was Arabella's. Then she scooped up her music and without even pausing to put it in the case, she shot out into the corridor.

She ran all the way upstairs to dormitory six.

She angrily hurled both the music and the leather case under her bed. Then she flung herself on top of the bed in despair.

Lying there, she could see the pile of school books standing on her white-painted chest of drawers. Standing there accusingly. It was all her revision, still waiting to be done.

She was not going to be in the concert, after all.

And now she was going to fail her exams!

## CHAPTER SIX

# JULIAN LEARNS THE TRUTH

'CHEER UP, Elizabeth! Have some sweets!' said Julian, as soon as she came down stairs. He produced handfuls of barley sugars and toffees and liquorice allsorts from his bulging trouser pockets. 'Just look what I made on my sweepstake!'

Elizabeth smiled weakly.

Everybody had been very kind.

Joan had been first into the dormitory to comfort her.

'You gave it your very best, Elizabeth. Nobody can do more than that. I'm proud of you. Now all we can do is accept the result.'

Other girls had come into the dormitory and said lots of nice things. Then her friends had dragged her outside and hustled her downstairs.

'Julian's looking for you, Elizabeth!'

'He made lots of sweets out of the sweepstake. Now he wants to share them out with everybody.'

'Come on, Elizabeth, you mustn't brood! Julian wants you to have first pick!'

Elizabeth plucked a favourite stripey allsort from Julian's hand. She popped it in her mouth. Then she chose two black ones and put them in her pocket. Everybody cheered. Then, grabbing sweets themselves, they all hurried off to their evening activities, laughing and chatting happily. The contest between Elizabeth and Arabella was over. It had been very exciting while it lasted!

Elizabeth and Julian were left alone.

From another pocket he produced two extra special expensive-looking chocolates, in crinkly gold foil wrappings. He was determined to cheer Elizabeth up.

'Come on. Have one of these. You've worked too hard. Need to get your strength back, Elizabeth!'

'Who put these in the kitty?' she asked. She unwrapped the chocolate and popped it in her mouth. 'Mmm. Delicious.'

'Arabella! She backed you to win. A sort of insurance policy, I suppose. She's lost them now.'

'Oh, well. That's some consolation,' sighed Elizabeth. She looked at her friend, in mild curiosity. 'However did you end up with so many sweets, Julian? How did you work it all out?'

'Simple,' he shrugged. 'Nobody much likes Arabella but everybody likes you. So I made your odds more tempting than hers and guessed everybody would want to back the bold, bad Elizabeth!'

'But you didn't think I would actually *win*?' realized Elizabeth, her face falling.

She had never seen Julian blush before.

'I had a little listen, a couple of times,' he confessed. 'It was a great surprise but I thought Arabella just had the edge on you.'

'She did,' admitted Elizabeth. 'You were right.'

She looked sad as she spoke. Julian at once tugged her by the hand.

'Come and see what I've got to show you. I've been keeping them a surprise. I want to know what you think. I've been busy, too, you know!'

He led her along to the craft room. Two or three boys and girls were working on their hobbies, completely engrossed. Otherwise, it was empty. Julian led the way to his drawer, in the corner. He took something out, wrapped in tissue paper.

'Look!' he said, lowering his voice. 'Do you like them?'

It was Mother Bear and Father Bear.

They were completed. Julian had sawn the piece of weathered oak in two and stripped off the remaining bark. From the natural shapes of the two pieces he had wrought a pair of carved animals. Father Bear was thick bodied and heavy jowled, with a stern but wise expression. The name WILLIAM was carved at the base. Mother Bear had a gentle face, full of kindness and understanding. Her name had been carved, too: RITA.

The wood had been sanded with great care, then polished until it gleamed. The carvings had taken Julian many hours to complete.

Elizabeth stared at them, in silence.

Julian was so clever. They were beautiful.

But as she looked at those two names, *William* and *Rita*, her own misery resurfaced. It gnawed at her.

William and Rita were leaving next week. Julian had used his time wisely. Now he had a beautiful memento to give them. The beautiful memento that *she* had been planning to give them, her music at the Leavers' Concert, had come to nothing.

She had not used her own time wisely. She had used it stupidly. Now she had nothing to give William and Rita. Instead, she might well fail the exams next week and be kept down in the first form like a baby.

'What's the matter?' asked Julian, glancing at her scowling face. He felt very hurt. 'Don't you like them? Don't you think they're any good?'

'It's not that, Julian!'

'Why are you sulking, then?'

Elizabeth could not bear Julian to think she was

sulking, or jealous in any way.

'The carvings are lovely, Julian. I think you are very clever. It's just that – oh, I've been so stupid—'

Suddenly tears sprang to Elizabeth's eyes and without warning she found herself blurting out her secret fears to Julian.

He looked at her in amazement.

'I am sure Miss Ranger did not mean it about keeping you down!' he exclaimed. 'She was just trying to make you work hard and catch up—'

'But I haven't worked hard and I haven't caught up!' said Elizabeth, in despair. 'And now there's no time left and it's hopeless . . .'

'Of course it's not hopeless, you goose.' He took hold of Elizabeth's arm and led her out of the craft room and into the corridor. He had a feeling that people could hear them, in there! 'Look, if you're really taking this work business seriously, you'd better dash off and do some right now. At least that will make you feel better!' he added, with a grin.

He was humouring her. Privately, he thought her fears were silly.

'I will! I will!' exclaimed Elizabeth. It had been such a relief to tell someone the truth, at last. Julian was so calm about things. She began to feel slightly better. They were quite alone in the corridor now. 'I'll go and do my French verbs. I'm going right now. I've got a secret place, you see. Oh, Julian,' she begged. '*Please* don't tell anyone about this. Promise!'

'I promise. Off you go, then!'

Julian watched as Elizabeth hurried off with a little skip. He shook his head and smiled to himself. The Naughtiest Girl was always full of surprises. You never knew what was going on in her head. That was one of the things he liked about her.

Whistling softly to himself, he went back into the craft room and replaced the wood carvings in his drawer. He was just leaving the room again, when someone spoke.

Daniel had caught snatches of what Elizabeth had been saying earlier. Now, he raised his head from his clay model and spoke to Julian.

'Poor Elizabeth!' Daniel was a sensitive boy. 'She's in a terrible stew about the exams, isn't she? I've never seen her in a state about school work before. It's silly of her not to have done any swotting.'

'Oh, she'll cope all right,' said Julian, airily. 'And don't you go noising this about, either. It's Elizabeth's private business and you're a nosey parker!'

'Sorry, Julian.'

Unfortunately, the very next day Daniel gave Elizabeth's secret clean away.

## CHAPTER SEVEN

# ELIZABETH HAS A NEW WORRY

DANIEL DID not mean to blurt out Elizabeth's private fears. But next morning, after first lesson, he heard some of the others criticizing her.

'Have you ever seen the Naughtiest Girl so gloomy in class?'

'She looks like the cat that's had the cream taken away!'

'It must be because Arabella won. She's in a sulk!'

'No, she's not!' butted in Daniel, unable to stop himself. 'She's worried about the exams, that's all. She's fearfully worried!'

'What? Elizabeth? We don't believe you!'

'It's true I tell you!' Daniel was determined to defend Elizabeth's good name. 'I heard her telling Julian. She doesn't want anybody to know but she's convinced she's going to fail!'

This titbit of news passed round the class in the course of the morning. They observed Elizabeth's behaviour with interest. She certainly seemed very absorbed in lessons today, taking copious notes all the time. When Julian made a paper dart and sent it skidding across her desk, in the middle of French, she barely noticed. Nor did she raise her head at Mam'zelle's cry.

*Zut alors, Julian!*

The rumours must be true, then. Elizabeth was really worried.

She was. But her worries were as nothing compared to Arabella's. After her great triumph of the previous day, she had woken up this morning in a state of panic. When Miss Ranger asked her some simple questions on the English set book, the oldest person in the form got every single question wrong. That was the moment when terror struck at her heart.

However, Arabella struggling in class was so commonplace that nobody even noticed. For Elizabeth to be having problems was far more noteworthy.

But by teatime, Elizabeth was in a much more positive frame of mind. Last night, in her secret den, she had revised all her French verbs. She had concentrated hard in lessons today and made lots of notes.

Straight after tea she would return to the oak tree for a good long session with her English set book. She could study it there, in peace. Miss Ranger had said they must be able to quote from it. She would spend at least an hour there and take extra cheese and biscuits with her, she thought, scooping some up and putting them in her pocket.

She hurried up to the dormitory to collect her English book.

She noticed the sheet music flapping about under the bed, where she had hurled it the previous evening. There was to be a Dormitory Inspection tonight.

'I'd better put it away,' she thought, shamefacedly. 'I've no time for piano practice any more.'

As soon as she hauled the music case from under the bed and opened it, she realized that she had picked up Arabella's by mistake! The cases were almost identical but, inside the flap, Arabella had written her name. And there were some chocolate marks, as well.

'When she hid those chocolate peppermints in it!' Elizabeth thought, disapprovingly. 'So she must have *my* case. I'd better go and get it.'

Arabella was still at tea. Her dormitory was empty.

Elizabeth quickly found her own music case. It was standing tucked between Arabella's chest of drawers and her bed. Elizabeth swopped the two cases over. Arabella's current music was lying loose on top of the chest of drawers. Like Elizabeth, she had not bothered to put it away yet.

'So she's not even realized we've got our cases mixed up!' thought Elizabeth. 'Well, as she's never noticed, I won't bother to say anything.'

She hurried back to her own dormitory with her proper case.

'I'll put *Greensleeves* away later. When I tidy up my cubicle for the Dormy Inspection!' Elizabeth decided, dumping the case on her bed. 'I really must rush now. This is wasting time!'

Soon she was ensconced in her tree house once more.

It was all very soothing. The leaves whispered and rustled around her. The big bough was as comfortable as any chair. It had branches protruding on which she could rest her feet, as she lay back against the warm, rough bark of the massive tree trunk.

She knew some of the book quite well and now she must study the remainder. She worked hard for the next hour. She broke off once or twice to feed the robin some biscuit crumbs. She memorized two passages from the book that Miss Ranger had told them were important. She smiled as she saw a squirrel scuttle past.

'Yes, you've got me back!' she told it.

She closed her eyes for a few moments. The doves were cooing again. Oh, she did love this special tree. It was so full of life! Perhaps she would share her secret with Joan one day, and Julian . . .

## ELIZABETH HAS A NEW WORRY

Her eyes opened wide. She could hear the murmur of voices, somewhere down below.

She peered down through the leaves. There were two men standing by the country road. They were looking at the tree and talking about it. Then they came and walked round its trunk, immediately beneath her.

They spoke again. This time she could hear exactly what they were saying. She frowned, puzzled by their words.

They were walking away now, in the direction of the village. They glanced back at the tree as they went, still deep in conversation. She could no longer hear what they were saying but she remained deeply puzzled.

'What did they mean about *a big 'un*? And something about some ropes?' she wondered. 'I don't understand . . .'

She remembered the strange white cross that was painted down below. She began to feel a sense of foreboding.

Elizabeth had a new worry now.

Then suddenly, from the direction of the school grounds, she heard her name being called.

It was Julian's voice.

## CHAPTER EIGHT

# AN EXAM PAPER IS LOST
# - AND FOUND

'ELIZABETH! YOO hoo! Where are you?' called Julian, hands cupped to mouth.

Harry joined in, as well.

'EE . . . LIZZZZZ . . . ABETH!  Come  on, wherever you are!'

'Special Meeting!' Julian shouted, to the empty air. 'We've all got to go inside! William and Rita's orders! Special Meeting of the first form!'

Elizabeth peered through the foliage. She could see the boys over by the school field. Now Harry was grabbing Julian's arm.

'Come on, it's no good, Julian,' he was saying. 'William and Rita told us to come straight back if we couldn't find her.'

The Naughtiest Girl watched the two boys run back to the school building. She felt ill at ease.

'Drat!' she thought. 'Whatever are William and Rita having a special Meeting of the first form for?

I don't want to go back inside yet.'

She wanted to stay where she was for a little while longer.

She hated the idea of leaving her tree on its own this evening. Was it something to do with what those men had said? Perhaps. If she stayed for a while, they might come wandering back. They might start talking again. She would listen carefully and try to make sense of what they were saying . . .

But she dare not stay longer. Not when William and Rita had called a special Meeting. Why was it only for the first form? That was very unusual. She had better hurry!

Poor Elizabeth then found herself stuck up the tree in any case – for ten whole minutes! The grounds were very busy at this time of evening. The juniors were coming in from play to have their cocoa. The older pupils were strolling back and forth with cricket bats and tennis rackets. Every time she tried to edge along the bough to climb down the wall and get back into the grounds, she would hear fresh voices!

At last the coast was clear.

She raced over to school, brown curls flying, and made straight for the hall. The doors were open. She slowed down to recover her breath, panting and dishevelled. A figure stepped forward.

'Stop! Elizabeth!'

It was Miss Ranger! She had been standing by the doors, observing the Meeting.

She took hold of Elizabeth's arm and surveyed her.

'There's no point in your going in now, Elizabeth. The Meeting's just ended! Wherever have you been? You know you should wash your face and brush your hair before you come to a Meeting! What *have* you been up to?'

'I – I was just out of doors, Miss Ranger,' she said, lamely.

She peered into the hall. She could hear benches being scraped back and the low buzz of conversation. William and Rita were leaving the platform. There were no monitors with them.

What a short Meeting! Miss Ranger was right. It had just ended.

'Why isn't the whole school here?' she asked, puzzled.

'Because something very unpleasant has happened which concerns only the first form. William and Rita are hoping it can be sorted out quickly. They would rather not have to bring it up at the big weekly Meeting.'

Miss Ranger hurried off then, looking very upset.

'Where did you get to, Elizabeth?' asked her classmates, as they came out of the hall.

One or two of them were looking at her with

considerable curiosity.

'Why didn't you want to come to the Meeting?'

'Are you all right?'

'Of course I'm all right!' replied Elizabeth, impatiently.

She pushed past them and found Julian, who was still in the hall. He was with Kathleen.

'We wondered what had happened to you, Elizabeth,' he said calmly. 'You've missed all the excitement.'

'What excitement? What was the Meeting about?'

'Something terrible's happened,' said Kathleen, her face pale. 'Somebody's stolen one of the first form exam papers.'

Elizabeth was shocked.

'How could somebody do that?'

'It seems they've been printed ready for next week and are in a drawer in the school office,' explained Julian. 'But the Beauty and the Beast counted them this evening and there's one missing. It's a copy of the paper we were all going to get for our English exam. Somebody got hold of their copy in advance!'

'What a cheat!' said Elizabeth, indignantly.

'Well, they haven't got away with it,' shrugged Julian. 'All the questions will have to be changed now. The joint heads must be furious! Shall we do a bit of detective work? That would be interesting.'

'I can't, Julian,' said Kathleen. 'I'm right in the middle of tidying up my cubie for Dormy Inspection. This Meeting's been a real nuisance.'

'Elizabeth?' queried Julian.

Elizabeth was also shaking her head.

Of course, it was terrible that someone had stolen the English paper. And it must be someone in their class! Who could it be? Normally, she would have been fascinated to do some detective work with Julian. They often solved things together.

But this evening she had something else on her mind. Something that was worrying her very much. A matter that she felt was of supreme importance.

She had quite a different mystery to investigate.

'I'm sorry,' she said. 'I want to go and talk to somebody about something. In fact, I'm off there right now.'

Kathleen looked puzzled as the Naughtiest Girl rushed away.

'Don't forget, Elizabeth! We've got Dormy Inspection, tonight. Don't go and disappear again!' she called out.

Julian just smiled and scratched his head. Dear Elizabeth. What was she up to *now*? It seemed to be something new. At least she didn't seem to have exams on the brain any more!

# AN EXAM PAPER IS LOST – AND FOUND

Elizabeth left the school building and hurried to the stables. She wanted to speak to the stableman. He was a real countryman and a fount of knowledge.

She would ask him what a white cross on the trunk of a tree might mean. She would also ask him if he had ever put ropes round a tree and if so, why. *We'll rope her up first thing in the morning* . . . That's what the men had said.

Of course, she mustn't let him suspect that she was asking about any *particular* tree. He might wonder how she knew so much about the oak tree when it didn't belong to Whyteleafe and was not even in the school grounds. She shouldn't really know anything about it at all!

But she had to speak to him, urgently. It was *her* tree and she had to know if anything were going to happen to it in the morning.

She desperately hoped not. Perhaps the stableman could give a simple explanation. Then she would hurry back and tidy up her cubicle for Dormitory Inspection.

Silly old Dormitory Inspection! This was much more important.

'Where has Elizabeth got to *now*?' said Miss Ranger, angrily. 'Her behaviour is very strange at the moment.'

The Dormitory Inspection was in full swing.

# WELL DONE, THE NAUGHTIEST GIRL!

Once a fortnight, the dormitories at Whyteleafe School were checked for tidiness. The class teacher concerned would accompany Matron on a tour of inspection.

All the other girls in number six stood to attention by their cubicles. Beds had been beautifully made, rugs straightened. The number of items on top of chests of drawers was limited to six, as school rules ordained. So far, Matron and Miss Ranger had been well pleased.

But now they were staring into Elizabeth's empty cubicle in annoyance. It was a mess. And the Naughtiest Girl herself was nowhere to be seen! Where was she?

She was climbing the stairs at that very moment, taking them slowly, one at a time. She was deep in thought and feeling trembly.

The stableman had not been at the stables. It had taken her some time to track him down.

But now, at last, she had the answer to her questions.

'It's not fair! It's horrible!' she raged to herself, over and over again. 'It's not in the least bit fair and I shall make them stop!'

She was already forming a plan in her mind.

She walked into dormitory six, her face very tense and pale.

In something of a daze, she noticed that Miss Ranger

and Matron were standing in her cubicle.

'Elizabeth! This is a disgrace!' said Matron. 'Look at all the books on your chest of drawers—'

'And don't add your English book to the pile!' scolded Miss Ranger, as she saw Elizabeth take the small volume out of her pocket. 'Your school books should be in your desk, not up here!'

'I've been reading it this evening for the exams,' protested Elizabeth.

She was still feeling in a daze.

'You should have been tidying up your cubicle!' said Miss Ranger, standing by the bed. 'What's your music case doing, just dumped on top of the bed? And you haven't even bothered to put your music away.'

The teacher gathered up the score and opened the brown leather case, intending to slip it neatly inside. But there was something in the way.

'Even your music case needs a tidy-up,' she complained.

She pulled out a crumpled sheet of paper that had been stuffed just inside the case.

She straightened it out and stared at it in disbelief.

'Elizabeth!'

The teacher's shocked cry brought everybody running to the scene.

Miss Ranger was holding something aloft, between

thumb and forefinger. She was waving it in front of the Naughtiest Girl.

Gasps of surprise echoed round dormitory number six.

It was the stolen exam paper.

'What was this English examination paper doing hidden in your music case, Elizabeth?' asked Miss Ranger.

The Naughtiest Girl gazed at the printed sheet in total astonishment. It was an exam paper, sure enough. Even from here she could see a list of questions about the English set book. She was dumbstruck.

'Is that why you have been reading so avidly this evening?' continued the teacher, in acid tones, glancing at the book in Elizabeth's hand. 'To plan your answers to the exam questions in advance?'

'No!' protested Elizabeth, angrily. 'Of course not, Miss Ranger!'

'I repeat. How did this exam paper come to be hidden in your music case?' asked the teacher.

Matron was trying to usher the other girls out of earshot. But they were hanging on to every word.

'Answer me, Elizabeth!' rapped Miss Ranger.

'I have no idea!' exclaimed Elizabeth, hotly.

'Come, come, Elizabeth. Think carefully before you speak. You must have *some* idea of how a stolen exam paper could be found in your music case,' said the teacher calmly. 'Just think about it for a moment. It must have got there somehow, must it not?'

Elizabeth's sense of outrage began to subside. Miss Ranger's comment was perfectly fair. How *had* it got in her case? She took a deep breath, to try to calm herself. It had been such a shock! The little girl frowned deeply for a few moments as she tried to think clearly.

Slowly, the truth dawned on her.

'Well, Elizabeth?'

The Naughtiest Girl had become pink with excitement.

'I – I think I know the answer,' she said. 'You see, my music case has been in somebody else's possession all day.'

'Somebody else's possession?'

Elizabeth's room-mates glanced at each other, uncomfortably. What a silly thing to say! The music case had been lying under her bed all day. They had noticed it there and wondered if she had forgotten about Dormy Inspection tonight.

'Whose possession, Elizabeth?'

'I – I'd rather not say, Miss Ranger.'

It sounded very feeble.

The teacher glanced at her watch.

'It is nearly bedtime. You are to tidy up your cubicle,

78

this instant. Then if, as you say, there is somebody else involved in this matter, you are to bring them to the staff room before you go to bed. I will wait to see you there. If for any reason you cannot find this other person, there is nothing more we can do about it tonight. Miss Belle and Miss Best will see you in the morning.'

It was clear, realized Elizabeth, that Miss Ranger found it very difficult to believe her story.

'Yes, Miss Ranger!' she replied, confidently.

Very soon the teacher would see that her story was true.

## CHAPTER NINE

# ELIZABETH DISAPPEARS

ARABELLA SAT primly on her bed in pyjamas, pretending to read a book. The curtains of her cubicle were drawn. She knew that would hardly deter Elizabeth. She was expecting her at any moment.

Next door, in room number six, Matron had supervised Elizabeth while she tidied up her cubicle. In those ten minutes, the dramatic news had spread like wildfire. The boys alone, away to their own quarters by then, knew nothing of the unfolding drama. But the news had very quickly reached Arabella's dormitory.

The excited chatter had raged all round her.

'The paper was in Elizabeth's music case! She was caught red-handed!'

'She tried to pretend someone else used her music case today. Miss Ranger says she'd better produce them!'

'I knew it was funny the way she didn't come to the Meeting! I *said* that was weird.'

'Poor Elizabeth! We knew she was in a bad way!'

'It was silly of her to waste all that time on the piano!'

'It's not a *bit* like Elizabeth to cheat. I'm so amazed!'

Arabella, already in pyjamas, had quickly drawn the curtain round her cubicle. She had peered inside her music case in horror.

The truth had dawned. They must have got their cases muddled up yesterday. Elizabeth had come and swopped them back this evening without checking inside and now everybody thought that she had stolen the exam paper.

Suddenly, now, the curtains parted.

'So there you are!' exclaimed Elizabeth, stepping into the cubicle. 'Just the person I want to speak to.'

Arabella's heart was thumping. She noted the fierce glitter in Elizabeth's eye.

'Am I?' she asked innocently, looking up from her book. 'And why would that be, Elizabeth?'

'You know perfectly well! It's about you stealing that exam paper and then putting it into *my* music case by mistake!' hissed Elizabeth. 'We've got to go and see Miss Ranger straight away. The two of us. You had my music case all day, not your own! You will have to confess to her.'

'I'm sure I don't know what you're talking about!' exclaimed Arabella, deliberately raising her voice. 'How dare you accuse me of stealing something. I haven't touched your silly music case!'

It brought Rosemary on to the scene at once.

'Elizabeth's saying I haven't had my music case all day, Rosemary. She says I've been using hers! Did you ever hear such nonsense?'

'Arabella's case has been here since yesterday evening. I've seen it!' protested Rosemary. 'Look, there it is! It's never budged.' She pointed to its position on the floor tucked between bed and chest of drawers. 'Whatever would she want *yours* for?'

Elizabeth stared at Arabella in disbelief. Arabella was refusing to own up. She must by now be perfectly well aware of what had happened. But she was not going to admit it.

'So you don't agree that you sneaked into the school office some time today and took that exam paper?' asked Elizabeth, scornfully. 'And then crept up here and hid it in the music case by your bed? Thinking it was your own! If I hadn't come in here after tea and swopped it for your proper case, the exam paper would still be there *now!*'

Arabella had gone very white.

Rosemary, thinking it was because of the outrageous things being said, turned on Elizabeth.

'You came and swopped it, did you?' she jeered. 'Did anybody see you?'

'Well, no. It's just that I . . .'

Elizabeth's voice trailed away. For the first time she

82

realized that she had not one single witness to support her story.

'It's just that you are sick with jealousy at Arabella being chosen for the concert!' said Rosemary, finishing Elizabeth's sentence in her own way. 'And not content with stealing the exam paper, you're now trying to pin the blame on *her* so that you'll play in the concert instead of her!'

Arabella was breathing heavily. She was racked with emotion.

Elizabeth had guessed the truth exactly. And, faced with the fierce candour of what Elizabeth had been saying, Arabella had come within an ace of confessing. Until Rosemary's words had reminded her of how much she stood to lose . . .

The Leavers' Concert! Her great moment of triumph was just one week away. So many times, Elizabeth had had the last laugh and she, Arabella, had been made to look stupid. All that would change now. People would look up to her. They would respect her. Perhaps they would even start to like her, the way they always liked Elizabeth. She had surprised herself, how well she could play the piano! She had worked so hard for her moment of glory next week. Nothing was going to rob her of that!

'I really don't know anything about a silly exam

paper, Elizabeth,' she said, her face expressionless. 'You seem to have made a mistake.'

The Naughtiest Girl looked at her, sorrowfully.

'You're a hopeless case, Arabella,' she said quietly. 'There is no point in talking to you.'

She left and returned to her own dormitory.

The room fell silent at her arrival but she cared not.

She went into her cubicle and drew the curtains. Then she lay down on top of the bed, still fully clothed.

She lay on her back, head resting on hands, staring at the ceiling. Outside, dusk began to fall. None of her room-mates came to see her, or said goodnight. Her friends were too embarrassed. Poor Elizabeth, they were thinking. So worried about the exams, to creep into the school office like that. And caught red-handed! Trying to pretend that it must have been somebody else!

Miss Ranger, too. Waiting in vain for Elizabeth to appear with 'somebody else'. Thinking exactly the same thing.

'They will have to think what they like,' decided Elizabeth, with a deep sigh. 'I can't prove my story is true and I expect Arabella will never confess. Never ever! But then life is not fair. No. Nothing is fair!'

The amazing sequence of events since teatime had convinced her of that. She was not thinking of her own plight but something of even greater concern.

# ELIZABETH DISAPPEARS

Soon she heard steady breathing from every corner of the dormitory. The others were all asleep at last. It was time to put her plan into action.

When the rising bell sounded next morning, Elizabeth did not appear from her cubicle.

Kathleen walked over and pulled back the curtain.

'Wake up, Elizabeth. It's late!'

Then she gasped.

The sun's morning rays slanted across Elizabeth's neat, empty bed. Kathleen could see at once that it had not been slept in.

Elizabeth had disappeared.

# CHAPTER TEN

# A HUE AND CRY

'ELIZABETH'S RUN away!' cried Kathleen, in great alarm. 'Look, she must have done. Her bed's not been slept in!'

The others rushed over.

'I don't believe it!' exclaimed Jenny, in astonishment. 'Perhaps she just got up early!'

'No, Kathleen's right.' Belinda checked the bed carefully. 'Look, the covers have never been pulled back. And do you notice something? One of the pillows has gone.'

'Yes – and so's the spare blanket!' realized Jenny.

They all looked at one another in horror. Poor Elizabeth! Overcome with shame, she had run away from Whyteleafe School. They had a sudden vision of her, wandering the dark country lanes with blanket roll and pillow, sleeping in ditches, trying to make her way back home.

'We should have been nicer to her,' moaned Kathleen. 'We should have been more understanding . . .'

As the word spread to the next dormitory, other

pyjama-clad girls thronged in. They gathered round Elizabeth's empty bed, pale and shocked. Nobody looked more shaken than Arabella who already had dark rings under her eyes from a bad night's sleep.

The first form girls held an emergency meeting on the spot.

'She'll never get home safely! It's more than a hundred miles. And she hasn't any money!' said Tessa.

'I wonder where she slept last night?'

'Some smelly old barn, I expect.'

'What should we do?' asked Belinda. 'Do you think we should go and report this to the Beauty and the Beast straight away?'

'It's not like Elizabeth to run away when she's got a problem!' decided Jenny, after giving it due thought. 'Perhaps this is just one of her pranks, to give us all a fright! Perhaps she's hiding around the school somewhere.'

'And if we go and tell the joint heads, she'll be in even deeper trouble,' realized Kathleen. 'More than she was already!'

'Yes, you're right!' exclaimed Arabella, eagerly. 'We mustn't worry any of the teachers about this at the moment. That would be silly. Let's search the school buildings.'

'Perhaps she's asleep in one of the storerooms?' suggested Rosemary.

The first form girls rushed to get dressed. Then they fanned out in all directions, scouring the school buildings.

Arabella scurried up and down the corridors, looking in the empty classrooms, opening and shutting each door with growing unease. Nobody had managed to find Elizabeth yet. Where *was* she?

'I expect she'll turn up at breakfast-time,' said Rosemary, to comfort her friend. 'She hasn't any money and she's bound to be starving hungry. It's not your fault, Arabella, if Elizabeth Allen has decided to do something idiotic.'

These were not the words to bring comfort to Arabella.

Elizabeth did *not* turn up at breakfast.

Sitting in the dining-hall, staring at that empty place, Arabella's serious unease turned to panic.

The Naughtiest Girl really had run away! And it was all her fault. She should have confessed about the exam paper while she still had the chance. Now Elizabeth felt hopeless about things and was sure that nobody would ever believe her. If only Rosemary had not butted in, thought Arabella, she might have admitted the truth. She had been on the point of doing so.

Now she was seized by a feeling of dread. Elizabeth

could be in danger. Something dreadful might have happened. Supposing she had been run over? And really, when she thought about it, Elizabeth was not *that* bad. She had her good points, after all. As she toyed with her breakfast cereal, Arabella's eyes kept straying to the door. How lovely it would be to see the Naughtiest Girl come strolling in through that open door, right now, laughing at them all and enjoying her silly joke . . .

*Come back, Elizabeth*, she kept thinking. *Oh, do please come back!*

But still Elizabeth did not appear and by the end of breakfast there was a great hue and cry. Daniel went racing off to see if she might be sleeping in the school stables.

'We must go and see the joint heads right away,' said Joan, turning pale, as soon as Kathleen had explained things to her. The second form monitor had looked across and noticed that her best friend's place at table was empty. 'Oh, poor Elizabeth! I am perfectly certain she would never have stolen an exam paper. She must be feeling very angry and upset at being misjudged.'

'Hear! Hear!' agreed Julian.

Kathleen reluctantly rose to her feet. She was beginning to feel very guilty.

'Will the heads ring the police, do you think, Joan?'

'I'm sure they will,' replied Joan. She looked across at

89

Julian. 'Do you want to come with us, Julian?'

He just sat there, spooning down the last of his cereal. He shook his head. He was frowning.

'I might follow on in a minute,' he muttered. 'I'm just trying to have a good think.'

There was a great buzz of excitement round the dining-hall as Joan and Kathleen went off together. By now, nearly everybody knew what had happened. Elizabeth Allen's bed had not been slept in. It looked as though she must have run away from school! Now Joan and Kathleen were going to report it to Miss Belle and Miss Best. The joint heads would have to telephone the police!

Julian put his spoon down, his brow deeply furrowed.

The Naughtiest Girl was always full of surprises. Even so, he found this one most baffling. If she *had* taken that exam paper she would have owned up at once except that she would never have taken it in the first place! She had been unjustly accused. But in that case, the last thing she would do would be to run away. Not the bad bold Elizabeth. She would stay to fight her corner, to the bitter end. It was such a riddle. There must be some other reason for her vanishing trick. Something different altogether . . .

He was trying hard to remember a remark she had made two days ago. It was to do with her swotting for the exams, without wanting people to know how worried she was.

'Got it!' he whispered suddenly. 'I remember what she said.'

*I've got a secret place, you see!*

A secret place! Was that why they couldn't find her for the Meeting yesterday? And was this now the explanation? Had the crazy Elizabeth been up all night, swotting for the exams in some secret hideout?

'And still there!' thought Julian. 'Probably fast asleep! But where is it?'

At that moment, Daniel returned.

'She's not in the stables,' he said, miserably. 'I think it was very catty of those girls last night, not accepting her word. Elizabeth would never cheat. No wonder she was upset. But it's all my fault,' he confessed. 'You see, I spilt the beans, Julian. About her being so worried about the exams. That's why they didn't believe her. I didn't mean to but I did.'

'Oh, do shut up, Daniel,' said Julian, absently. 'Can't you see I'm trying to think?'

When Joan and Kathleen arrived at the school office, they were amazed to see that Arabella had beaten them to it.

'Come in, please,' called the joint heads.

They each sat behind a desk and Miss Ranger stood by the window. She had arrived earlier to report back on the matter of the stolen exam paper. The culprit had been found.

'Elizabeth Allen? Oh dear. How very disappointing!' the joint heads had exclaimed.

Arabella, accompanied by Rosemary, was already in there. They were both seated.

Joan and Kathleen stared at them. Why had Arabella got there ahead of them? She seemed to be crying. Rosemary looked distressed, too, and was biting her lip.

'Please ring the police, Miss Belle!' Arabella was pleading, tearfully. 'I'm so worried about Elizabeth! I'm so frightened that something could have happened to her. And if it has, it's all my fault. I drove her to this. I drove her into running away! I could have owned up about the exam paper when I had the chance and I didn't.'

'You have owned up now, Arabella,' said Miss Belle, calmly. She nodded towards some more chairs. 'Sit over there, please, Joan and Kathleen. You may join us.'

The two headmistresses were very composed.

'We will have to contact the authorities, which will be very bad for Whyteleafe,' Miss Best began. 'Before we do so, we need to be quite sure the child has run away. Have you all had a good look for her?'

'We've searched high and low, Miss Best,' replied Kathleen, only just beginning to take it all in.

Elizabeth had been telling the truth all along. Somehow her music case *had* been in somebody else's possession yesterday. Arabella's! And it was Arabella who had stolen the English exam paper. She had come and confessed to Miss Ranger and the joint heads!

As Miss Belle and Miss Best asked further probing questions, Kathleen found it difficult to take her eyes off the fair-haired Arabella. It was strange to see her vain, doll-like face streaked with tears, to see her genuinely caring about somebody else for the first time, somebody other than herself.

'*Please* telephone the police,' she implored again.

The joint heads glanced at one another. It seemed that they had no choice.

'We'll speak to them right away,' said Miss Best, reaching out for the telephone.

'No!' cried a boy's voice, from the doorway. 'Please don't ring them yet!'

Julian walked eagerly into the room. Everybody stared at him.

'I might be able to find Elizabeth! I've got a hunch but I'll need some time! Could you just give me fifteen minutes, please? We can ring the police after that!'

Miss Best took her hand away from the telephone.

# WELL DONE, THE NAUGHTIEST GIRL!

She glanced at Miss Belle and then nodded. They both knew that Elizabeth's friend was a brilliant boy.

'Very well, Julian. Fifteen minutes.'

'And not a minute longer,' added Miss Belle.

## CHAPTER ELEVEN

# WELL DONE,
# THE NAUGHTIEST GIRL!

'DON'T WORRY, big brown moth. Don't worry, friendly little robin!' whispered Elizabeth, as down below the men took the ropes off the back of the lorry. *Don't worry, chattering squirrels and cooing doves and busy little insects and creepy-crawlies!* 'This is your house. I won't let them chop it down, I promise!'

Hidden in the oak tree, Elizabeth had the fierce light of battle in her eye. She had slept fitfully in its warm boughs. It had been a much lighter sleep than usual. The sleep of a soldier at the battlefront, ready for the enemy and poised for action. And since dawn she had been wide awake. She knew that the woodmen might start work very early. That was why she had not dared to sleep in her proper bed last night.

They had arrived at long last, not as early as she feared but early enough. They parked their lorry on the wide grass verge below and began to sort through their equipment. She was ready for them. She tensed every muscle now. She was preparing to make her stand.

At the same time, Julian was walking briskly round the grounds of Whyteleafe School. He was looking urgently about him. It was a chance remark of Daniel's that had given him his clue.

*The stableman hasn't seen Elizabeth since last night, Julian. She was asking him all about trees or something.*

So that was the person Elizabeth had rushed off to speak to last night. The stableman. To ask him about trees. Why *trees*?

Trees . . . secret place.

Could Elizabeth's secret hideout be in a tree? And in that case, which one? What sort of tree?

And then, in a flash of inspiration, Julian had remembered the piece of oak that Elizabeth had found him. That splendid piece of oak for his wood carvings . . .

But where had it come from? She had never explained. He had occasionally looked for oak himself and never found any. The reason being, as far as he could recall, that there were no oak trees in the school grounds. But there must be one somewhere, one that he had missed . . . And could that be where she had made her secret hideout?

He walked round to the back of the stable block, looking up at all the trees there. Then he stared at the meadow beyond. There was not an oak tree in sight. He hurried back by way of the cricket pitch. He was almost giving up hope.

Then, suddenly, he saw it.

'It's been right under my nose!' he realized. 'Only it's growing *outside* the school, on the other side of the wall. That's why I didn't notice it!'

He stood back and surveyed it. Elizabeth could have got into that tree by climbing up the boundary wall . . .

'And she has!' gasped Julian as Elizabeth's head suddenly poked out of the middle of the tree. She was shouting! She seemed to be looking down at some people in the road.

'Go away, please! Go away and take your horrid chainsaw with you! I'm staying here and I'm not going to budge. I won't let you cut this tree down. Never, ever! Don't you realize lots of little creatures live here? This is their home!'

Julian goggled for a moment – and then came to a swift decision. He turned away and sprinted back towards the school buildings. At top speed. His fifteen minutes was almost up.

'Julian!' exclaimed Miss Ranger, in relief, as he burst back into the school office, his face shining. 'You have some news?'

'I've found her!' he exclaimed. 'I know why she

disappeared now. It had nothing to do with the exam paper or anything like that!'

He told them all that was happening.

At first there were cries of joy and relief that Elizabeth had been found safe and well. But, after that, some anxious frowns appeared on the teachers' faces.

'That beautiful old oak tree? The one that we can see from the school grounds? It's being taken *down*?' said Miss Belle. 'Oh, Miss Best, we must do something about it. And quickly.'

'We certainly must,' agreed Miss Best. 'I will ring the tree department as soon as the council offices open.'

She rose to her feet and rapped out an order.

'Julian, you are to return to the tree immediately. You are to join Elizabeth there. She needs reinforcements. Under no circumstances are either of you to come down from that tree until we give you permission. And please tell Elizabeth that refreshments are on their way.'

'Oh, Julian, I'm so glad you turned up when you did,' said Elizabeth. 'I was getting so tired of arguing with those men. I don't think I could have stuck it out much longer up here. Not on my own. Not without any breakfast.'

'Another hour should do it,' grinned Julian.

Seated comfortably in the tree, the two friends munched the last of the delicious sandwiches that Joan and Arabella had brought out to them. They offered the robin a few crumbs.

It was morning break and quite a crowd of boys and girls was starting to gather below.

The woodmen had long since retreated. They had parked their lorry some distance away down the road. They were sitting in the cab, drinking tea from a flask, waiting helplessly for further instructions.

'They tried to tell me the tree needed to come down for a road widening scheme!' said Elizabeth, indignantly. 'A beautiful healthy tree like this with no disease at all! Who wants the silly road widened? Drivers can go a bit slower as they always have done and still have a lovely old tree to look at.'

The tree department people agreed with Elizabeth entirely. It turned out that the powers that be hadn't got all the correct paperwork, so the men weren't allowed to cut the tree down. Within the next hour, an official arrived and pinned a notice to the old oak. It was an emergency Tree Preservation Order. It would go to appeal, of course, but now Miss Belle and Miss Best were involved, Elizabeth was confident the tree would survive.

The doves cooed and all the little birds sang, as

though in gratitude. Elizabeth's heart sang loudest of all as, aching with tiredness, they were given permission to descend from the tree at long last. Everybody cheered.

'Well done, Elizabeth!'

Well done, the Naughtiest Girl!

## CHAPTER TWELVE

# GOODBYE TO WILLIAM AND RITA

NEVERTHELESS, ELIZABETH had been in breach of school rules. The big oak tree was out of bounds. She had visited it not once but several times. And she had spent an entire night away from her dormitory, causing everyone great alarm and anxiety. That was a most serious offence.

At the big school Meeting the next day, it all had to be written down in the Book. It was the last Meeting of the summer term and the last one ever for William and Rita. There were serious matters to discuss and the head boy and girl were determined that they should be dealt with fairly and wisely. All their conclusions would be written in the Book, offering help and guidance to future Meetings after they had gone.

'As soon as you suspected the tree was in danger, Elizabeth, you should have reported it to a monitor,' said William. 'Even though, to do so, would have meant confessing that you had been out of bounds.

Another time, you must try not to take matters into your own hands.'

'Yes, William,' agreed Elizabeth, contritely. 'I'm sorry.'

'On the other hand,' said Rita, busily writing in the Book, 'this was one of those very rare occasions when breaking a school rule had a beneficial outcome. If you had not been exploring the tree in the first place, you would never have discovered that it was to be felled. It would have been lost. Although you should not have acted alone, your action was brave and so that must go in the Book, too.'

The Meeting had to deal with Arabella's crimes, too. That was more difficult.

At the behest of the joint heads, Miss Ranger had started giving Arabella some extra lessons in preparation for Monday's English exam. She would have to spend the entire weekend on difficult exercises. There would be a completely new paper set, of course. The Beauty and the Beast had reasoned, correctly, that the girl must be beside herself with panic to have stooped so low. She clearly needed help. At the same time, cheating was a serious offence at Whyteleafe School and so was letting someone else take the blame. These were things that the Meeting must deal with.

There was also the very difficult matter of next week's

Leavers' Concert to think about. Should Arabella still be allowed to play – or should Elizabeth take her place?

'Why did you practise so hard for the concert, Arabella,' asked Rita, as the fair-haired girl stood up, 'when you should have been working for your summer exams?'

'At first I just wanted to be chosen to spite Elizabeth,' replied Arabella truthfully. 'She always seems to be better at things than me and then she laughs at me. I don't know why nobody likes me and everybody likes Elizabeth.'

'Elizabeth can be very naughty but she has a warm heart and that is why people like her,' explained Rita. 'She cares for others whereas you are sometimes thought not to.'

'It wasn't a bit warm-hearted of her to make such a contest of it,' complained Arabella. 'She knew I was better than her but she started practising so hard, I didn't dare slack off after that. I was so worried about the exams but I *couldn't* let Elizabeth beat me and I knew she wanted to. It was my big chance to shine, you see,' she blurted out. 'I did so want to be chosen. That – that was the only reason I took so long to confess about the exam paper.'

'Is this true, Elizabeth?' asked William. The whole school was listening, in fascination. 'That you knew

104

Arabella was better than you but decided to make a battle of it? Even when you both had exams coming up?'

For the first time, Elizabeth felt a twinge of shame.

'Yes, it is true,' she said, hanging her head. 'I did realize Arabella was better, quite early on. But I still wanted to beat her. Even though I'd been in the school play and she hadn't. And even though it meant skimping all my revision. And so, in a way, I suppose I stopped her revising, as well.'

Sitting down again, next to Julian on the first form benches, Elizabeth began to think deeply about things.

Poor Arabella! Elizabeth had been working hard and was starting to lose her fear of the exams. But she could tell that Arabella was as worried as ever. It must be dreadful to be the oldest in the form and always struggling near the bottom.

On the platform, with the other monitors, Joan put her hand up.

'Please, William, don't just blame Elizabeth! I think it was wrong of me but I heartily encouraged her at the time.'

'And I encouraged Arabella!' exclaimed Rosemary, jumping to her feet. 'I tried to mention the exams sometimes but most of the time, I just egged her on.'

The head boy looked from Joan to Rosemary and nodded.

'Thank you both for speaking up,' he said. 'There's an important lesson to be learnt here. The rest of the school, please take note. We always want to please our friends, don't we? We like to say to them the things that they want to hear. But sometimes the thing that is *best* for them is the very last thing that they want to hear. The finest friendship you can give someone is to stand up to them sometimes and tell them when you think they are doing the wrong thing.'

Joan at once nodded agreement. Rosemary sat down, feeling very ashamed at the way she always pretended to agree with Arabella, even when she knew she was wrong. Elizabeth glanced at Julian admiringly. He had told her several times that she was overdoing things with the piano business.

Rita wrote all this down. Then she, in turn, addressed the school.

'There is something else I would like to point out. To both Elizabeth and Arabella. But it applies to the rest of us, too. It is very easy to care about people whom we like. To care equally for those people whom we don't like is much more difficult but is something we must strive for.'

Shyly, Kathleen put her hand up.

# GOODBYE TO WILLIAM AND RITA

'Please, Rita, Arabella was really upset when she thought something had happened to Elizabeth. Even though she doesn't like her! She was crying.'

The Naughtiest Girl's eyes opened wide at this surprising piece of news. She turned to look at Arabella but the other girl turned her head away, embarrassed.

'Thank you for pointing that out, Kathleen,' said Rita. 'And this brings us to the final business of the Meeting. We have given everything a good airing and now we have to decide about the Leavers' Concert. Should Arabella still be allowed to represent the first form or should Elizabeth take her place?'

'This is going to be a very difficult decision,' added William. 'Rita and I will talk it over with the monitors.'

Everybody on the platform went into a huddle. There seemed to be a long argument going on. Elizabeth sat very tense and still. So did Arabella. All around them the hall buzzed with conversation, as the boys and girls discussed amongst themselves which of the two girls should be allowed to play.

Then William banged the gavel on the table for silence.

'We are finding it impossible to reach agreement,' he announced. He gazed towards the back of the hall where, as always, Miss Belle, Miss Best and Mr Johns sat in on the Meeting. They never joined in unless their advice was sought. 'We would like the heads to tell us what they think.'

Miss Belle at once rose to her feet. She was smiling.

'While you have been discussing this difficult problem, we have been discussing it, too. We have decided that you should let Elizabeth and Arabella use their own good sense in the matter. Let them discuss it together privately. Let *them* decide which of them should play at the Leavers' Concert.'

It was the end of summer term at Whyteleafe, the very last day of the school year. William and Rita and the others were leaving today! Exams were over and the results posted on the board.

Elizabeth had passed! She would be going up into the second form next term! She would be reunited with Joan. She would be going up with Julian and Patrick and Kathleen and Belinda and Jenny . . . and Arabella! Somehow Arabella had managed to scrape through the English exam and had passed in maths, and French as well. She had failed some other papers but because of her tremendous progress in music this term had been given some useful bonus marks for that instead. So she was being allowed into the second form.

'As a matter of fact, I really like my piano practice now,' she had confided to the music master. 'I never realized how satisfactory it could be, to find out that there's something one is really good at!'

Mr Lewis was delighted.

It was time for the Leavers' Concert.

He was up on the platform in the hall now, smiling at Sophie as she waited nervously with her flute. She would be the first to perform. All the parents had arrived and the hall was crammed full.

The girl from the junior class soon got over her nerves. She gave a faultless performance. Everybody applauded. William and Rita, sitting in the front row, sat very still. They glanced at each other, moist-eyed, for they knew that this concert would be their last memory of Whyteleafe.

'And now,' announced Mr Lewis, 'to represent the first form we have one of our most gifted pupils. Arabella Buckley.'

Sitting between her parents, near the front, Elizabeth watched Arabella as she walked on to the platform. She put her music in place on the grand piano which had been brought into the hall for this special occasion. How magnificent it looked. Arabella looked quite small against it. She looked different today, thought Elizabeth, her fair hair brushed and gleaming, a spot of colour in each cheek, her eyes sparkling.

As she started to play a deep hush descended over

the audience. The pictures came again to Elizabeth, conjured up by the music. Those lovely visions of green fields, grass blowing, clouds scudding across blue sky, wooded hills . . . What a fine player Arabella was!

William and Rita listened, enraptured.

All too soon it was over.

Children from other classes came and went. Richard played his fine new piece. Then Courtney Wood, the well-known concert pianist, performed for the rest of the programme, as planned.

It had been a wonderful Leavers' Concert this year and yet, for Elizabeth, it was Arabella's music that lingered in the mind. Had the head boy and girl enjoyed it as much as she had? She did hope so!

Afterwards, she and Julian went to say goodbye to them. They were deeply touched when Julian presented them with the little wood carvings.

'They are quite beautiful, Julian!' exclaimed Rita.

'Father Bear rather looks like me, doesn't he?' laughed William in delight.

He turned to face Elizabeth and smiled approvingly.

'So you and Arabella sorted it out then? How did you decide?'

'It was easy,' replied Elizabeth. 'I just thought Arabella's piece would be the best memento for you, better than mine actually. I – I'm just sorry that I haven't got anything of my own to give you.'

'But we heard your music drifting out one evening, Elizabeth, and that was lovely, too,' said Rita quietly. 'I will never be able to hear *Greensleeves* in future without its reminding me of you.'

Elizabeth blushed with pleasure.

'Naughtiest Girl in the school – Best Girl in the school!' laughed William. 'You have no need to give us a memento—'

He bent and kissed her on the cheek. Then Rita did likewise.

'Memento? Please don't be silly!'

'Dear Elizabeth! How could we ever forget you?'

# THE NAUGHTIEST GIRL

## Wants To Win

# CONTENTS

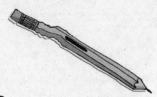

CHAPTER ONE

# THE REAL KERRY DANE

'STOP A minute, Daddy!' cried Elizabeth Allen, flinging herself in front of the luggage-trolley. 'Please – I need to get something out of my trunk.'

The long summer holidays were over. Elizabeth and her father were at the big London rail terminal where she would catch her train back to boarding-school. Mr Allen had business to do in London today, so had driven her up to the station by car.

They'd arrived more than half an hour early but, to Elizabeth's delight, her friends Julian and Joan were already at the station and keeping a lookout for her. She had rushed off to speak to them at once.

Now the three children caught up with Mr Allen as he laboured along with the laden luggage-trolley, looking for Platform 14.

'You'll never guess what Julian and Joan have just told me!' exclaimed Elizabeth, as her father braked. 'Kerry Dane's due at any moment. The real Kerry Dane herself!'

'And who might she be?' asked Mr Allen.

'Oh, *Daddy*!' Elizabeth was already clearing her tuck-box and sports things off the top of her school trunk. It was a smart brown trunk with E. ALLEN painted on it in black letters. 'You know – *Zara's Journey!* That wonderful film Mummy took me to in the holidays. Joan's seen it, too. Everybody has!'

'Ah. The one that you and your mother went to see twice? Starring the young girl that nobody's ever heard of?'

'Yes, Kerry Dane! She was an ordinary London schoolgirl until the film people found her, but now *everybody's* heard of her. Everybody except you, Daddy! And she's really marvellous.' Elizabeth dropped to her knees beside the trolley and managed to get her trunk open. She flung back the lid. 'I really admire her. She's exactly the sort of person that I would like to be.'

Elizabeth was hunting feverishly through her trunk, scattering its contents as she went. Books, garments and photo frames were starting to spill out. But she couldn't find what she was looking for. Where was it? Oh, surely she hadn't forgotten to bring it this term . . . ?

'You say she's due here? At the station?' asked Mr Allen, in surprise. 'Well, even if she is, Elizabeth, this is hardly the time or the place to start unpacking your trunk!'

'Not the station, sir,' explained Julian, his green eyes glinting with amusement at the sight of Elizabeth down on her knees, passers-by having to step round her. 'The big cinema next door. The film's playing to packed houses and we gather she'll be stopping by at ten o'clock to chat to all the fans in the queue.'

'She'll get wet then,' observed Mr Allen. 'It's raining.'

'There's a notice outside the cinema,' Joan rushed on. 'Julian spotted it coming in!' In her own quiet way, Joan was as excited as Elizabeth. 'We're hoping we'll have time to get her autograph.'

'Hooray!' cried Elizabeth, waving something in triumph. 'My autograph book. I was *sure* I'd packed it. It was right at the bottom. Isn't that typical? Sorry, Daddy.'

While the others quickly stuffed everything back into the trunk and closed the lid, Elizabeth stroked the white leather binding of her prized autograph book. She peeped inside. Some of the Leavers had written messages in it at the end of last term. And there were two very special entries from William and Rita, who had been the head boy and head girl. What a fine thing it would be to get Kerry Dane's autograph as well! It would be another treasured signature to add to her collection.

'We won't be long, Daddy,' she said quickly, as she

119

helped her father stack the rest of her belongings back on the trolley.

'Now, just a minute,' her father protested. 'I can't have you missing the train, you know. I'm not sure I can allow—'

'Oh, *please*, Daddy!' she begged. 'I'll never, ever get a chance like this again. We won't miss the train, I promise. We've got half an hour!' She turned and appealed to her friends for support. 'We wouldn't dream of missing the train, would we?'

'Certainly not,' agreed Joan.

'I absolutely couldn't *bear* to miss it!' vowed Elizabeth.

It was the simple truth. She had been looking forward for days to the train journey back to Whyteleafe School. There would be lots of people she knew on board and some new pupils as well. It was always very exciting. And she was going up a form. She was going into the second form! There would be an election for a new head boy and head girl as soon as they got back to school and second formers were allowed to vote in it!

'I'll make sure we're all back in good time. Platform 14, isn't it, sir?' said Julian, sounding his most grown-up. 'The cinema's just through the archway over there. Bang next door to the station!'

'And Joan's a monitor, so she'll make sure, too,' pleaded Elizabeth. She noticed that the other two had sensibly retained their raincoats when getting their luggage put on the train. 'I'll even wear my mac if you like, Daddy, so my school uniform doesn't get wet.'

'Very well,' relented her father. He knew how much Elizabeth hated wearing her old mac. He fished it out of a carrier bag and handed it to her. 'I'll get your luggage put on the train and meet you by the ticket barrier in fifteen minutes, then.'

'Oh, thank you, Daddy!'

The three friends raced out of the station and over to the cinema. Although it was early in the day, queues had already formed. The cinema illuminations shone down on the rainy pavements. ZARA'S JOURNEY, they signalled brightly, STARRING KERRY DANE. And there was the notice that Julian had spotted earlier:

### Announcement

We are pleased to announce a surprise visit from Miss Kerry Dane. She will be here to speak to the queues and sign autographs between 10.00 a.m.– 10.15 a.m. today.

The notice stood at the cinema's main entrance in front of the big glass doors. A policeman and a commissionaire in a bright red uniform were keeping the entrance clear.

'If you wish to see Miss Dane, please take your places in the cinema queue. Otherwise, pass along,' the doorman was saying. 'Miss Dane's car will be arriving at any moment.'

Excitedly, Elizabeth linked arms with her two friends. Her autograph book was safely stowed in her raincoat pocket.

'You didn't imagine it, then, Julian!' she said. 'Isn't it sporting of her to want to come and speak to the queues on a horrid wet morning like this?'

'She pops up at cinemas a lot,' ventured Joan. 'I've read about it in the papers. She says she really likes to meet her fans.'

'It's all good publicity, I suppose,' grinned Julian. 'It's clever not to announce it in advance, so she doesn't have to cope with a big crowd each time. I can't wait to see my cousin Patrick's face when I pull out Kerry Dane's autograph. I shall sell it to him for a tidy sum. He's been raving about her film all holidays!'

'Where should we stand and wait?' said Joan, anxiously. 'We're not allowed to hang around outside. We'll get moved on.'

'In the queue, of course!' replied Julian. 'We'll pretend we're waiting to go into the film like everybody else.'

The shortest queue was the one for the most expensive seats. It was sheltered from the rain by an awning. With Julian whistling nonchalantly, the three friends tagged on the back of it.

'I feel a bit guilty!' whispered Joan.

'It's only for a few moments,' Elizabeth pointed out. 'It must be nearly ten o'clock now.'

'As a matter of fact,' said Julian, glancing at his watch and then at the road, 'it's five past! And no sign of her car yet. If she's only staying till quarter-past, she'd better buck up!'

But Elizabeth wasn't listening.

'Look, Joan!' she was exclaiming. 'Do you remember this bit?'

The two girls had turned to gaze at the slim showcase fixed to the wall behind them. It contained, behind glass, a selection of film stills that portrayed dramatic moments from the story. The clip that Elizabeth was pointing to showed Kerry Dane, her golden hair matted and her face streaked with tears, stumbling down a mountainside with a small child in her arms.

'Yes!' agreed Joan, gazing at the still. 'My heart was in my mouth. I was convinced that little Stefan was going to die. After everything that Zara had done to get the younger children out of the war zone, to get them to safety. And they were so nearly home . . .'

123

Deeply engrossed, the two friends started to discuss the film. Together, they relived the story of how the brave refugee girl, Zara, played by Kerry Dane, had led a group of village children out of a war zone, narrowly escaping land mines and enemy fire. Then had come a terrible journey over the mountains, through storms and blizzards, with little food and no warm clothes, trying to reach the safety of her uncle's farm, in the next valley. Zara had given all her rations to the younger children and towards the end only kept herself alive by eating snow. And then Stefan, the smallest of the children, had fallen desperately ill . . .

'I liked the bit when Zara made a raft and rowed the children across the river, one by one,' sighed Elizabeth. 'You remember – when they found that the bridge had been blown up? Oh, wasn't she brave? A born leader. I'm sure Kerry Dane must be a brilliant person, in real life. It all seemed so *true* . . .'

'But where's she got to today?' came Julian's voice, sounding cross.

'Oh!' Elizabeth spun round to face Julian. He had been watching out for the car all this time. 'Is it getting late then?'

'It's nearly quarter-past.' He shrugged. 'I'm afraid our train goes in fifteen minutes.'

'Then we must get back to the station,' said Joan,

looking crestfallen.

'Surely we can wait another five minutes—?' protested Elizabeth.

And suddenly a cheer went up. A car had arrived, its brakes squealing loudly, its tyres spraying water.

A radiant figure jumped out of the back of the small blue car. The mane of golden hair was unmistakable. So were the huge brown eyes and sweetly smiling mouth.

'It's her!' everyone cried.

'It's Kerry Dane!'

It was a thrilling moment for Elizabeth and Joan. The real-life Kerry Dane – at last. And she looked as pretty off the screen as on it!

But then came a disappointment. She ran through the rain, straight past the queues and up the cinema steps. The doorman was standing at the ready, waiting to open one of the big glass doors.

Pressing forward, Elizabeth could see the cinema manager and his staff inside. They were lined up in the foyer, waiting to present a bouquet of flowers.

The urgent hand signal that the car driver gave to the young actress, as she turned to face the waiting crowd, told Elizabeth the worst. Kerry wasn't staying! The car was already moving off at speed, round to the back of the cinema, preparing for her to leave from a rear exit.

From the top step, the teenage actress gave a short

address. It was charming and very spontaneous:

'It's wonderful to see you all here. I hope you will enjoy watching *Zara's Journey* every bit as much as I enjoyed acting in it. If you like the film, do please remember to tell all your friends about it! I so badly wanted to meet some of you this morning and stay and chat. But what can I say . . . ?

'Well, I know one thing I can say! It's a lot easier coming over mountains and through blizzards and storms than it ever is trying to get through the London traffic!'

There was appreciative laughter from the crowd.

'So now I'm in big trouble!' she told them. 'I'm due somewhere else later, way outside of London. My driver, who is also my father, says I shouldn't be here at all – but I couldn't bear to let you down. Now all I can do is say bless you all. And run inside and give my thanks to the manager and his staff. Then on my way!'

It was such a friendly little speech that everyone swallowed their disappointment and applauded. Smiling and waving goodbye, Kerry Dane was ushered into the foyer. Most people pushed forward to witness her shaking hands with the cinema staff. What a beautiful bouquet!

But not Elizabeth. Elizabeth was hanging back. She

had taken her autograph book out, gripped with a sudden excitement.

'Let's race round to the back of the cinema!' she whispered. 'She's going to leave by the back way, it's obvious!'

Joan looked worried.

'Don't be silly, Elizabeth!' Julian smiled. 'We've only got ten minutes!'

'That's long enough! She'll be out in a minute! I want to get her autograph, even if you two don't!' she exclaimed hot-headedly. 'I'm not going to give up now!'

Elizabeth shot away. She rushed round the side of the building, following the route that the blue car had taken. The rain was getting heavier. She was splashing through puddles but she didn't care.

'Kerry Dane seems nice,' she thought, eagerly. 'I'm sure she won't mind! I just hope I'm in time. You can tell she's in a tearing hurry!'

It had hardly been the moment to stop and have a debate with Julian!

She could hear his voice somewhere behind her and the sound of running footsteps. He and Joan were chasing after her, trying to fetch her back! But for once, the Naughtiest Girl decided, she didn't care if she *was* living up to her nickname. She was not going to allow herself to be thwarted – she must get that autograph!

She had been running fast and was now somewhere at the back of the big cinema building. Blindly, she rushed into the first turning she came to, but it led to a dead end. She merely found herself staring at a fence and a row of black wheelie bins.

'Drat, it must be the next turning!' she realized, as she heard Julian and Joan go racing past, still calling her name.

Then, to her dismay, there came the sound of an engine starting up. She turned.

A blue car nosed into view across the top of her turning, coming from the next one along.

'She's leaving. I've missed her!' thought Elizabeth.

But, with a squeal of brakes, the car suddenly stopped.

Elizabeth stared, open-mouthed. Kerry Dane was leaping out of the back, still holding her big bouquet of flowers. She was running into the little cul-de-sac. She was heading straight for Elizabeth!

How could this be? For a moment Elizabeth wondered if her friends had somehow explained . . .

No! She was racing straight past Elizabeth without so much as a glance. Golden hair flying, she reached the nearest wheelie bin and flung back the lid.

The car horn was honking.

'Shut up, Daddy!' she cried out. 'I won't be a sec. I

can't take these stupid things with me. I've got to get rid of them!'

Julian and Joan reappeared, just in time to see Kerry Dane drop the bouquet in the dustbin and slam down the lid!

Elizabeth was stunned but nevertheless as the actress turned and came racing back, she rushed to meet her, her autograph book outstretched.

'Please, Miss Dane, will you sign this for me?' she gasped.

The girl turned on her in contempt. The transformation from her screen persona was now complete. Gone were the pretty smile and warm manner. The eyes glittered, the expression was hard.

'Of course I won't, you little pest!' She brushed Elizabeth's book away. 'Can't you see I'm in a hurry?'

The autograph book went flying out of Elizabeth's hand and landed in a puddle.

'My book!' cried Elizabeth furiously, as she dived to rescue it. 'You've made it all wet and messy!'

'Just like you, then!' Kerry Dane called back over her shoulder, as she ran the last few steps to the waiting car.

She scrambled on board and the car zoomed away.

Elizabeth stood there for a moment or two, clutching her book, speechless at the girl's rudeness.

'How mean!' said Joan, taking the book and gently wiping it with a tissue.

'Did you see what she did with those beautiful flowers?' asked Elizabeth, finding her voice. 'Lovely fresh flowers too – wasn't that a cruel thing to do?'

'We thought she would be such a nice person,' said Joan, every bit as shocked as Elizabeth. 'But she isn't. She isn't nice at all.'

'She's absolutely horrible!' stated Elizabeth.

Julian had not been under the spell of Kerry Dane's film, having never seen it.

'You told your father we were going to meet the real Kerry Dane,' he pointed out. He gave a wry smile. 'And now we have.'

'Daddy!' realized Elizabeth, in horror. 'The train! Now we're going to miss the train!'

'No, we're not,' said Julian, glancing at his watch. 'Not if we run!'

'I'll give Daddy the flowers to take back for Mummy!' exclaimed Elizabeth, darting back to the dustbin. 'That will cheer him up!'

Five minutes later Elizabeth had cheered up considerably herself. She had said goodbye to her father and now they were safely aboard the train.

'You see, Julian! I told you we had plenty of time!'

It had been an embarrassing episode. It had been

humiliating. Kerry Dane had turned out to be a completely different person in real life. A hateful person! But Elizabeth had no intention of talking about it to anybody. She could forget all about her now.

She was going back to Whyteleafe, the best school in the world.

The train moved off, then immediately juddered to a halt. Somewhere, right at the back, a late arrival climbed aboard the First Class section laden down with luggage.

Then came the sound of banging doors and another blast from the guard's whistle . . . and at last they were on their way.

CHAPTER TWO

# BELINDA SURPRISES ELIZABETH

'I'VE ALREADY decided who I'm going to vote for!' announced Elizabeth some time later, as the train rattled merrily along.

The rain had stopped and the sun was trying to come out. Her raincoat was stowed on the luggage rack and her damp curls were almost dry again in the warm railway carriage. Her father had been too surprised by those lovely fresh flowers to be cross with her. Elizabeth felt at peace with the world again.

Some of her classmates were on the train. They had caught up with their holiday news and then discussed going into the second form. Mr Leslie would be their new form teacher. Julian was pleased about that. Mr Leslie was the science master and a great favourite with the boys. But the girls liked him, too.

'He's quite strict about school work, though,' Joan had told the others. Being older than Elizabeth, Joan was already in the next class and was now a second form monitor. 'He expects quite a lot from us and is always saying that we're not first formers any more!'

'And neither are we!' Elizabeth had said proudly.

And her thoughts had turned to the forthcoming election for a new head boy and girl. As second formers they were allowed to vote, unlike the first formers and the babies in the junior class!

'I've been thinking about it all holidays,' she said excitedly. 'You know, the election for the new heads.'

'I can't imagine anyone but William and Rita running the school Meetings,' confessed Jenny. 'They were both so marvellous, weren't they? They were always so fair and came to the right decisions. And we could all look up to them!'

'Yes, the new ones will have to be people the whole school can look up to!' agreed Martin.

'So who are you going to vote for, Elizabeth?' asked Belinda.

'For head boy, I think Thomas,' she replied firmly.

Everybody at once murmured agreement.

'Yes, he'd be excellent,' nodded Julian. 'He's got real leadership qualities. And who's your head girl then, Elizabeth?'

Elizabeth hesitated. She didn't want to rush what she was going to say. It was important to her.

'I've thought about it a lot,' she said. 'At first I couldn't think of *anyone* who'd be able to step into Rita's shoes! And then gradually it dawned on me – Emma!'

Elizabeth's suggestion created an instant buzz of interest.

'Emma?' said Belinda.

'Isn't she a bit quiet?' mused Jenny.

But Joan was nodding her head. She had gone into the next carriage earlier, to talk to her friend Susan. And she'd noticed Emma sitting with some new junior pupils who'd looked rather scared and homesick. Joan had admired the way that the senior girl was finding time to chat to them and was getting them to smile.

'I think I agree with you, Elizabeth,' she said eagerly. 'I do believe Emma would be just right. In her own special way, that is.'

'Yes. Excellent,' said Julian, after thinking about it.

But Martin looked doubtful.

'She seems sort of shy to me,' he said. 'Especially as she'd have to speak up in front of the whole school all the time. And make sure to hold everyone's attention! Emma's nice but she's sort of soft-spoken . . .'

'Strong underneath, though!' decided Julian. 'There's no softness there, if you ask me. I think Emma's got authority but it's the best sort. It's quiet authority . . .'

'Rita wasn't exactly loud, Martin!' Elizabeth pointed

135

out, rather impatiently. 'I bet Rita was very like Emma before she was elected head girl. Was she, Belinda? You must have been at Whyteleafe then.'

Belinda had been at Whyteleafe longer than the others. She had joined in the junior class. She frowned now, deep in thought.

'Why, Elizabeth, I do believe you're right! I remember overhearing some of the teachers say that Rita was a bit too young and as quiet as a mouse and might not be able to keep order! But they were proved wrong. Rita was nervous at the first Meeting or two. But after that she was such a success she stayed on as head girl for two years running.'

'There, Martin!' said Elizabeth.

'Lucky the teachers don't have any say in it then, isn't it?' laughed Julian. 'I think all schools should be run by the pupils, the way ours is.'

'What about Nora?' asked Jenny, suddenly. 'She wouldn't be nervous of going on the platform.'

'She'd be good in some ways,' said Belinda, her mind now made up, 'but I don't think she'd be as good as Emma . . .'

They discussed it further. By the end, Elizabeth felt well satisfied. Everyone seemed to agree that Thomas was the right choice for head boy. And apart from Martin, who didn't know who he wanted, and

Jenny, who still favoured Nora, everyone seemed to agree with her about Emma.

Because of the way that Whyteleafe School was run, in Elizabeth's opinion it was extremely important to get the right head boy and head girl. And she'd set her heart on Thomas and Emma. She felt that this discussion was a promising start.

Then suddenly, near the end of the train journey, Belinda raised something which made Elizabeth's scalp prickle with excitement.

'We haven't even talked about our *own* election! For a monitor to replace Susan. Now she's going up into the third form, we'll need someone new. We've got Joan, of course, but the second form always has two.'

She was looking straight at Elizabeth!

'We all think you should be the other monitor, Elizabeth,' explained Jenny. 'We talked amongst ourselves at the end of last term and everyone agreed. Would you be willing to stand?'

'I – I—'

Elizabeth was quite lost for words. Speechless with pleasure! She had already been a monitor once and William and Rita had promised that her chance to be a monitor would surely come again. But she'd never expected it to come so soon!

'You see, Elizabeth,' Joan said gently, having been in on the secret, 'everyone thinks it was very fine the way you stood down in favour of Susan last term. And that it's only fair you should take her place now she's going up.'

'Not to mention all the things you've done for the school. Even if we *do* always think of you as the Naughtiest Girl!' laughed Kathleen. 'We were really proud of you last term, Elizabeth. We were proud that you were in our form!'

'So *would* you be willing to stand?' repeated Jenny.

'Oh, yes, please!' exclaimed Elizabeth, glancing across at Joan in delight. Their classmates wanted her to be a monitor again, with her best friend Joan! The two of them would be second form monitors together. 'There's nothing I'd like better!' she added.

What a wonderful surprise. What a marvellous term this was going to be!

They all piled off at the station and watched their luggage being loaded on to the school coach. Julian gave Elizabeth's back a pat. There was an amused gleam in his eyes.

'Well, well. It looks as though the Naughtiest Girl is going to be made a monitor again. At the first Meeting. When will that be? This Saturday? Can she

138

last that long without misbehaving?'

'Of course I can, Julian,' replied Elizabeth, refusing to be amused. 'I'm going to jolly well make certain of that!'

That, at least, was her intention.

## CHAPTER THREE

# A GRAND ENTRANCE

ON THE coach they joined all the other boys and girls who'd been on the train. There were plenty of new first formers and junior class pupils. They were losing their shyness now and chattering away, excited to think that they'd be seeing their new school very soon. Mr Johns and Miss Thomas, who had both accompanied the train from London, checked names off on a list. Elizabeth and Joan looked round eagerly, wondering if there were any new pupils for their own class.

'Good. All aboard. Off we go!' said Mr Johns.

Soon the coach had left the town far behind and was labouring up the steep hill towards the school. A white station taxi overtook them on the hill. There were two large suitcases on its roof rack. Julian, always alert, watched it turn in through the gates of Whyteleafe School, ahead of them.

'I wonder who's in that taxi from the station?' he said to Elizabeth. 'There would have been room for them on the coach.'

'Perhaps it's a new teacher,' responded Elizabeth absently. She hadn't even noticed the taxi overtake them.

She was thinking instead about the coming Saturday. She was imagining the scene at the first school Meeting of the year. The results of the election for head boy and head girl would be announced. Thomas and Emma would take their rightful places at the special table on the platform. As a monitor, Joan would be seated on the platform already. Then any new monitors required would be chosen by their respective classmates. Elizabeth would proudly leave the second form benches and take her place up on the platform with Joan and the rest.

Together with the other monitors they would be helping their fine new head girl and head boy to govern the school . . .

The coach pulled up.

'We're here now, everyone.'

That was Emma's voice. The senior girl was standing at the exit, helping the teachers. Some of the new pupils were clambering about, peering out of the windows, trying to get a good look at their new school.

'No kneeling on seats, please,' she said, quietly but firmly. 'All the new children are to leave the coach first. Before you do so, please show me your hand baggage.

141

Nothing is to be left on the bus! The girls will then please line up outside with Miss Thomas and the boys with Mr Johns. You will be shown to your dormitories and have a wash before dinner. Your main luggage will be sent upstairs later.'

Obediently, the new pupils queued up to leave the coach, showing Emma their hand baggage as they went. They were longing to get inside the building now, to see their new living quarters.

So, too, was Elizabeth. She waited impatiently for the last of the younger children to be ushered off the coach. She knew that she and Joan were to be in the same dormitory this year. But who would they be sharing with? And which room?

Just as their turn came to get off the coach, a small fair-haired boy reappeared and clambered back on board. He looked rather scared.

'Please, miss,' he said to Emma, blinking, 'I think I've left my teddy bear behind. I was sure it was in my carrier bag.'

'Don't look so frightened, Rupert!' replied the senior girl. 'We must try to find it quickly. We can't keep Mr Johns waiting.'

Elizabeth glanced around the empty seats at the front. Suddenly she spotted a furry paw sticking out from under one of the seats.

'I can see it!' she laughed, diving forward to pick it up. 'It's fallen on the floor!'

She handed it to the grateful boy. What a dear little face he had, she thought. He looked a rather dreamy child.

'There you are, Rupert,' smiled Emma. 'Say thank you to Elizabeth. And my name's Emma, by the way.'

'Yes, miss.'

As the bewildered child ran to join the other new juniors, Emma turned to Elizabeth with a gentle laugh. How pretty she looked when she laughed! thought Elizabeth. And how clever of her to have memorized the boy's name already. There were so many new ones this term.

'Well spotted, Elizabeth,' she said. 'I think we're all going to have to keep a motherly eye on Rupert. He's rather young for his age.'

'He thinks you're a teacher, Emma!'

'He'll soon find out that I'm just an ordinary pupil, like him,' laughed the senior girl.

Elizabeth gave Joan a meaningful glance.

They disembarked.

'I very much hope that Emma won't be an ordinary pupil for much longer!' she said. 'Don't you, Joan?'

'Yes, she's certainly got my vote!' agreed Joan.

'I can't understand why Jenny thinks Nora might be better!' complained Elizabeth.

To their delight, the two friends found that they had been put in Room 14. And they were sharing with Jenny and Kathleen.

'What a lovely sunny room!' exclaimed Elizabeth. She ran to the window. 'And look at the view! We can see right across the grounds. Does anybody want this bed in the corner, or can I have it?'

'I like this one by the door,' said Kathleen.

'And I'm happy with this one by the window,' said Jenny good-naturedly.

The four girls went off to the bathrooms to wash and tidy up before dinner. When they got back to Room 14, they found their luggage waiting for them. It had been brought up from the coach.

'What's in your tuck-box. Elizabeth?' asked Kathleen, hungrily. 'Let's see!'

Elizabeth showed them the big chocolate cake that she'd brought from home, to be shared out at teatime.

'I know I'll be starving again by then!' she said happily. 'I'm going to practise my table tennis this afternoon, after we've unpacked. If I can find someone to practise with!'

Second formers were eligible to play table tennis and

to be chosen for school teams. Elizabeth had always loved the game and she knew she was good at it. She was pleased that she was old enough now to play it at Whyteleafe. She was longing to make one of the teams and play matches against other schools.

As they all looked in each other's tuck-boxes, the four girls got hungrier and hungrier.

'That strawberry cake, Joan!' sighed Elizabeth. 'It's almost unbearable to look at it.'

'Mummy and I made it together,' said Joan proudly.

Luckily, before they could be tempted further, the dinner-bell went.

'Hooray!'

In fact, it was the second dinner-bell. They had somehow missed hearing the first one.

The girls raced downstairs to the dining-hall, quickly realizing that everybody else was already inside. Dinner was always served late on the first day of term, to allow time for all the pupils to get back. This made the boys and girls very hungry indeed. They knew there would be an extra special meal today, with plenty of delicious meat and gravy and fresh vegetables from the school gardens. No wonder all the other pupils had got there early.

'What kept you?' frowned Julian. There was a strange look on his face.

He had saved Elizabeth and Joan places at a big table by the window.

'What's the matter with you, Julian?' laughed Elizabeth. 'We didn't hear the first bell, that's all.'

But she quickly realized that there was something unusual afoot. All their classmates were in a huddle round the table, talking in low voices. Julian's cousin Patrick kept looking round, as though expecting something.

It wasn't just happening at their table, either. An air of expectancy hung all around the dining-hall.

'Whatever's going on, Julian?' she asked.

'I've had a horrible shock, Elizabeth.' There was still that funny expression on Julian's face. 'You and Joan are going to get one, too. You'll never guess in a thousand years!'

'Sssh!' said Patrick, rather bossily. 'Keep your voices down! You know we've been told not to make a fuss. Mr Leslie says we are all to behave perfectly normally.'

'Just because somebody's famous, they don't want to be stared and gawped at,' said Arabella, primly. In fact her hands were shaking slightly as she folded her napkin. She seemed hardly able to control her excitement. 'Mr Leslie's just been over to our table and had a word with us about it.'

# A GRAND ENTRANCE

'Famous?' asked Elizabeth. She settled down in her seat between Julian and Joan. 'What's being famous got to do with anything, Julian?'

'Look for yourself, Elizabeth,' he muttered, as the doors swung open. 'Look who's here!'

The three friends were facing the swing doors. They had a perfect view as an elegant figure swept into the dining-hall, her golden hair brushed to a gleaming halo, her smile radiant. It was a grand entrance. Miss Belle and Miss Best, the joint headmistresses, bustled the girl quickly across to the senior pupils' table. A boy called Paul was already on his feet, pulling out a chair for her.

All round the dining-hall, conversation ceased.

The clatter of knives and forks was stilled.

'What's *she* doing here?' whispered Elizabeth, indignantly. 'And whatever does she think she's doing wearing our school uniform? I don't understand!'

It was Kerry Dane.

## CHAPTER FOUR

# ELIZABETH SHOWS RESTRAINT

'ELIZABETH, CAN'T you guess?' asked Julian. He tried not to laugh. The expression on Elizabeth's face was really comical!

The chatter in the dining-hall had suddenly resumed, on a rather forced note, as the children remembered that they were supposed to take no notice of the new arrival and on no account to be rude and stare! It was a tall order but they were managing it well, even the younger ones. Two exceptions, at the second form table, were Patrick and Arabella. In spite of their fine words, they had actually swivelled round to get a better look. Patrick's eyes were almost out on stalks.

Elizabeth lowered her gaze and busily piled vegetables on to her plate. She was trying to collect her thoughts. What an astonishing turn of events! For a moment, in her bewilderment, she'd wondered if a scene for some new film was being shot at Whyteleafe School. But a quick glance towards the seniors' table showed no sign of cameras, or cameramen, or special lighting . . . It was every bit a real-life happening.

Kerry Dane, golden-haired, elegant in a brand new Whyteleafe uniform, was sitting with the other seniors, chatting, smiling, making friends . . .

'She's a new senior pupil, Elizabeth, that's what!' Julian was whispering. 'I'm very much afraid she's come to Whyteleafe! She must have been in that taxi which passed us. She must have been somewhere on our train.'

'So *that's* why she was in such a rush this morning!' realized Joan, with a slight gasp. She, like Elizabeth, could hardly believe her eyes. The vision from the silver screen, the girl they had queued up to meet in London that morning, who had turned out to be such a disappointment, was sitting in this very dining-hall. She was now a member of their school. 'She had to catch the train. The same train as us!'

Elizabeth glowered.

'Just look at her now!' She tossed her curls in the direction of the senior table. Kerry was talking animatedly to her new friends. 'If only they knew what she's really like!'

Julian grinned. He hissed from behind his hand:

'She'd have a surprise if she knew where those flowers were now!'

'Not as big a surprise as Mummy must have had when Daddy brought them home! Mummy does love flowers so!' replied Elizabeth, cheering up.

# ELIZABETH SHOWS RESTRAINT

The three friends started to laugh.

'Hey, pass the roast potatoes please, Elizabeth.' That was Harry's voice. 'What are you three laughing and whispering about?'

'Oh, nothing!' Elizabeth said quickly.

'Isn't it wonderful that she's decided to come here?' Belinda was exclaiming. 'Of all the boarding-schools her parents could have chosen, they chose Whyteleafe. I feel so proud.'

'It's going to be good for the school,' chimed in Kathleen, her rosy cheeks dimpling. 'And she's so nice. Wasn't she good in that film? Did you see it, Elizabeth?'

'Yes,' replied Elizabeth, at the same time giving both Julian and Joan a warning nudge.

Her feelings were still very raw. So far, the three friends had kept quiet about their adventure. And Elizabeth wanted to keep it that way. She wasn't going to tell her classmates about the humiliating episode in London. It had been such a horrible experience, asking Kerry Dane for an autograph!

But there was something else, too.

She knew that if she didn't guard her tongue carefully she would soon be rude about Kerry Dane. And they would think her very catty. At the moment, everybody believed that Kerry must be like Zara in the film. Elizabeth had believed that herself. They would find out soon enough, but this, reasoned Elizabeth, was hardly a good time to start upsetting her classmates. They were planning to elect her as a monitor at the end of the week!

'So what did you think, Elizabeth?' pressed Kathleen.

'She's a very good actress,' replied Elizabeth. 'Brilliant, I'd say.'

Julian was amused.

It was not often that the Naughtiest Girl showed such restraint. She really *was* on her best behaviour. She must want to be a second form monitor very badly!

After dinner, as soon as the three friends came out of the hall, Elizabeth gave full vent to her feelings.

'I don't feel in the least bit proud that she's come to Whyteleafe!' she declared. 'I wish she hadn't bothered! Why didn't she want to stay on at her London school? After all, she must be in the middle of studying for her certificate. It's a funny time to change schools.'

'Why go back to school at all, after you've been in a film and become famous?' wondered Joan. 'You'd think she'd want to leave school now and try to be a full-time actress.'

'Perhaps she's not quite old enough to leave school,' Elizabeth pointed out. 'Or perhaps her parents think she should take her exams first.'

'But why Whyteleafe?' mused Julian, pushing his

untidy black fringe back. He was puzzled. 'Why not some big famous school somewhere, with its own theatre and all that sort of thing. Somewhere really posh. We're only a small school, buried away in the countryside!'

Elizabeth thought this over carefully. As far as she was concerned, Whyteleafe was the best school in the whole world. But it was a fair point.

'You're right, Julian. Somehow Kerry Dane and Whyteleafe School just don't go together.'

'Perhaps she wants to be a big fish in a small pond?' suggested Joan, gently.

'She certainly wants to be noticed,' said Julian, shrewdly. 'That warning from Mr Leslie about how she wants to be treated like any other pupil and not made a fuss of . . . Really! So why didn't she just slip quietly into the dining-hall at the same time as the other seniors?'

'Yes! Why didn't she? Instead of making a grand entrance!' Elizabeth could feel a temper coming on. 'She wants to be the centre of attention, all right. She doesn't belong here. I'm longing for everyone to find out how horrible she is and then perhaps she'll go away again!'

'But we must let them find out for themselves, Elizabeth,' said Joan, quietly. 'You've decided that, haven't you? At the moment I don't think anyone would believe us if we told them what she's really like.'

'Don't worry, Joan.' Elizabeth linked arms with her friend. She had instantly calmed down. 'I know I mustn't lose my temper or say anything silly. But I've just thought of something – you don't think she might recognize me, do you? That would be a bit awkward!'

'She won't recognize *any* of us,' declared Julian, who had been thinking about it. 'We were wearing raincoats over our school uniform. There was nothing to connect us with Whyteleafe at all. And she certainly wouldn't recognize *you*, Elizabeth. Your hair was all plastered down by the rain. As a matter of fact, you looked a sight! Anyway, she didn't even bother to look at you.'

'Thank you, Julian,' said Elizabeth. What a mean, horrid person the girl was. Oh, her lovely autograph book! All spoiled now.

But she felt relieved, all the same. She had to make sure that she continued to keep her temper. It would make life very much simpler if Kerry Dane did not recognize her.

'I still find it odd, her coming to Whyteleafe, though,' mused Julian. 'You put it exactly, Elizabeth. She doesn't belong. Whyteleafe and Kerry Dane just don't mix. But now,' he continued airily, 'let's forget all about her, shall we? There's Harry looking for me. Isn't it time we all went and unpacked?'

'It certainly is,' agreed Joan. 'Come on, Elizabeth.'

Elizabeth needed no second bidding. Kerry Dane or no Kerry Dane, she was going to get on with her life! She was a second former now. She had a lovely new room. She was longing to get her things out of her trunk and arrange them just how she wanted. After that, she would go and practise her table tennis and work up an appetite for tea.

Her mouth watered at the thought of the delicious chocolate cake in her tuck-box.

And Kathleen had some excellent news for them.

It was to do with the choosing of the new heads of school.

## CHAPTER FIVE

# JULIAN IS PUZZLED ABOUT SOMETHING ELSE

'YOU'LL BE pleased when you hear my news, Elizabeth,' said Kathleen, as she came into Room 14. 'I've been talking to some of the seniors and looking at the notice-board.'

Joan smiled gently.

'I don't want to sound too monitor-ish, Kathleen, but you should have been up here unpacking. You know it's all got to be done by three o'clock.'

'Sorry, Joan!'

Jenny had unpacked her trunk already and left the room. Elizabeth and Joan had almost finished. Elizabeth was standing back and admiring the way she had arranged her ornaments and photograph frames. It was very satisfying to have been given a much larger chest of drawers this year and to be allowed to put extra things on top. How glad she was to be a second former now.

'What news, Kathleen?' she asked.

# JULIAN IS PUZZLED ABOUT SOMETHING ELSE

'It looks as though your wish is going to come true, Elizabeth,' smiled the rosy-cheeked girl. 'You know, what we were discussing on the train. It looks very likely that Thomas and Emma will be the new head boy and head girl.'

'How do you know?' Elizabeth asked eagerly.

She and Joan exchanged delighted looks.

'There's a notice up about it!' explained Kathleen. 'And their names have been written up there. Some of the seniors are backing them. And there are no other names up at all!'

Elizabeth clapped her hands with pleasure.

They'd all been sure that Thomas would be made head boy. But – how pleasing – some of the top class agreed with her about Emma!

'Great minds think alike!' she said, gleefully. 'Oh, I think Emma's going to make a very fine head girl.'

'So we may not even need an election then!' said Joan, happily. 'If no more names are put up Thomas and Emma will just be appointed the new head boy and girl on Saturday and take the first Meeting.'

Now that William and Rita had left, Joan could think of no two nicer heads. As a monitor, she was looking forward to working with them and helping them in the running of the school.

And so was Elizabeth.

Knowing that she was going to be chosen as a monitor at the Meeting, she could hardly wait for Saturday to arrive.

She hummed happily to herself as she looked for her table-tennis bat. She would go and take a look at that notice herself sometime!

'And there are no other names up, Kathleen?' she asked. 'You're sure?'

'Quite sure!' laughed Kathleen.

Elizabeth spent the afternoon practising her table tennis. She had three quite even games with Patrick and then a long session with Harry. She found that she was able to beat Harry easily!

By the end, he was quite out of breath. A few people had gathered to watch them.

'I'm going off to have a shower now!' he told Elizabeth, as he left. 'You're a great player, though. I'm really impressed.'

'I'm impressed, too,' said a quiet voice.

A senior girl had stepped forward. Elizabeth spun round to see who had spoken. It was Emma!

'I think you might be school team material, Elizabeth,' she said. 'I'm running some coaching sessions this term. Would you like to put your name down?'

'Oh, I'd love to!' replied Elizabeth eagerly, hardly able to believe her ears. 'Thank you, Emma.'

# JULIAN IS PUZZLED ABOUT SOMETHING ELSE

'If you come with me, I'll show you the list.'

The senior girl led Elizabeth along to the main school notice-board. Proudly she signed up for the table-tennis coaching sessions.

'Oh, good. The first one's tomorrow!' she exclaimed.

But she realized that Emma was staring rather dreamily at the notice next to it. She followed Emma's gaze.

There it was, just as Kathleen had said:

## APPOINTMENT OF HEAD BOY AND HEAD GIRL

Pupils in the second form and above may propose names. Please write the candidate's name in block capitals, with the name of the proposer in brackets. *Do not put anyone's name forward unless you have first obtained their permission.* IF MORE THAN ONE NAME IS PUT FORWARD FOR EITHER POST, AN ELECTION WILL TAKE PLACE ON SATURDAY IN TIME FOR THE FIRST MEETING OF TERM.

The notice was signed by Miss Belle and Miss Best, the joint headmistresses of Whyteleafe School. There were only two names entered:

# THE NAUGHTIEST GIRL WANTS TO WIN

## EMMA GLOVER [John Terry]
## THOMAS HILL [Philippa Dearing]

Elizabeth smiled.

'Some of us were really hoping you might be made head girl!' she blurted out. 'With Thomas as head boy! It's really good that it seems to be all decided!'

'Oh, I wouldn't say that, Elizabeth,' replied Emma lightly, a flush coming to her cheeks. She was feeling very excited but was trying her best to hide it. 'I was very honoured when John and some of the others asked me if I would allow my name to go forward. But there's plenty of time for other names yet. There may have to be an election.'

'I'm sure there won't be!' said Elizabeth, confidently. 'Everybody in the school respects John and Philippa's opinions. I shouldn't think anyone would want to go against them. I know I certainly shan't.'

'Thank you, Elizabeth,' said Emma. 'And I'll see you tomorrow, then? I think I can help you a bit with that service.'

Feeling extremely pleased with life, Elizabeth went off to find John Terry. He was one of her favourite people at Whyteleafe. He was in charge of the school gardens and she knew that was where she would find him.

## JULIAN IS PUZZLED ABOUT SOMETHING ELSE

'Hello, Elizabeth!' he greeted her. He straightened up, trowel in hand. 'Look at what all the weeds have been doing while we've been away! Happy to be back, then?'

'Very!' said Elizabeth. 'And even happier that you've persuaded Emma to stand as head girl. Won't she make a fine one?'

'Some of us think so,' he said.

'Only some of you?' asked Elizabeth.

'Well, there are those that are worried that she's not forceful enough. I don't agree with them.'

'Nor do I!' said Elizabeth.

'But a few of them *are* worried.'

'Like Jenny then,' laughed Elizabeth. 'She says the same thing. But it's silly, isn't it?'

John nodded, wisely, and returned to his weeding.

At teatime, Elizabeth was told that Jenny had gone along to see Nora. She had gone to ask her permission to put her name forward as head girl.

'What did she say?' asked Elizabeth, when Jenny appeared.

'She refused,' said Jenny, with a sigh. 'She said she doesn't feel she can stand in Emma's way. Isn't that noble of her? Now I don't suppose there will be an election at all. It might have been fun. I was looking forward to it!'

161

'Well, never mind, Jenny,' said Elizabeth. 'She would have lost anyway. Want a piece of chocolate cake? Doesn't it look scrumptious?'

Teatime on the first day back was always very enjoyable. The children were permitted to bring their tuck-boxes to the dining-hall and share some of the good things that they'd brought from home. They were allowed to go and chat to people at other tables. There was quite an informal atmosphere on the first day of term.

'Kerry Dane was with Nora when I went to see her,' Jenny confided, watching hungrily as Elizabeth divided up the cake. 'They seem to be quite friendly. She's really nice, you know. She's *just* like Zara in the film. She asked me all about myself.'

'Yes, everybody's saying how nice she is!' agreed Belinda.

'Hurry up with that cake, Elizabeth!' said Julian. He had been out all afternoon, helping Robert with the school ponies. 'It looks very good.'

'Wait a minute, Julian!' scolded Elizabeth. She had counted the number of children at the table. She wanted them each to have a piece. 'I'm trying to get the slices all exactly the same size.'

While completing this task, Elizabeth became aware of a sudden buzz of excitement around the table.

# JULIAN IS PUZZLED ABOUT SOMETHING ELSE

She looked up, quickly.

Kerry Dane had just strolled into the dining-hall, arm in arm with Nora. They were heading this way! Kerry was giving Jenny a friendly little wave.

'Hello, Jenny!' she said, as she reached the table. 'You promised to introduce me to some of the second formers. So here I am!'

There was a moment's awestruck silence. The radiant, golden-haired 'Zara' was in their midst! For a split second, Elizabeth herself was affected by it. Even without make-up, and wearing just an ordinary Whyteleafe uniform, Kerry Dane had a mesmerizing presence. She really did have star quality.

'What a lovely spread!' she said as she gazed round at the open tuck-boxes. 'Nobody told me that we could bring things in. I haven't got a tuck-box!' she added, screwing up her eyes and pretending to sob. 'Why didn't anybody tell me?'

The children laughed. The young star certainly knew how to put them at their ease! Soon they were all talking at once, introducing themselves. Jenny, flushed with pride at the unexpected visit, offered Kerry some shortbread.

'Do you like popcorn?' Patrick was asking eagerly.

But now Kerry had turned and walked over to Elizabeth.

Elizabeth froze, her head lowered as she pretended to divide up the cake, though in fact the task was complete. She drew in a sharp breath.

The moment had come. Would Kerry Dane recognize her?

'Hello!' Kerry was saying. 'Nora tells me you're Elizabeth, otherwise known as the Naughtiest Girl in the school.' She gave a friendly little laugh. 'But that you're really one of our best pupils. A completely reformed character!'

Steeling herself, Elizabeth looked up and met Kerry's gaze full on. But she need not have worried. Julian's surmise had been correct.

There was not a flicker of recognition.

Kerry had no idea that the two of them had met that morning, in such very different circumstances! Already her gaze was falling from Elizabeth's face to her real interest – the lovely big chocolate cake. And her mouth was watering.

'How do you do,' said Elizabeth politely.

'I would do very well with a piece of that gorgeous cake. I'm afraid chocolate is my great weakness!' replied the star, sweetly. 'Can you spare a piece?'

She was looking full into Elizabeth's eyes again, willing her to agree. In the electric silence between them, Elizabeth could feel the invisible force of that will. Kerry Dane wanted a piece of the chocolate cake. And whatever Kerry Dane wanted, must be given to her.

'I'm sorry,' Elizabeth replied, meeting that fierce gaze. 'I'm afraid it's all spoken for.'

For a fraction of a second, a cold hardness crossed Kerry's face, the exact look that Elizabeth had seen before. For that brief moment, the mask slipped and the real Kerry Dane showed through.

'Oh, Elizabeth, how mean!' Arabella was exclaiming. 'You can have my piece, Kerry—'

'No, have mine,' Patrick added.

'No, mine!' said Martin.

As some of the boys and girls clamoured for the privilege of giving up their slice of chocolate cake, Kerry turned and faced them, at her most charming once again.

'I wouldn't dream of letting any of you give me your cake!' she smiled. 'How silly of me to ask! Really greedy of me. Nora will take me over to our own table and we'll see what's on offer there! But before we go—'

She looked directly at Jenny.

'There's something Nora wants to say to you, Jenny. I think you're going to be pleased.'

Elizabeth, Joan and Julian exchanged surprised looks. For the first time they realized that Nora, usually a calm, sensible person, had a rather silly, over-excited expression on her face.

'If you really think I would make a good head girl, Jenny,' said Nora, her cheeks flushed, 'then I will let my name go forward, after all. I might as well.'

'Oh, good!' exclaimed Jenny, although she was rather taken aback. Less than ten minutes earlier, Nora had been so definite about not standing. 'I'm so pleased, Nora. I'll go and put your name up after tea. Oh, what fun! We'll be able to have a proper election now.'

'Always the fairest way,' smiled Kerry Dane. 'I do think Nora's made the right decision. She's told me how important the post is. The more candidates the better! May the best girl win!' she added lightly.

Elizabeth ground her teeth.

'I hate her!' she said to Julian and Joan, later. 'What does she know about our school? It's not a bit fair of her to flatter poor Nora like that.'

'Yes,' agreed Joan. 'I think you're right and that's what's happened. She must have talked Nora into standing. Against her better judgement.'

'And she's bound to get beaten,' nodded Elizabeth. 'If any of the seniors really wanted Nora, they would have put her name up themselves. It's obvious they've decided they want Emma.'

'But it's not just the seniors who vote,' Julian pointed

out. 'I think we should run an election campaign for Emma, don't you? Just to help her on her way!'

'Oh, Julian, what an excellent idea!' exclaimed Elizabeth. 'We can make a banner. And we can get Belinda to do some posters. She's good at art!'

'I think your idea's a very good one, Julian,' said Joan, after due thought. 'The whole school is so taken in by Kerry Dane, the very fact that she approves of there being an election will tend to bring Nora a few votes. We must do all we can to help Emma.'

'The whole school won't be taken in much longer!' declared Elizabeth, confidently. She was feeling cheerful again. 'Kerry Dane won't be able to keep up her act of being like Zara in the film for ever! Did you see the way the mask slipped when I wouldn't give her any chocolate cake? Greedy pig! Did you see the look she gave me?'

'Well, no, she had her back to the rest of us,' said Julian, looking amused. 'I can imagine it, though! But I was right about her not recognizing you, wasn't I, Elizabeth?'

'Yes, Julian!' laughed Elizabeth. 'You were right as usual!'

The three friends set off for the art and crafts room, eager to start the preparations for Emma's election campaign.

As they walked along, Julian dug his hands in his

pockets, deep in thought. He was frowning slightly.

'There's something that puzzles me about Kerry Dane.'

'You mean, why she's come to a little school like ours?' asked Elizabeth. 'Yes, it is puzzling.'

'Well, that, of course. But something else. Why should she work on Nora and get her to stand for head girl?'

'Well, she's probably jealous of Emma for being so nice,' volunteered Joan.

'But if you ask me,' said Julian, darkly. 'What she'd *really* like is to be head girl herself.'

The two girls looked at Julian in surprise.

'She's new. She can't be!' exclaimed Elizabeth. 'Oh, Julian, what a ridiculous idea!'

## CHAPTER SIX

# THE NAUGHTIEST GIRL WANTS TO WIN

'GOOD MORNING, children,' said Mr Leslie, the next day, 'and welcome to the second form all of you who have come up this term. Please find yourselves a desk and get settled down. Then I'll give out the new timetable.'

Elizabeth stared round her new form room with pleasure. It was large and airy with windows on two sides. Those pupils already in the second form, like Joan and Jake and Howard, were seated back at their old desks. The rest of them, from the first form, had to find their own.

'Can we really sit anywhere we like, Joan?' whispered Elizabeth, making straight for the empty desk next to her friend's. 'When I first arrived in the first form we had to remain standing until Miss Ranger told us where to go.'

'You're a second former now, Elizabeth!' laughed Joan.

Elizabeth felt very pleased as she settled down next to Joan. Carefully she stacked her books in her desk. It was true. She really *was* in the second form at last. And very soon now – after this week's Meeting – she would be a second form monitor!

She was going to enjoy having Mr Leslie as her class teacher, although she would miss Miss Ranger, of course. She was also going to enjoy having a new timetable and learning new things. But most of all she was going to enjoy the Meetings and being a monitor with Joan. They would sit on the platform each week, as second form representatives, with all the other monitors. They would sit in a row, just behind the new head boy and girl.

Whyteleafe was a very unusual school. It was largely governed by the children themselves. The weekly Meetings were like a school parliament, where problems were discussed and grievances aired. When any cases of wrong doing were reported to the Meeting it then became more like a court, with the monitors as the Jury and the head boy and girl as the Judges. Miss Belle and Miss Best, the joint headmistresses, sat in on the Meetings, together with Mr Johns, the senior master, but they were mere observers. It was left to the pupils themselves to decide how things should be dealt with.

And Thomas was going to make an excellent head

boy, Elizabeth felt. He could be relied upon to be totally fair, as William had been. Emma would be just the same, as head girl; she was truly worthy to step into Rita's shoes. Oh, they must make absolutely certain that it was Emma who became head girl, now there was to be an election!

'You are not to lose your new timetables,' said Mr Leslie, as Joan handed them round the class. 'There's just one each and none left over!'

Elizabeth stuck hers down inside the front cover of her rough book. She studied it carefully. They were going to have more science lessons this year, with Mr Leslie. And more French with Mam'zelle. There were to be more games lessons, too. And they would still have Miss Ranger for English. Good! She would be able to choose between various outdoor sports this term. And on rainy days they'd be allowed, during games lessons, to play either chess or table tennis.

'Table tennis. Hurray!' thought Elizabeth. 'I do hope I get in a team!'

After school today Emma would be holding the first coaching session. Elizabeth was looking forward to it eagerly.

But, before that, there was something else to look forward to.

The three friends had been very busy in the craft

room last night. They had made a beautiful banner. Julian had fixed it to a light wooden frame, so that someone could hold it aloft and march along with it.

At dinner-time, the election campaign could begin in earnest. And so it did.

'Roll up, roll up!' shouted Julian, his hands cupped to his mouth. 'Join on the end if you support us. Roll up! Roll up!'

Julian stood by the open doors as boys and girls emerged from dinner. He was shouting encouragement.

It was a merry sight, as the Naughtiest Girl came marching on to the scene.

Elizabeth was striding this way, holding aloft a bright banner. It said:

## VOTE FOR EMMA
## EMMA FOR HEAD GIRL!

With Harry banging a toy drum beside her and Joan just behind, they began to parade round the big sunny lawn. From the second form, Belinda and Kathleen quickly joined on. Then a gaggle of excited juniors, who all adored Emma, tagged on behind. They started singing at the tops of their voices: 'Roll up! Roll up for Emma . . . !'

Each time Elizabeth circled the lawn, the procession

grew longer. Soon there were more than twenty pupils in the parade, while others stood round applauding. Some of them were seniors, like John Terry and Philippa Dearing. It was beneath their dignity to join the parade but they were happy to clap and cheer.

'Well done, Elizabeth!' John Terry called out, each time she marched past him.

When the bell went for afternoon lessons, Elizabeth and Julian returned the banner to a cupboard in the craft room.

'Wasn't that good, Julian!' said Elizabeth, her face flushed with excitement.

'Very!' His eyes glinted with amusement. 'Pity some of them aren't old enough to vote. But we've made a grand start!'

'We must do it every day until the election,' vowed Elizabeth. 'I'll ask Sophie to play the flute tomorrow! We'll remind people every day who they should vote for! And Belinda's promised to make posters later today.'

After school, Elizabeth collected her table-tennis bat and hurried to the coaching session. She was the first to arrive.

'I saw your parade at dinner-time,' confessed Emma. She looked very pleased, if slightly embarrassed. 'Elizabeth, I was very touched.'

'Nora hasn't got a chance!' replied Elizabeth, in her usual forthright way. 'We respect her but most of us think she's a bit too bossy to be head girl!'

Emma quickly turned to hide a smile. And just at that moment, several other children arrived – including Julian's cousin, Patrick.

'Hello, Elizabeth,' he said, in surprise. 'I didn't know you'd put your name down for coaching.'

'Emma suggested it,' replied Elizabeth, sweetly.

Patrick frowned. He couldn't help liking Elizabeth but he was very competitive. It would be rather annoying if a girl – and especially the Naughtiest Girl – managed to bag a place in the table-tennis team ahead of him. Emma clapped her hands.

'Right, everyone. First of all, I'm going to go through Elizabeth's service action with her. She needs some help with it. I want you all to gather round the table and watch, in case there are some tips for the rest of you.'

By the end of the session, Elizabeth's service action had already improved. In spite of the fact that Emma had helped him with his forehand smash, Patrick was annoyed when Elizabeth managed to beat him 21–18 in a practice game.

'No wonder you want Emma to be head girl,' he said, as they went off to tea.

'Patrick! How dare you? She helped us all equally!'

'Sorry! Sorry!' he said quickly, seeing the tempestuous look in Elizabeth's eye. 'Only joking.'

'I should think so,' replied Elizabeth. 'But honestly, Patrick, who else *could* be head girl? Aren't you going to vote for her yourself?'

'I don't know yet. I'm not sure that she's got enough presence. But then I don't think Nora's quite right, either.'

'She's quite wrong!' replied Elizabeth witheringly.

After tea, Elizabeth helped Belinda put up her little posters round the school. She thought they were very effective. Written in large letters, in brightly-coloured crayons, were some simple slogans.

X
VOTE ON SATURDAY
X EMMA X

DON'T FORGET
XX EMMA XX

EMMA FOR HEAD
USE YOUR VOTE
X

'They're really eye-catching, Belinda,' said Elizabeth admiringly, as they fixed one to the door of the third form common room. 'Everybody's going to notice them!' She gave a little sigh. 'But I do wish Jenny hadn't put Nora's name forward. It's unsettling, somehow, though she can't possibly win.'

'I agree,' replied Belinda. She surveyed her handiwork, feeling quite pleased with it. 'None of the boys wants to stand against Thomas. It's just taken for granted that he's going to be head boy. But now Nora's standing against Emma, it's sort of raised doubts in people's minds. It's started lots of discussion and made them worry whether Emma will be forceful enough, even though they don't think Nora's right.'

'Yes,' said Elizabeth, 'it would have been better if Emma could have been elected unopposed. But as Jenny told me last night, nobody's got an exclusive right to be head girl and they shouldn't be frightened of an election. It's a fair point. We've just got to make sure that Emma gets a huge vote on Saturday. On her merits! I'm sure she will! As a matter of fact, Belinda, I'm quite enjoying this election campaign.'

'Yes, it's fun!'

Going upstairs, at bedtime, Elizabeth smiled as she saw some tiny notices on doors. They were written in Jenny's handwriting. They said simply VOTE FOR NORA. She thought they looked rather feeble, compared with Belinda's efforts.

And when she got to Room 14, she found Jenny in a chastened mood.

'I'm not getting a lot of support for Nora,' she confessed, as the girls sipped their bedtime cocoa. 'I'm sure Kerry will vote for her and one or two other seniors. But I think she may only get about twenty votes altogether.'

'Serves you right, Jenny!' laughed Elizabeth.

Joan was gentler about it.

'Poor Jenny,' she said to Elizabeth, when they went with Kathleen to clean their teeth.

'And poor Nora!' added Kathleen.

'Yes,' agreed Elizabeth. *And it's all Kerry Dane's fault for interfering. What does she know about Whyteleafe School?*

Elizabeth was longing for Kerry's mask to crack, for the rest of the school to see the young actress in her true colours. Only then could she tell her classmates about the adventure that she, Joan and Julian had had in London. And how the three of them had known all along that she was not nearly as nice as she seemed. That she was, in fact, perfectly horrid.

But three whole days passed by.

And, by Friday evening, Elizabeth was getting impatient.

'I don't know how Kerry Dane's managing to keep it up!' she complained to Julian, as they came indoors together after a ride on the ponies. 'She's so nice to everybody all the time, especially the older forms. Everybody thinks they're getting to know her properly. They keep saying she's even nicer than the part she played in the film. Really!'

'Yes. I hear she's offered to do something for the Earthquake Bazaar!' observed Julian. 'You know, the sale that the seniors are going to hold, to raise money for the earthquake victims. She's running the sweet stall, or something. Arabella's been making some fudge for it.'

'I know,' said Elizabeth, grinding her teeth. '*And* she's offered to get someone important from the film world to come and open it. Everybody thinks she's marvellous! How *does* she keep it up? It must be a terrible strain for her. I simply can't think why she bothers.'

'Hallo!' said Julian suddenly, as he looked down the corridor. 'What's going on? There's quite a crowd round the notice-board.'

Elizabeth and Julian hurried over and pressed forward to get a good look. There was a buzz of excited chatter all around them. Everybody was gazing at the election list for head boy and girl.

Miss Belle and Miss Best would be taking the notice down tonight. But another name had been added, at the last moment!

A third nomination for head girl had been added to the list. The name was written clearly, in a senior boy's bold handwriting:

KERRY DANE [Paul Kirk]

Elizabeth backed away from the notice-board, laughing out loud in shock.

Julian whistled to himself.

'There's your answer, Elizabeth,' he said. 'All is explained.'

## CHAPTER SEVEN

# A VERY CLOSE RESULT

ELIZABETH LISTENED to the babble of voices all around her. Everyone seemed to be talking at once. There were many conflicting opinions.

'Paul persuaded her! She shouldn't have listened to him!'

'She didn't really want to stand. She says she's too new.'

'And she is. Much too new! If she'd been here a while, and been a monitor, I'd definitely vote for her. She'd make a marvellous head girl. But—'

'But why not? Paul says the important thing is just to get the very best person. If people were so sure about Emma, why would Nora bother to stand?'

'Yes! And seeing there's going to be an election *anyway* . . .'

'I say, wouldn't Hickling Green be envious if we had Kerry Dane for head girl! They're such a lot of stuck-up snobs! And you know, I can just see her on the platform, taking the Meetings with Thomas. She's got such presence!'

'Yes, she has. But it wouldn't be right – it's got to be a real Whyteleafean. It's got to be Emma or Nora.'

'I agree with you, Candida!'

'Yes! I'll be voting for one of the old stagers.'

'Me, too. Emma, in fact . . .'

'But she *would* have made a marvellous head girl.'

Elizabeth and Julian walked away.

'*A marvellous head girl?*' exploded Elizabeth. 'She'd be a disaster! Oh, Julian, do you think she's been planning this?'

'I'm sure she has,' frowned Julian. 'From the moment she saw the chance to provoke an election and unsettle things. What a schemer!'

'Julian, you don't think . . .' The idea filled Elizabeth with horror. 'You don't think there are enough people who'd be *silly* enough . . . to get sort of carried away and vote for her on the spur of the moment? So that she ends up being elected?'

It was like looking into the abyss.

'There'll be some,' said Julian, thoughtfully. 'But not a majority, I'm quite sure. You heard what everyone was saying. Most people feel strongly that she's much too new. They may be dazzled by her but they are going to vote for Emma or Nora.'

'Good! Then we've got to make sure it's Emma!' said Elizabeth fervently. 'Let's have one last parade tomorrow, Julian. The best parade yet! Straight after breakfast. Just before the election!'

Voting was at ten the next morning. The school Meeting would follow at eleven.

At bedtime, Jenny looked unhappy.

'I am surprised,' she said, 'that Kerry's allowed her own name to go forward! She came to talk to me about it. She said she didn't want it to happen but other people were insisting. And, after what she'd said to me about Nora standing, she couldn't really refuse, could she? But she told me not to worry. She's promised to vote for Nora herself, and she's going to tell everyone she meets to vote for Nora, as well! Isn't that sweet of her?'

Elizabeth didn't believe a word of it. But out loud she said, 'So what's the matter, then?'

'Oh, nothing!' Jenny replied quickly.

Jenny was too proud to admit to Elizabeth that Kerry Dane had forgotten her name already. She'd kept calling her Jane! It had left Jenny feeling rather uneasy. There was something odd about the whole thing but she couldn't quite put her finger on what it was.

Saturday morning dawned bright and sunny. The election campaign for Emma reached its climax. Elizabeth organized the final parade with great flair. Sophie came with her flute and all the juniors brought tambourines. And Richard agreed to strum his guitar! For the last hour before the voting began, Elizabeth marched her band around and around the outside of the school buildings, holding the banner aloft.

Each time they passed below dormitory windows, Harry banged the drum and Julian shouted, 'Wake up! Wake up! Don't forget to come and vote!'

And the juniors chorused, 'VOTE FOR EMMA! VOTE FOR EMMA! ROLL UP, ROLL UP AND VOTE FOR EMMA!'

Cheerful faces appeared at windows. There were smiles and waves.

Elizabeth found the whole thing very exhilarating. Afterwards, she said, 'I'm sure Emma's going to win, Joan. I just feel it in my bones!'

'Let's hope so,' replied Joan gently. 'At least there should be a good turnout now! Come on, Elizabeth. We mustn't forget to cast our *own* votes. It's nearly ten o'clock.'

Miss Belle and Miss Best were in charge of the election, which took place in the dining-hall.

As Elizabeth joined the queue of people waiting to cast their vote, her confidence grew. What an excellent turnout! If most of these people were voting for Emma, then Kerry Dane was in for a big disappointment.

When she reached the head of the queue, Miss Belle

ticked her name off a list and Miss Best handed her a voting paper. Elizabeth then walked through to a special table, picked up one of the pencils there and firmly marked a cross against Emma's name. As she carefully folded her ballot paper, she squinted along the table and saw that a third former was marking his cross in the same place. Good!

Under the watchful eye of the joint headmistresses, Elizabeth posted her voting slip into the big ballot box. It was a very satisfying feeling, to have cast her vote. The Beauty and the Beast, as the children called the heads, both smiled at her warmly.

'I wonder if they know I'm going to be made a monitor today?' wondered Elizabeth. 'I seem to be in their good books.'

She met up with Joan and Julian outside the hall and the three friends wandered along to their common room together. Some fourth formers, walking along the corridor ahead of them, were talking loudly.

'I was going to vote for Kerry,' one of them was saying, 'but I changed my mind this morning. Kerry persuaded me to vote for Nora. She's just so positive she'd be best!'

'Oh, how funny. She said something to me, too. She's very persuasive, isn't she! I really had to fight with myself to stick to my guns and vote for Emma.'

'Isn't it decent of her not to expect people to vote for her but to ask them to vote for Nora instead?'

The three friends heard this in some surprise.

'So it's true, then!' said Elizabeth. 'Jenny told me that Kerry had promised to campaign for Nora. I didn't believe she really would.'

'How very odd,' said Joan.

Julian said nothing. He looked worried.

'Well at least Kerry Dane can't possibly win herself now!' declared Elizabeth.

While the votes were being counted in the hall, all the boys and girls had morning break. Then they went to their rooms to get spruced up for the Meeting. Elizabeth was in a state of high excitement by now.

Kathleen came and brushed some fluff off the collar of her blazer for her. She was smiling and rosy-cheeked as usual.

'Well, the suspense will soon be over!' she said. 'I'm sure Emma will have won. And we know Thomas has, because nobody stood against him. And then we'll be able to get on with all the proper business of the Meeting. You're still quite happy about being a monitor again, Elizabeth?'

'Kathleen, need you ask!' exclaimed Elizabeth, with a happy laugh.

The Meeting had arrived at last. She was looking forward to it.

They filed into the school hall and took up their new places on the second form benches. Elizabeth sat next to Julian. Joan left them and took her place up on the platform, with the other monitors. The hall was filling up very quickly. Elizabeth glanced across to the senior benches. Emma was sitting there, next to John and Philippa. Kerry Dane was sitting beside Paul, her hair brushed to a beautiful golden sheen.

At the back of the hall sat Mr Johns and the Beauty and the Beast, as always, although they would take no part in the Meeting.

When everybody was seated, Thomas walked into the hall.

A cheer went up as the tall, fair-haired boy mounted the platform and stood behind the special head boy and girl's table. He held up his hand for silence. In his other hand, he held a piece of paper.

The election results!

A hush descended over the hall as Thomas started to speak. Elizabeth realized that she was clenching her hands into tight little fists and that her heart was beating faster than usual.

'I am very proud to be the new head boy of Whyteleafe School,' he told them, in his clear, pleasant voice. There was a deadpan expression on his face. It gave nothing away. 'And now, without further ado, I am going to read out the results of the election for our new head girl. She will then be able to take her place on the platform beside me and the business of the Meeting can commence.'

He opened up the piece of paper. Elizabeth held her breath.

'The number of votes cast for each candidate was as follows: Nora – 29 votes. Emma – 34 votes. Kerry – 35 votes.'

Elizabeth gasped. Was she having a bad dream?

Thomas was giving a signal to someone on the senior benches.

'I declare Kerry Dane the new head girl. Would you come up on to the platform, please, Kerry? And would everybody give Kerry a round of applause, please.'

The school buzzed with surprise and then began clapping.

What a close result! It could hardly have been closer. But as Kerry ran lightly up to the platform, many of the first formers and juniors looked crestfallen. They had never seen Kerry Dane's film. She was such a remote figure to them – not like Emma.

Elizabeth turned and looked at Julian in disbelief.

'It isn't possible,' she whispered, in horror.

# A VERY CLOSE RESULT

Julian was busily doing some calculations on his fingers.

'I'm afraid it is, Elizabeth,' he whispered back. 'How very clever of her. Very cunning indeed.'

Elizabeth tossed her head. She wasn't listening. She was glancing across at Emma. The senior girl was trying to smile but was fighting back the tears. It would have been such a privilege, such an honour, to serve Whyteleafe School as its head girl. She had so longed to be chosen. John Terry placed an arm round her shoulders to comfort her. There was an angry expression on his face.

Suddenly Elizabeth was incandescent with rage. Her temper boiled over.

She got to her feet.

'It's not fair! I don't know what's happened but it's not fair!' she hissed at Julian. 'I'm going!'

She marched off towards the exit.

Julian didn't hesitate. He jumped up and followed her. 'Me, too, Elizabeth,' he said, catching her up.

Trembling and upset, Joan scraped her chair back and left the platform with quiet dignity.

With Elizabeth leading the way, the three friends walked out of the Meeting.

CHAPTER EIGHT

# NEW MONITORS HAVE TO BE FOUND

'SILENCE, PLEASE, everyone,' said Thomas, banging loudly on the table with the gavel that William and Rita had always used. 'Will you settle down at once and pay attention?'

It was Thomas's first big test as head-boy. The hall was in something of an uproar. The Naughtiest Girl had marched out of the Meeting, with two of her friends! What a surprise.

Thomas could have turned to the Beauty and the Beast for advice but he had no intention of doing so. He must handle this himself. He thought hard about what William or Rita would have done. They would have handled it with a light touch. He must follow suit.

'That's better,' he smiled, as the Meeting came to order. 'I'm afraid that elections can make people very emotional sometimes, especially when the result is extremely narrow. Let us take no notice of what has happened. Elizabeth and her friends will soon calm down and come back to join us. But now I want the

Meeting to get straight down to business . . .'

However, Kerry Dane had other ideas. She was not going to be deprived of her moment of glory by those three people walking out, or by Thomas wanting to get on with the silly Meeting. She had a speech all prepared!

'First of all, I'd like to say a few words, if I may, Thomas.'

She walked forward to the very front of the platform. She felt exultant, as she stood before the assembled school, her beautiful hair making a halo of golden light around her head. It felt so right, somehow, that she, Kerry Dane, should be up here, with all those faces gazing at her. Now she was mistress of all she surveyed. This was what she was used to, ever since becoming famous. This was how it should be!

'I want to tell you all how humble I feel,' she began. 'I never, ever dreamt of being elected. I never expected an honour like this. You had two such fine candidates for the position of head girl. I am merely a new girl. I am so proud that, in spite of this, I am the person who has been elected – and I promise to serve Whyteleafe School to the very best of my ability. Thank you.'

The children listened, mesmerized.

She made an impressive sight and it was an impressive little speech.

191

There was applause. Patrick, Arabella and Martin exchanged smug looks. They had all voted for Kerry, and some of their classmates had criticized them. How wrong they were. Even the first formers and juniors began to feel more cheerful. Kerry seemed a nice person. They would just have to get used to not having Emma as head girl . . .

Kerry stood there, acknowledging the applause. She was in a happy state, wanting it to go on and on.

The applause was dying away now with only the die-hards like Arabella continuing to clap.

But still Kerry stood there.

'Ahem,' said Thomas, politely. 'Time to start, Kerry.'

She seemed not to hear.

Looking a little cross, Thomas had to bang the gavel again to bring the Meeting to order. Only then did the newly-elected head girl come and take her seat beside him. She had almost forgotten where she was.

'Right, first things first,' Thomas told the Meeting. 'Will you all give your money in, please? Richard will come round with the school box.'

Kerry Dane watched in surprise as the wooden box was passed along the rows. Into the box went all the money that the children had brought back from home after the summer holidays.

'At Whyteleafe School,' Thomas explained to the

new pupils below, 'it is not thought fair for some children to have more money than others. You will find that at every Meeting, any money you've been sent will be collected up. After that, each child in the school receives two pounds pocket-money for the week. You are then allowed to make Special Requests if you need extra money for something important. Every request is listened to carefully and then the Meeting decides.'

While the box was going round, Kerry pulled out her wallet and counted the banknotes inside. She saw Thomas glance at them.

'Obviously, Thomas,' said Kerry, sweetly, 'this rule doesn't apply to us? Not to the head girl and head boy of the school?'

'I'm afraid it does, Kerry,' he said tersely. 'Seniors do have more calls on their purse than the younger children, so you will find that no reasonable request is ever turned down. But in the meantime –' he looked at the banknotes hard '– all of those must go in the box.'

Kerry managed to conceal her shock. What a ridiculous system! She would have to find some way of getting round it.

In the meantime, when the box came to the platform, she had no choice but to place all her money inside under Thomas's watchful gaze.

Soon, the week's pocket-money had been handed out

to every pupil in the school and it was time to hear Special Requests for extra funds.

Julian's cousin was one of the first on his feet.

'I think Patrick *should* be allowed the money for a new table-tennis bat, Thomas,' Kerry decided. 'He tells me he's a very keen player.'

She was beginning to enjoy herself again. It was lovely to have so much power over the other children. Some of them would find their requests refused, if she didn't like the look of their faces!

Thomas did not agree at all that Patrick needed a new table-tennis bat but he had to let it pass. Kerry obviously did not understand the rules about Special Requests. It would all have to be explained to her. Now Patrick had been given an unfair advantage over other children who were also hoping to get into Emma's table-tennis squad.

But it would not be right to have an argument with Kerry in front of the entire school. It would undermine her authority.

As more Special Requests came and went, Thomas was keeping an eye on the doors at the back. Surely the Naughtiest Girl would have cooled down by now? He very much hoped so.

She and her two friends should really come back to the Meeting quickly. He expected to see them slip quietly back into their seats and show that they had now accepted the verdict of the ballot box. However regrettable, thought Thomas, that verdict had turned out to be.

Elizabeth had raced off to the school vegetable gardens. When Julian and Joan caught her up, she was marching up and down one of the little paths.

She walked up and down like that for some minutes, in order to work off her temper.

When at last she grew tired, the three of them sat on a sunny bench, just in front of the greenhouses.

'Let's have an apple,' said Joan, in her gentlest voice.

She picked three rosy apples from one of the little trees nearby. They each took a bite. As Elizabeth tasted the sweet, sharp tang of the fruit, she gazed around sorrowfully. These dear gardens, how she loved them. How she loved helping John Terry with the weeding and planting and hoeing.

Dear Whyteleafe School, the best school in the entire world. What happy times she had had here. But now, surely, it could never be the same again?

'It's the worst thing that's ever been,' she said miserably. 'And how did it happen? I just don't understand. Emma seemed to have so much support. You were wrong for once, Julian! You were so sure that

most of the school wouldn't vote for Kerry, however much they admired her.'

'I wasn't wrong at all,' replied Julian, patiently. 'You obviously haven't done your sums, Elizabeth. Most of the school did not vote for Kerry Dane. She only collected about one third of the vote. She always knew that would be the best she could hope for. That was why she got Nora to stand. And *that* was why she went round persuading people to vote for Nora.'

'You mean . . . ?' Elizabeth frowned, trying to work it out.

'Julian means that Kerry guessed that a majority would never vote to elect a new girl,' explained Joan. 'But if she could split that majority in two, as evenly as possible—'

'She could squeeze through the middle and maybe win!' finished Julian. 'And that's exactly what happened. It was a master stroke, begging people to vote for Nora. It made some of them worry about voting for Emma and change their minds. And it made some of them, who may have been thinking of voting for Emma, but who didn't have strong principles about not electing a new girl, think "I don't want to vote for Nora but what a fine person Kerry is. I shall give her my vote." So she picked up some extra votes for herself as she went along. That's what made all the difference!'

'She would never have had a chance, if she'd just stood against Emma,' sighed Joan. 'She would have been very soundly beaten. But, as it turned out, she was able to split the vote three ways. What an impossible schemer! I realized what she had done as soon as Thomas read the result out. I felt such contempt for her that I just had to leave the platform, even though a monitor should never do a thing like that. I just had to.'

'It's not fair,' exclaimed Elizabeth. 'It's horrific!'

Julian threw his apple core so it landed on John Terry's compost heap. Then he glanced at his watch.

'Should you two be sitting here?' he asked. 'The Meeting must be racing along. They'll be getting to the bit about the second form monitors soon.'

Joan and Elizabeth looked at one another.

'I'm not going back in there,' said Joan bravely.

'Nor me,' stated Elizabeth.

Her face crumpled and tears of anger came to her eyes.

'I don't want to be a monitor any more. Not with her as head girl! I couldn't bear, as a matter of fact, ever to sit on the same platform as her!'

'Those are my feelings exactly, Elizabeth,' declared Joan.

* * *

'Now,' said Thomas, gazing around the hall, 'we come to the last business of the day.'

Complaints and grumbles had been dealt with. There had only been two.

'We have to sort out the second form monitors,' he continued. 'As you know, you are allowed two. Joan is still in the second form and can remain as a monitor, if you so wish. Or you may elect a new person, if you prefer. Susan has gone up into the third form this term. So a new monitor will have to be chosen to take Susan's place. Do you want to choose one new monitor, or two? What have you decided, second formers?'

Belinda rose to her feet. It had been agreed that she would be the spokesperson for the form. It had also been agreed what she should say. The words were written on a piece of paper.

Her cheeks hot with embarrassment, Belinda glanced round to see if there was any sign of Elizabeth and Joan coming back. For the past few minutes she had been looking out for them constantly. But they had not returned to the Meeting.

'Well, Belinda?' prompted Thomas.

Feeling awkward, Belinda read out the prepared statement.

'We, in the second form, have agreed unanimously that we would like Joan to continue as a monitor for

199

another term. For our other monitor, we are all of the same opinion. We would like to appoint Elizabeth.'

As she sat down a buzz of conversation ran round the hall. The second form wanted Joan and Elizabeth as monitors. But both girls had walked out of the Meeting! This was going to be an unusual situation. What would happen now?

'Please!' said Arabella, putting her hand up.

'You wish to say something?' asked Kerry Dane eagerly, from the platform.

Arabella stood up. She was feeling outraged at the way that Elizabeth, Joan and Julian had walked out of the Meeting earlier. Just because their favourite hadn't won! The election had been fought fair and square and Kerry had won. She was going to make such a fine head girl. Perhaps she would be able to get Arabella a part in a film one day. She had almost hinted as much! It was extremely horrid and rude of Elizabeth and the others to walk out like that.

'When we've chosen monitors before, they've always had to stand up at the Meeting and agree,' she pointed out. 'But how can we elect Elizabeth and Joan if they're not here?'

'Shut up and sit down, Arabella!' hissed Daniel, crossly.

'You know they've agreed,' whispered Belinda,

looking anxious. 'You know Joan's agreed to stay on and Elizabeth wants to be the new one.'

'What do the rules say about it, Thomas?' Kerry asked sweetly. 'Is there anything written about it in the Book?'

The Book was a large volume that stood on the table between them. It contained a record of everything important that had happened at Meetings and the many rules that had been agreed upon over the passage of time. Together, Kerry and Thomas pored over the Book together and soon found what they needed. They discussed it briefly with the monitors behind them and then Thomas turned to face the school. He looked upset.

'It appears to be an established rule that people must be here to be elected. The Meeting also feels that Elizabeth and Joan have ruled themselves out by such bad behaviour. So we've decided that the second form must now choose two new monitors. First find out if your choices are willing to stand, then write both names on a piece of paper.' He handed Kerry some slips of paper to take down to the second formers. 'We shall then count the votes and have a result very quickly.'

When Elizabeth and Joan went into dinner later, they learnt that Belinda and Daniel had been elected in their place.

They accepted the news bravely. Both girls were determined never to sit on the same platform as Kerry

Dane, or recognize her as head girl in other ways.

'I expect next week's Meeting will have to decide on some sort of punishment for us,' Joan sighed to her friends, after dinner. 'It's a very serious offence to miss a whole Meeting.'

'See if I care!' pouted Elizabeth.

'I don't expect the Meeting will punish you two,' said Julian, airily. 'They'll decide that you've been punished enough by losing your monitorships. They'll have to find some punishment for me, of course.'

Julian dug his hands in his pockets. His green eyes glinted.

'Whatever it is, it'll be worth it! It was good to make a stand. I really enjoyed it.'

'Yes,' nodded Elizabeth. 'I didn't mean to lose my temper. But it was good to show her what we think of her.'

Julian smiled to himself, in spite of everything. Life was never dull with the Naughtiest Girl around.

At bedtime that night, Elizabeth discovered that Jenny was very upset.

'I feel it's all my fault, Elizabeth. I should never have asked Nora to stand! It's worked out all wrong. Much as I admire Kerry, I never expected her to be elected as head girl. She just doesn't seem right for it.'

# NEW MONITORS HAVE TO BE FOUND

'She doesn't seem right for anything!' said Elizabeth coldly. She had no need to keep her feelings to herself any longer. 'She's really hateful. I'll tell you all about it some time. But I expect you'll find out soon enough.'

'Really?' Jenny looked intrigued. She frowned. 'In a way, I suppose, she doesn't seem right here at Whyteleafe at all.'

Elizabeth felt tired after all the strains of the day. She climbed into bed. But it was nice that Jenny was beginning to see sense. She had already forgiven her.

'Kerry's completely wrong for Whyteleafe,' she said sleepily. 'What Julian and Joan and I can't understand is what she's doing here at all!'

## CHAPTER NINE

# EMMA SPEAKS TO ELIZABETH

IT WAS wet on Sunday. Elizabeth spent much of the day practising her table tennis. She hung around the green tables downstairs, getting as many games as she could. Soon she had perfected the new service that Emma had taught her. She then went on to improve her forehand smash. Patrick was practising hard, too.

They'd both discovered there was to be a match next Saturday, a friendly against St Faith's. It would be the first fixture of the new school year. And Emma and Mr Warlow would be choosing the squad after this week's coaching session. Elizabeth was determined to get in the team!

She found the forehand smash particularly satisfying. She was still feeling angry and upset. She had left Joan sitting in the common room, hard at work with some knitting. Joan had decided to make a child's scarf for the Earthquake Bazaar which the seniors planned for next Sunday. It would be a comfort to try to help the earthquake victims in some small way.

## EMMA SPEAKS TO ELIZABETH

'It will take my mind off things, Elizabeth,' Joan had said, an expression of quiet fortitude on her face.

It upset Elizabeth that she was not to be a monitor, after all. But it upset her even more that Joan had been stripped of the post.

'Kerry Dane's been too clever for us so far, Joan, but we're not going to let her win!' Elizabeth muttered darkly. 'We'll find some way – *some* way – of showing her up for what she is!'

By Sunday afternoon, Elizabeth was hitting the table-tennis ball with great venom and accuracy. It was an excellent way to relieve her feelings.

'Phew!' said Harry, as Elizabeth won their game with a beautiful smash.

'Your return just sat up and begged for a forehand smash, Harry!' laughed Elizabeth. 'You should try to spin it and keep it low, that's what Emma says. You ought to come to the coaching sessions, they're fun!'

'I'm not good enough,' said Harry. 'But you're getting brilliant. I'm sure you'll get into the team, Elizabeth.'

Most of her classmates were being very nice to her this weekend. She had worked so hard to get Emma elected. They felt sorry that she'd lost control of her temper and with it her chance of being monitor. It was sad about Joan, too. Belinda and Daniel, the new monitors, felt especially unhappy.

At that moment one of the seniors appeared.

'Ah, found you, Elizabeth,' Philippa smiled. 'A treat for you! A telephone call from your mother. Would you like to run and take it?'

Philippa felt sorry for the Naughtiest Girl too and the trouble that her emotions had got her into the previous day. It was nice that her mother had rung!

'I wonder what Mummy wants?' Elizabeth thought, as she hurried along to the little room called the Telephone Room. It was just a tiny box room with a comfortable chair and a low table. On the table was a coin-in-the-slot payphone.

Boys and girls from the second form upwards were allowed to receive calls from their family on a Sunday, and even to make outgoing calls if they were important. It was an exciting privilege. But Elizabeth had not expected to receive a telephone call so soon! The receiver lay on the table, waiting to be picked up.

'Hello, Mummy!'

'Hello, Elizabeth dear.'

Mrs Allen had rung about the flowers.

'Thank you! It was such a lovely surprise when Daddy brought them home. They're still as fresh as ever, even now. I've arranged them in the big vase on the hall table. I wish you could see them!'

'I can just imagine them, Mummy,' said Elizabeth,

closing her eyes and doing so. Mrs Allen loved flowers so and made wonderful arrangements. 'I'm glad you're pleased with them.'

'It must have been very interesting for you to meet Kerry Dane like that!' her mother was saying. 'I was so surprised that she didn't want to keep the flowers herself—'

'I think she had too much to carry, Mummy,' Elizabeth said hastily. The Naughtiest Girl had not, of course, told her father that the bouquet had been rescued from a dustbin. There'd hardly been time to explain all that! It was simpler just to say that the actress hadn't needed them. 'I expect she gets lots of flowers,' she added.

'It was still extremely kind of her to make us a gift of them,' continued Mrs Allen. 'I thought you would like to know how pleased I am. And, of course, I hope to find an address to write to. I would like to drop a thank-you note to Miss Dane. I expect she has an agent in London . . .'

'Oh, Mummy, I shouldn't bother to do that! I'm sure she would just find it embarrassing. Please don't bother to write a note!'

But her mother had become distracted.

'Oh, there's the doorbell!' said Mrs Allen. 'I have some friends coming to tea. They will be very impressed when they hear about the flowers. Thank you again, Elizabeth. How lovely to speak to you on the telephone.'

Elizabeth replaced the receiver and left the Telephone Room. It was a nice surprise to get a telephone call from her mother. But how she would hate it if Mrs Allen found out the agent's address and sent him a note for Kerry Dane!

If only she knew where she was! One day, when this was all over, she would tell her mother the whole story.

'Where's my table-tennis bat?' she asked John McTavish when she returned. He was having a knockabout with Daniel, now that the table had come free.

'I expect you took it with you to the Telephone Room, Elizabeth!' laughed John. 'We haven't got it!'

'Yes, so I did! And I've left it there, too. How silly of me!'

Elizabeth retraced her footsteps. She would pick up her bat and then go to have a shower before tea.

The door of the Telephone Room was ajar. Somebody else was already in there, she could hear them speaking. The telephone was in use again!

Elizabeth hovered outside the door, wondering if the person would mind her just creeping in to get the bat.

Then, as she recognized the voice, she stiffened.

It was Kerry Dane.

She was gloating. Elizabeth could hear every word.

'Mummy, it was brilliant of you and Daddy to find Whyteleafe School for me. I didn't believe you when you said you'd found a school like this where the pupils are in charge! No stupid teachers will ever boss me around again . . .'

Then, a few moment's silence. Followed by laughter.

'Yes, of course it was cheeky of them at Horton High! Trying to behave as if I was still an ordinary schoolgirl. Trying to act as if I wasn't famous. It's different at this place. You said it would be. We can do what we like. And you'll never guess. I've been made head girl! Instead of being bossed around by grown-ups, I'm in charge of the other pupils, with a boy called Thomas. It's going to be such fun, telling everybody what to do! There are one or two silly little rules, that's all. I'll tell you why I've rung, Mummy. Can you get some cash to me . . .'

More silence. And then, the voice became sulky:

'Oh, don't be silly, Mummy. I can't be bothered to explain about the other cash. Why's it difficult? Can't you send banknotes by registered post?' Kerry was becoming increasingly petulant. 'I need to be able to buy myself treats when I want to, Mummy!'

Elizabeth tiptoed away. She had heard enough! Her table-tennis bat could wait!

She raced off to find Joan and Julian.

Breathlessly, she told them everything she'd overheard.

'So *that's* why she's come to Whyteleafe School!' whistled Julian.

'Yes, she thinks there's no discipline here. That this is a soft school where she can do exactly what she likes!' said Elizabeth, outraged. 'But that's not how things work at Whyteleafe. A person like that can't be allowed to be head girl! It's an insult! Surely we can do something—'

'There's nothing we *can* do, Elizabeth,' said Joan calmly, 'except be very, very patient. It can only be a matter of time now before her true nature reveals itself.'

'I'm not sure I can just sit around and wait for "time"!' exclaimed Elizabeth furiously.

Julian ruffled her hair and grinned.

'Always the bold, bad Elizabeth!' he observed. 'I'm afraid we haven't any choice, whether we like it or not.'

There was strawberry ice cream for tea that day but Elizabeth hardly tasted it as she spooned it down, silent and inwardly smouldering.

# EMMA SPEAKS TO ELIZABETH

Looking across from the seniors' table, Emma saw how unhappy she seemed.

The senior girl came and sought her out later. Emma was still very unhappy herself but she was determined not to let it show.

'Cheer up, Elizabeth!' she said lightly. 'I know how disappointed you must be feeling about the election result. But we must put a brave face on things, you know!' She smiled. 'We can't have people thinking we are bad losers, can we?'

'It's nothing to do with being a bad loser!' Elizabeth blurted out. 'It's just that Kerry Dane doesn't go with Whyteleafe School and she's certainly not a worthy person to be its head girl!'

'Sssh, Elizabeth!' said Emma, unhappily. 'You really mustn't go around saying things like that. I forbid it. The election is behind us now and we have the result. Kerry is our new head girl and I want you to tell me that you accept it.'

'I don't accept it, Emma,' replied Elizabeth, firmly. 'I'll *never* accept it. I can't even bring myself to go to the next school Meeting. Not if she's still head girl!'

Emma's eyes widened.

'Stop it, Elizabeth! Of course Kerry will still be head girl at the next Meeting! And of *course* you must go! If you miss another Meeting over this you will show

211

a complete lack of self-discipline. You will be setting a bad example to the younger pupils in the school.'

Elizabeth tried to turn her eyes away.

'Look at me, Elizabeth,' said Emma, gently. Elizabeth met her gaze. 'I want you to make me a promise. Even if privately you can't accept Kerry as head girl, you are to *promise* not to miss another Meeting. Do you give me your promise?'

Elizabeth could see that she was making Emma unhappy. She swallowed.

'All right,' she mumbled. 'I promise.'

That night she took out her autograph book and gazed at its spoiled white leather cover, with tears in her eyes. Then she opened it. She found the words that Rita had written at the end of last term, a beautiful line of poetry.

'Kerry Dane isn't good enough to step into Rita's shoes,' thought Elizabeth. 'She never was and she never will be. Only Emma will do! It's an outrage!'

But if the three friends tried to explain that to people, they'd only think, as Emma had gently tried to point out, that it was a case of Elizabeth and Co being bad losers.

Julian and Joan were right. They would have to bide their time.

'I only hope my patience can last out,' thought

212

Elizabeth, restlessly, as she tossed and turned and tried to get to sleep. 'I only hope nothing unexpected takes place, to push me over the edge.'

But that was exactly what happened.

It was after school, the following Friday.

It had turned out to be a very good week for Elizabeth, in other respects. She was enjoying her new lessons in the second form. And, although it was horrid not being a monitor after all, Belinda and Daniel were both very kind about it. They kept saying that they weren't really cut out to be monitors and Elizabeth and Joan would have been so much better. She was also pleased that Miss Ranger had made her top in English this week.

But the best thing of all about the week was that she had got into the table-tennis squad! After the second coaching session, Mr Warlow's list had gone up on the notice-board – and there was her name! Patrick was only first reserve, in spite of his excellent new bat.

Tomorrow, Saturday, they'd travel by minibus to St Faith's and play their first match. How exciting that was going to be!

Before that, however, Elizabeth was trying to steel herself for the weekly Meeting. It was taking place on

Friday this week. That morning, a dark cloud had descended over her head. When lessons were over, she went for a walk around the school grounds, trying to calm herself.

'I just dread going into the hall today!' she muttered to herself. 'Even though I promised Emma I would. It will be too unbearable to sit there in silence and watch Kerry Dane being a drama queen. Acting the part of being a fine head girl! Everybody looking up to her! I really cannot bear it . . .'

Suddenly Elizabeth stopped. She had heard a funny little sound. She looked all around.

There it was again! It seemed to be coming from the shrubbery.

It was the sound of someone sobbing.

## CHAPTER TEN

# ELIZABETH IS DEFIANT

'WHAT'S WRONG, Rupert?' asked Elizabeth, diving in amongst the bushes. 'Why are you hiding? Has somebody been bullying you?'

The small new boy gazed up at Elizabeth, his cheeks stained with tears. He had hidden so that nobody would think that he was a cry-baby. Slowly he brought his sobs under control. Elizabeth gently dried his eyes with her clean white handkerchief.

'Well, have they?'

Rupert shook his head.

'Then why have you been crying?' coaxed Elizabeth. 'What's the matter?'

'Mustn't talk about it,' he muttered. 'Mustn't let people know I'm greedy.'

His lip trembled and he started sobbing again.

'I'm not greedy!' he wailed. 'I was going to share them with all my friends!'

'Share *what*, Rupert?' asked Elizabeth. 'You are allowed to tell me about it. And it will make you feel better. Share *what* exactly?'

The words came tumbling out.

'My chocolate soldiers grandfather sent me for my birthday! I was going to share them out at teatime. But she wouldn't listen to me. She took them away from me! She took them away!'

'Who did, Rupert?'

'Kerry did!'

Elizabeth stared at him in disbelief.

'The head girl?'

Rupert nodded solemnly.

'When?'

'This afternoon. She needs them for the earthquake.'

The earthquake? Elizabeth frowned. Of course. The Earthquake Bazaar, next weekend. Kerry Dane was in charge of the sweet stall. But what a mean, horrid way to behave! She had no right to force the little boy to give up his birthday present for it!

Rupert looked scared and put a hand to his mouth.

'I promised not to tell anybody. Or else she'll tell everybody in the whole school I'm a very greedy little boy!'

Elizabeth bent down and gently placed an arm round his shoulders.

'You're not greedy, Rupert. Now listen to me. You're to go and wash your face and hands. It will soon be

216

time for the Meeting. You're to stop worrying about this. It's just a – a horrid little mistake. Remember how I found your teddy bear for you, on the bus? Well – I'll make sure you get your chocolate soldiers back, too! Off you go!'

The fair-haired boy looked pleased and grateful.

'Oh, thank you!'

Elizabeth stood and watched him walk back to the school buildings. He turned and waved. Calmly she waved back but her cheeks were flushed with anger. What a despicable way for a head girl to behave. What an abuse of power!

'The real Kerry Dane,' Elizabeth thought. 'The mask has started to crack at last!'

She reached a decision. She had promised Emma to attend the Meeting.

Well, she would keep her promise!

'And I know exactly what I'll do when I get there,' thought Elizabeth, with a cheerful gleam in her eye.

'Silence!' shouted Thomas, banging the gavel loudly. 'I am trying to start the Meeting!'

The head boy was angry. The children were refusing to settle down. They all kept chattering and turning round to look at Elizabeth Allen.

It was such an amazing sight.

# THE NAUGHTIEST GIRL WANTS TO WIN

The Naughtiest Girl was seated on the second form benches but she was facing the wrong way! She was sitting with her back to the platform.

'What does Elizabeth think she's doing?' wondered Emma, in dismay.

Elizabeth sat stiffly on her bench. Instead of facing the head boy and girl and the monitors, she had turned her back on them and sat facing the other way. Her arms were folded stubbornly, in silent protest.

'Quiet, everybody!' cried Thomas.

The children forced themselves to stop looking at Elizabeth. The chatter died to a whisper and then to complete silence.

'Thank you,' said Thomas. 'We have a lot of business to get through today. But before we begin, would Elizabeth please be kind enough to stand up and face the right way. I wish to speak to her.'

Elizabeth did so.

'What is the meaning of this tomfoolery, Elizabeth?' he asked.

'I do not wish to face the platform,' announced Elizabeth, in clear ringing tones. 'I do not accept Kerry Dane as head girl. She has proved herself an unfit person and I think she should resign.'

The school listened in astonishment. Julian and Joan exchanged troubled glances. What had provoked this? They had all agreed they would have to be patient. Did Elizabeth know what she was doing? Was she not being very hot-headed?

Next to Thomas on the platform, Kerry Dane cast her eyes down. Her heart was bumping with anger. Who was this dreadful girl they called the Naughtiest Girl? What was this all about?

'I see,' replied Thomas, calmly. 'That is a very dramatic statement, Elizabeth. Perhaps you would be good enough to explain to the Meeting your reasons for making it.'

'I will be very pleased to, Thomas.'

Elizabeth pointed accusingly at Kerry Dane.

'Kerry thinks that this is a school where she can do whatever she likes. She has behaved today no better than a common bully. Little Rupert was sent some chocolate soldiers for his birthday, by his grandfather. This afternoon Kerry Dane forced him to hand them over to her for her stall at the Earthquake Bazaar.'

A shocked gasp ran round the hall.

Kerry Dane leapt to her feet at once, a pained expression on her face.

'Elizabeth, how could you say such a thing?' she asked sorrowfully. 'How could you even *think* such a thing? I am very, very hurt.'

She then looked down at the juniors, sitting cross-legged on the floor at the front of the hall. Her eyes lighted on the smallest one, with very fair hair.

'Stand up please, Rupert,' she said, in a kindly voice. 'I think we need to sort this out together, don't you?'

The small boy rose.

But he was left standing there, nervously blinking, as the young actress came to the edge of the platform and looked straight past him. With arms out-flung, she began to address the school, a radiant expression on her face, her lips sweetly smiling.

'First of all, this is exactly the right moment to say thank you! Thank you all for the wonderful response you've made so far! All the lovely things you've been bringing me for the sweet stall. Every day you come and see me and bring your goodies, knowing the money raised will help the earthquake victims. I find your generosity very touching. And I found Rupert's gift today perhaps the most touching of all . . .'

She then looked down and fixed her eyes on the small boy, who was now beginning to feel frightened and overwhelmed.

'Look at me, please, Rupert.'

The small child gazed up at the figure towering over him.

'Now, Rupert, where did Elizabeth get this funny idea from? Have you been making up naughty stories?

Did you regret it afterwards, giving your chocolate soldiers away? Was it something you did on the spur of the moment because you felt sorry for the earthquake victims? But you were so insistent at the time, Rupert! Don't you remember? You told me you thought it would be a very greedy thing to keep them. Didn't you?'

Rupert gazed up into those mesmerizing brown eyes. He was blinking non-stop, overcome with confusion. He was like a frightened rabbit in the thrall of a stoat.

'Now, think hard, Rupert. Don't you remember?' repeated Kerry.

She was daring him to contradict her. His sense of confusion increased.

'I – I can't remember exactly. I s'pose I must have done. I don't know. Elizabeth asked me why I was crying and I s'pose . . .'

Arabella whispered to Patrick behind her hand.

'Elizabeth making up naughty stories, more like it!'

Kerry was finishing Rupert's sentence for him.

'You knew you'd given me your soldiers but then you wished you hadn't and it made you cry. But you didn't dare tell Elizabeth how silly you'd been, so you made up a naughty little story instead! Now, please don't start crying again! There's no need to get upset about it. We all make mistakes.'

'You may sit down now, Rupert,' intervened Thomas, feeling sorry for the child. 'And don't be a cry-baby. Nobody's going to punish you. Think carefully in future before you give things away. Make quite sure that you really want to do so. Only babies give things to people and then want to have them back! You're a big boy now, remember.'

'Yes, Thomas.'

The child hastily sat down, feeling tearful and totally confused.

Elizabeth had listened to the whole exchange in stunned silence.

What a brilliant actress Kerry Dane was. What an Oscar-winning performance!

Thomas now spoke to the Naughtiest Girl, while the whole school listened with avid interest. Julian and Joan were feeling only total dismay.

'We already know, Elizabeth, that you have found it very difficult to accept the results of last week's election. And that you have lost your chance to be a monitor because of it. But you must know that the way you just spoke to our new head girl is not something that can be tolerated. She has been properly elected and she must be shown respect. You will please make a public apology to Kerry.'

'I certainly shall not,' said Elizabeth defiantly.

## ELIZABETH IS DEFIANT

Thomas bit his lip. He felt worried and upset but he dared not show it.

'Then you must leave the Meeting at once.'

Elizabeth barely heard him. She was already striding out of the hall. Her eyes were misted with anger and there was only one thought on her mind.

## CHAPTER ELEVEN

# THE NAUGHTIEST GIRL WINS THROUGH

'I DON'T believe Kerry Dane for one instant!' she thought. 'I'm going to get Rupert's chocolates back for him!'

Elizabeth raced upstairs to the seniors' common room. She knew that she was strictly forbidden to enter without permission, but she didn't care. There was nobody to stop her. The entire school was seated safely at the Meeting.

'I know where they keep everything for the Bazaar!' thought Elizabeth. 'It's going to be quite easy to get Rupert's soldiers! I promised him!'

Elizabeth was quite positive that Rupert had been telling her the truth. It was Kerry Dane who'd been telling the naughty little stories, as she called them! But how could the school know how awful she was? That she had actually taken a junior's birthday present away from him? Even for a good cause, it was such an unbelievable thing to do!

But that, Elizabeth felt quite sure, was exactly what had happened.

'Goodness only knows why', thought Elizabeth, as she slipped into the big common room and headed for the cupboard in the corner. 'But I'll see that Rupert gets his birthday present back if it's the last thing I ever do at Whyteleafe!'

At her boldest and most reckless, Elizabeth found the key to the cupboard. She knew where it was because she'd been here with Daniel when he'd handed in some pottery for Philippa's craft stall. She turned the key in the lock.

The cupboard door creaked open.

The shelves were neatly labelled: Craft Stall . . . White Elephant . . . Sweet Stall . . .

The shelf set aside for the sweet stall was already nearly full. There were sweets of every description, some of them shop sweets, many of them home-made. There were jars of home-made peppermints, toffees and coconut ice. There were at least three sugar mice. There was Arabella's fudge, too. Elizabeth recognized the box. How busy all the children had been, eager to please the young film star.

She frowned, beginning to feel uneasy.

'It's true what she said, then. The children *have* been giving her stacks of things for the sweet stall. The shelf's almost full and there's still a whole week to go before the Bazaar! So there's hardly any danger of her stall not being a success, then . . .'

It made her mean behaviour seem more unbelievable than ever.

'I know!' Elizabeth said to herself. 'Perhaps there isn't very much chocolate. Everybody's giving her sweets but she wants to have some chocolate things to go with them.'

Elizabeth then checked each item on the shelf, very carefully.

And then she realized something.

It wasn't that there was not *very much* chocolate.

There was no chocolate at all!

'Even Rupert's chocolate soldiers aren't here,' she realized, in surprise. She relocked the cupboard and carefully replaced the key in its hiding place, puzzled. 'What *can* she have done with them?'

Elizabeth came out of the seniors' common room and closed the door. She looked up and down the corridor.

'It must be that she simply hasn't bothered to put them in the cupboard yet,' Elizabeth decided. 'Yes, that will be it! They must still be somewhere in her room.'

Slowly, hesitantly, she walked along the corridor until she came to a door. It said: HEAD GIRL,

PRIVATE. She hesitated for many seconds. Much as she hated Kerry Dane, it seemed a very wrong thing to do.

But then she thought of Rupert, and his tears, and the terrible injustice he had suffered.

She turned the handle and eased open the door of Kerry Dane's private quarters.

The Meeting was in full swing. On the platform, the head boy and girl had just been in a huddle with the monitors and come to a decision. Kerry and Thomas returned to their special table. It was Kerry's turn to pick up the gavel and bang for silence.

'Quiet, please, everybody!' she smiled. What a satisfying sound that gavel made. How quickly it brought the Meeting to order! She was beginning to enjoy herself again. 'The Meeting has now decided on the matter of punishment for the three pupils who walked out of last week's Meeting,' she announced. 'We have listened to the representations made by Belinda and Daniel on behalf of the two girls. And the Meeting has agreed that the losing of the monitorships is sufficient punishment for their last week's behaviour. As far as Elizabeth's behaviour today is concerned, the Meeting has decided that she is not a fit person to represent the school at table tennis.'

Kerry had to fight hard to conceal her glee. This was all such fun!

Julian and Joan looked at one another in dismay. They had been sitting there, discussing Elizabeth's latest walkout in growing alarm. They had hoped all week that Elizabeth would not lose patience and do something reckless. But she had! She had tried to catch Kerry Dane out on quite the wrong thing! The story that Rupert had told Elizabeth was really rather preposterous. And, even if there had been a grain of truth in it, Kerry Dane had been much too clever to be caught out!

'Poor Elizabeth,' whispered Joan. 'We warned her to be patient.'

'The Naughtiest Girl doesn't know the meaning of the word,' Julian whispered back. 'Something like this was bound to happen.'

'Now we come to the matter of the boy,' the head girl continued. 'Would you stand up, please, er—'

Julian got lazily to his feet, a mocking expression in his eyes.

'My name's Julian,' he said. 'Julian Holland.'

'Yes, well – er – Julian. The Meeting has decided that you must apologize in front of the whole school and—'

'No!' shouted a voice from the back.

Elizabeth came running into the hall, panting for

breath. She was holding something aloft. She halted and everyone turned round to look at her.

'You're the one who must apologize in front of the whole school, Kerry Dane,' she cried out. 'You must apologize to Rupert for your despicable behaviour. For stealing his chocolates and pretending you wanted them for the Bazaar. When all the time . . .'

Slowly, deliberately, Elizabeth began to walk towards the platform. There was a high colour in her cheeks and a scornful expression on her face. She was holding aloft a floral patterned wastepaper basket. It had come from Kerry Dane's room.

'. . . you wanted to eat them yourself.'

The head girl turned white as she recognized the wastepaper basket.

What happened next was very un-head-girl-like.

With a cry of fury, she leapt down from the platform and raced towards Elizabeth, her golden mane flying out behind her. Her face was contorted with rage.

'How dare you go into my private room!' she screamed. 'How dare you go poking around in my wastepaper basket—!'

She took a wild swing at Elizabeth. It knocked the wastepaper basket out of her hands and sent it flying to the ground.

Glittering tinfoil wrappings scattered in all directions.

There were loud gasps throughout the hall.

Julian nipped across and picked one up. Quickly he straightened it out. A soldier's face appeared and then the body, dressed in bright red tinfoil uniform. Silently, Julian held it up and displayed it to the shocked, silent children all around him. At the back of the hall, Miss Belle and Miss Best and Mr Johns had gone very pale.

'The wrapping from a chocolate soldier, I presume,' he said drily.

'It's mine!' cried Rupert, his little voice piping up from the front of the hall. 'It's all eaten! I didn't give them to her. I didn't, I didn't. She took all my soldiers!'

'And this stupid school has taken all my money!' blazed Kerry Dane. 'I need to be able to buy chocolate when I crave some, don't I? As soon as some more money comes through, I'll replace your silly little soldiers. They weren't even all that chocolatey!'

Gradually she began to regain her composure. The whole school watched, open-mouthed, as she turned on her heel. Slowly, majestically, she walked back to the platform. Her chin was thrust forward, her head held high.

'I would like to remind you all of something. I *am* the head girl of this school, you know.'

She remounted the platform and took her place

beside Thomas. She did not even notice the horrified expression on the head boy's face, or on the faces of the monitors behind him.

'Now, to more important matters,' she began. 'The question of Julian Holland—'

Suddenly a strange sound filled the hall. It was a sound that had never before been heard at a school Meeting. It was started by some of the fourth formers.

It was the sound of booing.

Within moments the whole school joined in the booing and hissing, drowning out the sound of Kerry Dane's voice.

'Resign!' cried the children.

'Resign! Resign!'

Elizabeth, Joan and Julian exchanged joyful looks.

'We want Emma!' cried the Naughtiest Girl. 'Emma for head girl!'

The booing stopped. Everybody clapped and cheered and stamped their feet, taking up Elizabeth's cry.

'We want Emma!'

'We want Emma!'

Kerry Dane gazed at the sea of faces in disbelief. She had suffered the disapproval of many teachers at her last school and it had annoyed her. But this was something very much worse. The disapproval of other pupils, of her school mates, was really horrid. It was humiliating.

She sank down in her chair, deeply shocked.

Thomas picked up the gavel and brought the Meeting to order. He knew that even William and Rita would, at a moment like this, have needed help from the joint headmistresses and the senior master. He looked to the back of the hall.

'Please, can you give the Meeting your advice?' he asked them. 'What should we do?'

Miss Best rose to her feet.

'The Meeting must follow its own advice, Thomas. It could hardly be clearer! Might we suggest that you now declare the Meeting closed? Next week, when Kerry has resigned and been replaced by her runner-up in the election, the slate can be wiped clean and a fresh start made.'

'Thank you, Miss Best,' replied Thomas, looking pleased.

He smiled across at Emma and his smile was returned.

Shortly after, Kerry Dane came down from the platform for the last time. She knew that she had no hope of ever returning to it.

## CHAPTER TWELVE

# A LOVELY MEETING

IT HAD been a chastening experience for the young film star. But the days that followed were worse. The seniors tried to be friendly towards her but they found it very hard after what had taken place. Even kindly Emma found it difficult, although she tried her best.

The rest of the school, with few exceptions, shunned her.

To the many children who had seen *Zara's Journey* in the school holidays and admired her as Zara, the shock of discovering her true nature had been very severe; just as it had been, that day in London, for Elizabeth and Joan. Kerry was left to her own devices a great deal. She had plenty of time on her hands to think and to contemplate. She was not used to this. She began to feel unhappy and to think about her real self and whether she liked what she found.

In the days before the next school Meeting, Elizabeth by contrast was in very sunny spirits. She was allowed to play in the table-tennis match after all, and did well. Belinda and Daniel insisted on standing down as second form monitors. Mr Leslie agreed that Joan and Elizabeth should take their places and be monitors after all.

Thomas, with Emma as the new head girl, called in all the monitors early in the week, to decide how much money the children should be allowed at the next Meeting. They would need a lot more than usual, for the Earthquake Bazaar.

Elizabeth was proud to have her opinion asked and to be part of the running of the school. She knew that she was going to enjoy every moment as a second form monitor with her best friend Joan.

But she was beginning to notice how much time Kerry Dane spent on her own. For the very first time she began to feel slightly sorry for her.

One day, after school, when Elizabeth and Julian came back from a pony ride, they found her on her own as usual, by the stables. She was stroking one of the ponies.

'Hello, Kerry.'

The three of them stood and talked for a while. Elizabeth was as forthright as ever. She knew no other way.

'I was shunned when I first came to Whyteleafe, Kerry, so I know just what you're going through!' she said cheerfully. 'I was very spoilt, like you, and I made it my business to be as horrid as I could.'

'Did you?' asked Kerry in surprise.

'She wanted to be sent home, that's why,' explained Julian, glancing at Elizabeth in amusement. He never knew what his friend was going to say next. He always had to expect the unexpected. 'That's how she got her nickname, the Naughtiest Girl in the School. She didn't want to be at boarding-school! She's not really horrid, by the way.'

'You mean, she isn't like me?' commented Kerry, drily.

'No, I wasn't anything like you!' Elizabeth declared truthfully. 'But I *did* behave badly. And I definitely remember that nobody liked me.'

'So what happened then?' asked Kerry.

'Oh, it doesn't last,' replied Elizabeth, airily. 'Not if you mend your ways.'

Kerry patted the horse once more and then walked slowly back to school.

'I don't think she's a person who can *ever* mend her ways,' smiled Julian, as they rubbed down the ponies. 'She's too far gone for that.'

'Perhaps she'll make a tiny little start some time,' said Elizabeth hopefully. 'You never know.'

And at the Meeting the next day, that was exactly what Kerry did.

She sat, pale and silent, on the senior benches while Thomas and Emma moved smoothly through complaints and grumbles. When, finally, they reached Any Other Business, she raised her hand.

'Yes, Kerry?' asked Emma, encouragingly.

Kerry rose. She was trembling slightly. She was suffering from stage fright, something she'd never experienced before. But she was determined to go through with this. She held aloft a large box of chocolate soldiers. She had borrowed two weeks' allowance in advance, to be able to buy them. It had been hard work finding them, too.

Her words came out in a rush.

'I'd like to present Rupert with this box of chocolate soldiers. And I'd like to apologize to him in front of the whole school for what I did.'

At a nod from the platform, the little boy came running over and took the box. His face was shining.

'I'm sorry they're not exactly the same as the other ones, Rupert,' said Kerry.

'They're bigger! They're better!' Rupert beamed, his faith in Whyteleafe School restored. 'I will share them, I promise!'

There were approving murmurs around the hall. Some people clapped. From her monitor's chair up on the platform, Elizabeth saw the look on Julian's face and laughed. It was satisfying to think he could sometimes be wrong.

It had turned out to be a lovely Meeting.

Soon after that, Kerry Dane had a birthday. It was no longer a legal requirement for her to remain at school. She had received a batch of letters from her agent in London and amongst them was another film offer. In consultation with her parents, it was decided that she should forego her certificate exams and leave school. She could now become a full-time actress.

From the joint headmistresses' window, on the day she left Whyteleafe School, the Beauty and the Beast watched her walk towards her father's small blue car. Her hair was as golden as corn in the sunshine as she stood waiting for her luggage to be loaded aboard.

'All that glisters is not gold,' sighed Miss Best, looking at that halo.

'She certainly glistered though, didn't she?' observed Miss Belle. 'If, alas, not gold.'

'She was not with us very long,' continued Miss Best, 'but I would like to feel that she leaves Whyteleafe a better person than when she came.'

'Elizabeth Allen saw to that!' smiled Miss Belle. 'I will never understand how it was that Elizabeth and her friends divined her true nature long before the rest of us.'

'Nor me,' agreed Miss Best.

But it was no mystery to Kerry Dane. Not any longer. Amongst the batch of letters that her agent had forwarded from his London office, had been a very odd little note:

*Dear Miss Dane*
*Thank you so much for the beautiful flowers you gave to my daughter Elizabeth last week. She was about to catch her train to boarding-school and so passed them to her father to bring safely home. They are very much appreciated and still as fresh as ever.*
*Yours sincerely*
*Audrey Allen*

Slowly, the truth had dawned.

Cringing in embarrassment at the memory of their encounter, Kerry had gone to find Elizabeth and to apologize. She was playing chess with Julian.

'It's all right, Kerry,' Elizabeth had replied. 'But it just shows you should always be nice to everybody you meet. Even old tramps and beggars in the street. You never know where you might meet them again.'

'Yes, I can see that,' had been Kerry's humble reply. 'I suppose it's cruel and silly to be horrid to someone for no good reason.'

'Especially when it's the Naughtiest Girl,' thought Julian, with a smile.

# THE NAUGHTIEST GIRL

## Marches On

# CONTENTS

CHAPTER ONE

# JAKE IS GRUMPY

ELIZABETH ALLEN was enjoying life in the second form at Whyteleafe School. By early October she could barely remember what it had felt like to be a first former. How young the new first formers looked now, how small for their age! Surely, she would say in amazement to her best friend Joan, *they'd* never been that small when they were first formers? Joan would smile gently and assure her that a year ago they must have looked every bit as small.

Being a second form monitor with Joan this term made Elizabeth feel all the more grown-up. She was delighted to be a monitor again and refused to let her friend Julian put her off her stride.

'How long will the Naughtiest Girl last this time?' he asked her, an amused light in his green eyes. 'One week? Two weeks? Or till half-term, perhaps?'

'Wait and see, Julian Holland. You might get a surprise. It's exciting being a monitor. Thomas and Emma have got really good ideas. I've not the slightest intention of blotting my copybook!'

It was a long time since Elizabeth really *had* been the school's Naughtiest Girl – but the nickname had stuck. And how Julian loved to tease her about it!

Privately Elizabeth now considered Whyteleafe the best school in the world. She liked the way the pupils made most of the rules themselves, through the weekly Meeting, which was a kind of school parliament. And she loved the monitors' get-togethers that Thomas and Emma, the new head boy and girl, had introduced. All twelve monitors now met Thomas and Emma once a week for tea and biscuits in their study. They helped to plan the main Meeting and were encouraged to put forward ideas. It was known simply as the Monitors' Meeting, or MM for short.

'Don't forget we've got an MM before tea, Elizabeth!' Joan reminded her friend one day.

They were still outside, after Games. Elizabeth was loitering near the main hockey pitch, where members of the school's first eleven were having a team practice. There were some important matches coming up soon.

'I know, Joan,' replied Elizabeth. 'I'm looking forward to it. Wasn't it good last week?'

There had been three MMs so far and Elizabeth had enjoyed each one. She wanted to play her full part in the smooth running of the school. She was determined to be a dynamic and successful monitor. She took her responsibilities to heart.

'But we haven't got time just to stand around,' Joan said softly. 'We've got to wash and change and smarten up . . .'

'I'm not just standing around, Joan!' Elizabeth pointed out, patiently. 'I'm looking at Jake and his poor ankle, that's all. I'm worried about him, aren't you? We *are* his monitors, after all. I think the least we can do is go over and have a few words with him. He looks so grumpy! Come on, let's try and cheer him up.'

Only then did Joan realize that her friend was gazing not at the team practice but at a forlorn figure sitting on the grass, with his ankle heavily strapped. Joan knew Jake well. He had been in the second form even longer than she had. He was a big, strapping boy for his age. He was a brilliant hockey player and at the end of last season had been selected for the school's first hockey team. He was the youngest pupil ever to have made it into the first eleven. He had played superbly.

'Poor Jake!' she agreed. 'All right, then. But we'd better not talk to him for too long.'

Elizabeth was already striding ahead.

It was sad to see the big boy sitting there, staring miserably into space, while his team-mates practised running and passing and shooting goals. He had returned to school from the summer holidays a different boy, thought Joan. It seemed he had fallen badly on the last day of the holidays and injured his ankle. It had been strapped up for nearly a month now and he was still limping heavily. The injury seemed to have affected his confidence, too. He was much quieter this term than Joan had ever known him.

'Cheer up, Jake!' Elizabeth was telling him, with her bright, friendly smile. 'We just want you to know how proud we are to have a second former who's already in the first hockey team. And already a star! It's such an honour for us. It won't be long now before that ankle of yours is better and it won't be a moment too soon! Mr Warlow says there are some very important matches coming up and the team's not the same without you. We can't wait to see you in action again, I can tell you. The whole second form will be cheering you on from the sidelines!'

Even at the best of times, Jake was the strong, silent sort of boy. He seemed taken aback by such effusiveness. His cheeks turned red.

'Oh, leave off, Elizabeth,' he said grumpily.

'Don't be embarrassed, Jake!' said Joan, tactfully. 'We just want you to know that our thoughts are with you. It's such a shame for you, not being able to play games. We do hope the ankle will be better soon.'

'Thanks, Joan,' mumbled the big boy.

'It's got to be!' declared Elizabeth, in her boisterous way. 'I am going to wish and wish and WISH your ankle to get better, Jake! Just you wait and see!'

The boy shrugged and made no response.

'Come on, Elizabeth. We must dash now!' Joan tugged at Elizabeth's arm. 'We mustn't be late for the MM!'

As they went indoors, Elizabeth sighed. She'd hoped to cheer Jake up but instead she seemed to have made him grumpier than ever!

'He seemed surprised at my coming over and talking to him,' she frowned. 'I got the impression that he'd quite forgotten I'm one of his monitors this term.'

'He probably had,' laughed Joan.

'Do you think it would be a good idea if all monitors had a special armband?' continued Elizabeth. 'Shall we bring it up at the MM and see what Thomas and Emma say?'

'Don't be hasty, Elizabeth,' replied Joan. 'We can't bring ideas up just to please ourselves. We go to the MM as representatives of form two. We'd need to find out what lots of other people in the form think about it first – and there isn't time.'

'Here come Kathleen and Jenny!' exclaimed Elizabeth. 'We can ask them what they think while we're getting ready.'

The four girls shared dormitory number 14, a big sunny room on the first floor. As Elizabeth and Joan prepared to go to the Monitors' Meeting, they talked to the other two about the armband idea.

'Do you think we really need monitors to have an armband?' said Kathleen, her cheeks rosier than ever after an hour on the games field. 'Everybody knows who they are.'

'I'm not sure they always do,' pouted Elizabeth.

'It's a good idea in some ways,' reflected Jenny. 'But it would mean the school having to spend money to get them made. The Beauty and the Beast might think it's a waste of money!'

Miss Belle and Miss Best were the joint headmistresses. They weren't greatly in favour of unnecessary fripperies and frills.

'We could make our own,' suggested Elizabeth.

By the time she had finished chattering and brushing her hair and (at Joan's suggestion) sponging a jam mark off her school skirt, it was getting late. The two friends hurried off along the corridor to go to the meeting – and bumped straight into Julian.

He had come looking for Elizabeth. He was still wearing his tracksuit after Games and was disappointed to see her looking so smartly dressed.

'Oh, why have you changed, Elizabeth? We were planning to go for a pony ride before tea!'

Elizabeth's hand flew to her mouth.

'Oh, Julian, sorry! How awful of me. I forgot I had an MM today. Can we go for a ride tomorrow, instead? But, listen, there's an idea I want to tell you about. I need to know your opinion . . .'

At that moment, two other second form boys appeared.

'Harry . . . Martin . . . I need your opinions, as well.'

Elizabeth stood there in the corridor and declaimed her idea about the special armbands for school monitors. Joan looked anxiously at her watch.

'Well, Julian, what do you think?' ended Elizabeth.

Her friend threw back his head and roared with laughter.

'What a horrible idea, Elizabeth! Do you want to be mistaken for a member of the secret police or something?'

Harry and Martin started tittering. Elizabeth . . . armband . . . secret police. What a joke!

'All right, all right. I was only asking!' protested Elizabeth.

She suddenly went off the idea, herself. It had fallen flat. All the fizz had gone out of it. Although she hated being teased by Julian, she always valued his opinion. By the time the two girls had reached the door of Thomas and Emma's big study, her mind was made up.

'I don't think we'd better say anything about the armband idea, Joan,' whispered Elizabeth. 'It doesn't seem to have a lot of support.'

Joan murmured her agreement.

Privately, she was thinking about Jake. It might have slipped the big boy's mind that Elizabeth was one of his monitors but how could he have escaped the fact? Elizabeth was so keen! She was so determined to be a successful and dynamic monitor. There was really no need for her to think about wearing an armband!

It was much more likely, reasoned Joan, that the boy was upset at being reminded about his injury, by a monitor or anybody else, no matter how kindly meant. It only made him more grumpy. Elizabeth had better go easy in that quarter, she thought.

Out loud, she simply said:

'I expect there will be a lot of other things to talk about.'

'Yes!' replied Elizabeth eagerly. 'I wonder what Thomas and Emma have got in store for us to discuss this week? I expect it will be something interesting!'

## CHAPTER TWO

# THOMAS AND EMMA
# AIR A NEW IDEA

'HELLO, ELIZABETH! Hello, Joan!' The head girl ushered
them in with a smile. 'You'd better grab your tea and
biscuits before you sit down. We're all crammed together
like sardines as usual.'

'Sorry we're a bit late, Emma!' apologized Elizabeth.

The study was packed. The two friends had to squeeze
past all the other boys and girls to get to the table where
their mugs of tea awaited them. The mugs stood next to
a plate of biscuits. Elizabeth chose her biscuits with care
– a shortbread and a chocolate digestive.

'If you can *find* anywhere to sit down!' laughed
Thomas. The tall, fair-haired boy was standing by the
window, waiting to start. 'Last to arrive had better sit
on the floor if they can't find anywhere else!'

Joan managed to find a perch on the arm of a chintz-
covered armchair normally reserved for visitors. Then
Donald stood up and insisted on giving Elizabeth his
place on a wooden bench that had been brought in.

'I'll sit on the floor next to Peter,' smiled the older boy. 'I don't mind at all. Budge up a bit, Peter.'

Peter was the youngest there. He had gone up from the junior class to the first form this term and had been made a monitor.

Elizabeth sandwiched herself on to the bench between Eileen and Richard, who were also monitors now. What fun these get-togethers were, she decided. She sipped her tea slowly and gazed round the room. All twelve monitors had turned up, as in previous weeks.

Whereas the main Meeting in the school hall each week was a formal affair, these little MMs were just the reverse, everybody squashed into a small space, the atmosphere relaxed and jolly.

'Thank you all for coming!' began Thomas. 'I see we've got a full house, as usual. And that's good because Emma and I want to give something an airing. It's a completely new idea. We need to know whether you like it yourselves – and whether you think your classmates would approve. Emma – you explain the thinking behind it.'

Emma finished her tea, placed the cup down and swung round in her chair to face them all.

'Tom and I were talking the other day about how we all like to win honours. It's part of human nature. If we're good at games, we try to get into the teams. And if we're good at lessons, we try to come top in class. However some boys and girls are not especially good at games or brainy either but they may have other fine qualities. We thought, is there a way *they* can be given recognition at Whyteleafe too? Some honour they can compete for on equal terms? What do you think?'

The monitors received the idea with enthusiasm.

'You mean, people who do something unselfish?' asked young Peter.

'A noble deed?' exclaimed Elizabeth, eagerly.

'An act of bravery?' suggested Donald.

'Exactly!' said Emma, pleased to see how quickly the monitors were warming to the idea. 'All of those things. Hands up all of you who think such a prize would be popular with the boys and girls in your form.'

At once every hand in the room shot up.

Thomas smiled as he looked round at the forest of hands.

'Good!' he said. 'In that case, Emma and I would like to announce the plan at this week's Meeting. Let's work out the details. How often should we give out the honour? Perhaps once a term, do you think?'

'Yes! And keep it separate, so award it at half-term!' suggested Eileen.

'But what will the honour be called, Thomas?' asked Donald.

'Now, there's a good question,' smiled Thomas. 'Let's put our thinking caps on.'

After that, the discussion raged for several minutes. Elizabeth was aglow. She liked the head boy and girl's idea. Now they were all being asked to think of the name for the new honour. It was so exciting to be in at the very beginning of things like this. A new tradition at Whyteleafe School . . .

Suggested names for the honour came thick and fast.

'The Bravery Award!'

'The Gold Star for Good Conduct!'

'No – the Gold Star for Courage . . .'

'What about the Good Deed Award?'

In the end, it was one of the fourth form monitors, Eric, who came up with the best name. He was a thoughtful, learned-looking boy. He got to his feet, adjusted his spectacles and cleared his throat.

'May I say something? I'll never forget some of the things that William and Rita told us about courage at camp last term. They knew the true meaning of courage, didn't they? And they explained it so well. I'm sure the whole school would wish to remember them.'

'They were the finest head boy and girl that any school could hope for,' said Thomas, humbly. 'Emma and I are going to have to work hard to live up to their example.'

Emma nodded, her eyes misting over.

'And so, Eric?' she asked.

Before Eric could reply, Elizabeth suddenly guessed what he was going to say. A thrill ran through her and she clapped her hands. She couldn't stop herself, shouting it out loud –

'The William and Rita Award!' she cried. 'That's what you're going to say, isn't it, Eric?'

'Yes! That's it, exactly. You've taken the words right out of my mouth, Elizabeth!'

There were surprised gasps all round and then everyone began to cheer. The William and Rita Award. Excellent!

Thomas and Emma looked at each other in delight.

'That's a lovely name for the honour, Eric,' smiled Emma. 'Quite brilliant.'

'Perfect!' exclaimed Thomas.

And the whole room agreed.

It turned into a long session after that. There was so much to discuss! But it was all very fruitful. By the end of the session, not only had the name of the award been decided but so had all the details of how the winner would be selected. These would be announced in full at the school Meeting.

'Until then, this is all hush-hush,' Emma reminded them. She placed a finger to her lips. 'Not a word to anyone. We don't want this leaking out in dribs and drabs. It must be announced in the proper way when the whole school is assembled.'

Elizabeth and Joan were used to this. Things that the monitors discussed at MMs often had to remain confidential, until the head boy and girl were ready to make them public.

'It's so lucky that we're friends, Joan!' remarked Elizabeth, as they went into the dining-hall for tea. 'We can talk to each other as much as we like about things that are said at the MMs. I'd die if I couldn't talk to somebody about them! I wonder whoget the first William and Rita Award? I wonder if it will be anyone in our form? Wouldn't that be an honour!'

She was still bubbling over with it all when she sat down for tea. Julian had saved her a place by the window, at one of the second form tables.

'Hello, Elizabeth!' Julian wore his usual grin. 'How did the meeting of the secret police go, then? What are you looking so excited about? Did you decide anything interesting?'

'As a matter of fact, we did,' Elizabeth blurted out.

'What then?'

'It'll be announced at the school Meeting,' said Elizabeth. 'But my lips are sealed till then. Oh, sorry, Julian. I shouldn't have said anything, should I?'

A look of annoyance had crossed her friend's face.

'It's not *my* fault,' she added. 'It's a rule!'

'Since when has the Naughtiest Girl worried her head about rules?' asked Julian, waspishly. 'If this monitor business is going to turn you into the school goody-goody, I will feel very badly let down, Elizabeth Allen.'

'Sorry, Julian,' Elizabeth repeated.

Then he gave her hair a friendly tweak and smiled.

'Only joking,' he said airily. 'No leaks allowed from the Cabinet Office, eh? Has to be announced at the full sitting of parliament? Fair enough.'

Daniel Carter, sitting opposite, was looking solemn.

'Julian, Elizabeth would love to tell you what happened. You can see that just by looking at her face! I'm sure she *would*, if she could. Gosh, I can't wait for the Meeting, to hear what it is. I wish I'd been at the MM, Elizabeth. They *do* sound fun.'

The wistful expression on Daniel's face gave Elizabeth a sudden pang.

For the first few days of term, Daniel had been appointed as a form monitor in Elizabeth's place, while she had been in disgrace about something. But as soon as Elizabeth had been vindicated, the boy had of course stood down to enable her to have her monitorship back. Poor Daniel!

But before Elizabeth could brood about it, another boy called down the table to her. It was Julian's cousin, Patrick. The two cousins liked to keep their distance as they did not get on particularly well.

'Please stop gabbing, Elizabeth, and pass the bread rolls up this end! I'm starving! I've been practising my ping-pong for the last hour!'

Elizabeth smiled and passed the bread basket along the table.

Patrick smiled back.

'Don't forget it's squad practice tomorrow,' he reminded her. 'I'm going to beat you for a change!'

They were both in the school table-tennis squad but Patrick was only the team's first reserve. He was a very competitive boy and was striving with all his might to become a full team member, like Elizabeth.

'You *wish*, Patrick!' Elizabeth called back cheerfully.

After that, she tucked into her tea with gusto.

She gave no further thought to Daniel's comments, nor Julian's. It would be some days before she would have good reason to recall them.

## CHAPTER THREE

# ELIZABETH HEARS ABOUT
# A BRAVE DEED

THE TABLE-TENNIS practice, the one that Patrick had mentioned, took place after lessons the following day. Mr Warlow, the sports master, had asked all team members and team reserves to attend. He and Emma, who was table-tennis captain, wanted to check that everyone was in good form for a match on Saturday. It would be an away match against Hickling Green School, their old rivals, to take place alongside a hockey fixture. Hickling Green had a very strong hockey eleven. Mr Warlow feared that Whyteleafe might do badly in the hockey match, especially with Jake out of the team. But he had high hopes of his table-tennis squad! It was a good one this term.

Elizabeth would not have been allowed to miss the practice, even if she'd wanted to. And, of course, she would not have dreamt of missing it. She was looking forward to the trip on Saturday. Miss Belle and Miss Best had hired a full-size coach to accommodate both teams and their supporters. It would be so exciting if they could beat their old rivals, thought Elizabeth, and they would be sure to get a lovely tea afterwards.

However it was a great disappointment to have to put off going riding with Julian for the second day running.

'Don't worry, Elizabeth, it's not your fault,' he said, good-humouredly. 'It's just a pity we're not allowed to go riding after tea this term, with the evenings drawing in. I'll fix up a ride with Robert, instead.'

'Let's go and feed the ponies after tea. At least we're allowed to do that!' suggested Elizabeth. 'I haven't seen them for days and I'm missing them.'

'Good!' said Julian. 'I like that idea. Off you go to your ping-pong, then. Don't wear yourself out. See you at tea!'

It was a busy practice session. Emma and Mr Warlow spent most of the time coaching the boys and girls. They were shown how to improve their footwork, as well as their batting technique. They were then split up to play a proper practice game, paired according to ability. Elizabeth was asked to play against Patrick. The two were evenly matched although Elizabeth was considered to have the edge.

She usually beat Patrick. But today he was determined to reverse that situation. He had been working on his

game furiously, for days.

And he knew that both Emma and the teacher were keeping a watchful eye on all three tables, checking everybody's current form. It made him very focused.

But Elizabeth was equally aware that they were being kept an eye on. And she was very focused, too.

They both played exceptionally well.

Patrick served first and took the lead, 3–2. Then Elizabeth served and lost only one of her service points to lead 6–4. After that the lead passed from one to the other, backwards and forwards, the scores tending to go with service. The rallies were long, fast and furious.

The score reached 20–20!

Now they had to change service on every point. The first to lead by two clear points would win the game. In the tension of the moment, Patrick's service faltered. It twice missed the table and he lost the point. 21–20 to Elizabeth. Then Elizabeth did a safe medium-paced service, nothing fancy. Patrick returned to her backhand. She gave back a spinning lob that just caught the edge of the table. Patrick had to swoop low and only just managed to return it.

It was a weak, loopy return. It bounced high on Elizabeth's side of the table. She changed to forehand grip, swung her arm back and then—

Whooosh!

## ELIZABETH HEARS ABOUT A BRAVE DEED

A beautiful forehand smash to the far corner! Patrick dived . . . too late. He missed.

'22–20!' Elizabeth cried in delight. 'I've won! I've won!'

The ping-pong ball hit the far wall and came rolling slowly back towards Patrick's foot. In his fury and frustration, and in the heat of the moment, he stamped on it.

Crunch!

The ping-pong ball was flattened.

The sudden sound made Emma glance round.

'Oh, Patrick, you clumsy boy! You've trodden on the ball!'

Already regretting his temper, Patrick stared at Elizabeth imploringly. He was silently begging her not to give him away! She was the only person who had seen him deliberately stamp on the ball.

Emma was scooping the poor ball up from the floor, examining it.

'It's past repair, I'm afraid,' she said.

'Oh, what a shame,' said Elizabeth, innocently.

'I'll replace it, Emma,' Patrick said, quickly. 'I'll go to the village and buy a new one with my own money. I'll go straight away if you like. Has the session ended now?'

'Oh, Patrick, you are a good sport,' said Emma. 'Will you really? As a matter of fact, we're getting rather low on balls at the moment. Would you like to go with him, please, Elizabeth? You've both got some time before tea.'

At Whyteleafe School, pupils were allowed to go down to the village. But it was a strict rule that they went out in pairs and not on their own.

'The sun's coming out!' said Elizabeth cheerfully. 'I'll be glad of a walk to the village.'

As the boy and girl strolled out through the school gates and along the quiet road to the village Patrick looked sullen and shamefaced.

'Thanks for not giving me away, Elizabeth,' he said.

Elizabeth felt slightly sorry for him.

'Cheer up,' she said. 'I've got an awfully hot temper myself, so I know just what it's like to lose it!'

Patrick did not reply. The fact was that, in spite of their occasional clashes, he could not help liking and admiring Elizabeth. He often wished that she would like and admire *him*. It was annoying the way she seemed so much to prefer his cousin Julian. And now he felt angry with himself for losing his temper like that. It had been childish.

'It's all right for you to lose your temper, Elizabeth,' he said. 'You're only a girl.'

Elizabeth couldn't help smiling to herself. It was a typical Patrick remark – and just one of the reasons why

266

she much preferred his cousin Julian!

Patrick did not speak again until they reached the shop.

'The truth is, Elizabeth,' he confessed, as they stared in the shop window, 'that I really thought I might beat you today. You've been so busy with this monitor business. You haven't been practising so much lately. I was so hoping that they'd notice me. How well I was playing . . . Then maybe I'd get a chance to play in a match soon.'

'You *were* playing well, Patrick,' said Elizabeth, truthfully. 'And the game could easily have gone the other way. And I'm sure they did notice you and that you'll be given a chance, sooner or later.'

A little bell on the shop door tinkled softly as they pushed it open and went inside. It was a lovely, old-fashioned shop with a warm musky smell. The table-tennis balls were in a cardboard box, jammed between the shuttlecocks and the birthday cards.

Patrick picked out a shiny new white ping-pong ball, took it to the counter and paid for it. Elizabeth followed him out of the shop.

They stood outside on the pavement wondering whether there was time to go across to the sweet shop, on the opposite side of the road. They decided there was not.

Then suddenly a car squealed to a halt in front of them and a mother burst out of the car, with a small red-headed child. They seemed to be in a great state of excitement. They were looking this way.

Something strange was going on.

The little girl was pointing at Patrick! She was whispering to her mother. Her eyes were very big and round. Her cheeks had gone very pink.

'Are you *sure*, Sandra?' the woman kept asking. 'Are you really sure it was him?'

'Yes, Mummy. It was, it was, it was!'

'Look at his face. You are quite sure?'

'Sure as sure can be, Mummy!' squeaked the child, getting more excited by the minute. 'Cross my heart. It was him!'

Then an extraordinary thing happened. To Elizabeth's amazement, the woman ran up to Patrick and embraced him! There were tears of emotion in her eyes.

'Thank you!' she exclaimed. 'Thank you for saving my little Sandra's life! Every day when we come to the shops, I tell Sandra to look out for you, in case she should see you again. We so wanted to be able to thank you!'

Patrick stood there, blushing.

And then the woman picked the child up and thrust her at Patrick.

268

# ELIZABETH HEARS ABOUT A BRAVE DEED

'Give the young man a kiss, Sandra. Tell him you're sorry for being such a silly girl and giving us all a fright. Say thank you, nicely.'

Patrick's blushing increased tenfold as the little girl planted a kiss on his cheek and lisped her thank-yous.

The woman then set the child down on the pavement and turned to speak to Elizabeth.

'I don't suppose your friend's ever told you he's a hero?'

'No!' exclaimed Elizabeth. 'Whatever happened?'

'My Sandra ran out of this shop last week when my back was turned!' the woman explained. 'She ran across the road to go to the sweet shop. That's what happened! And your friend here—' The woman patted Patrick's arm, overcome with emotion. 'There was this car, you see,' she gulped. 'It came speeding round the bend. It didn't see my Sandra. And your friend – he was so brave. He ran into the road and pushed her out of the way, just in time! And he could have been killed himself. And he didn't even stop to let anybody thank him. He just ran off.'

'Patrick!' gasped Elizabeth.

Politely, Patrick bowed to both the mother and child. Then he backed away.

'I'm afraid we're in a bit of a hurry!' he said. 'Come on, Elizabeth.'

He took her arm and marched her swiftly away. Elizabeth could sense the boy's embarrassment. He would never have dreamt, she thought, that his brave deed might come out in this unexpected way. He was walking so fast, he was almost running!

'Thank you again,' the woman called out. 'I just had to stop the car when Sandra saw you. I didn't mean to embarrass you! You're a real hero, young man. I'll never forget you as long as I live!'

Worried that the woman would take Patrick's discomfiture for rudeness, Elizabeth looked back and gave mother and daughter a friendly wave. Elizabeth's face was flushed with excitement. Her eyes were shining.

'Think nothing of it!' she called. 'It was a pleasure.'

And, as soon as she and Patrick had gone a safe distance, she jerked at his arm and made him halt.

'Patrick! I am absolutely amazed!' she said, gazing at him. 'What a wonderful surprise! I know it's a horrid thing to say but I had no idea that you could be such a brave person. I'm really ashamed of myself now. What a fine thing to do! And to think that when it happened you didn't even wait to be thanked!'

She gazed at him, wide-eyed. She was seeing him in a completely new light.

'Oh, Patrick. I do admire you for this.'

He lowered his gaze, crimson with pleasure.

'Lot of fuss about nothing,' he muttered.

They walked on in silence, each wrapped in their own thoughts. Patrick glanced at Elizabeth from time to time, as they wandered along. Her lips were parted and there was still that thrilled expression on her face.

She was thinking about the William and Rita Award! Surely, now, no other candidate could possibly match Patrick's claim to it? It was almost as though the very award itself had been designed with Patrick's deed in mind. What an honour for the second form if the very first William and Rita Award came their way!

'What are you thinking about, Elizabeth?' asked Patrick, at length. 'Why are you so quiet?'

They were turning in through the school gates. They could hear a distant bell ringing for tea.

'I'm still thinking about your brave deed, of course. And – Patrick, I can't explain yet – but there's a reason why the whole school is going to need to know about it soon!'

'WHAT?' exclaimed Patrick.

He pulled her to a stop. He gripped her arm.

'Don't you dare, Elizabeth! Nobody's to know about this. No one, you understand? You're to promise me at once that you will never say a word to anyone!'

Elizabeth looked at him in dismay. She pouted.

'Why not, Patrick? Why ever not? Quite apart from

this – er – special thing, it's right that people should know! I'd like *everybody* to know what you're really like. What a good, brave person you are. And how you've never once showed off about what you did.'

Patrick flushed, basking in Elizabeth's praise.

'Why must I keep it secret, Patrick?' Elizabeth repeated.

The boy thought long and hard, staring at the ground. When he replied, the words were carefully chosen.

'Look at it this way,' he said. 'If a boy in a Whyteleafe uniform was down in the village one day, and performed a brave action, why would nobody know about it? At least one other person should know about it, shouldn't they? I'm not admitting anything and certainly not to a monitor but isn't there a rule at Whyteleafe School? Isn't there a very strict rule that must never be broken?'

'Oh!' gasped Elizabeth. 'Of course! You went down to the village on your own, Patrick! That's it, isn't it? You didn't pair up with somebody else, the way you're supposed to.'

Patrick did not reply. Instead, he let go of Elizabeth's arm and strode on up the school drive.

He looked back over his shoulder.

'Come on, Elizabeth. You're going to be late for tea.'

She hurried after him. She was thinking things over

carefully. She caught up with him, outside the doors of the dining-hall.

'Patrick, I can see you're in an awkward situation. But believe me, I'm sure this boy would be forgiven, just this once, for breaking an important school rule. Once everybody knew what a hero he'd been.'

'He's not interested in being a hero, Elizabeth, and that's final. A hero to you, if you like. I don't mind that. But nobody else. So now please shut up about it.'

Swallowing her deep disappointment, Elizabeth went in to tea. Julian and Joan were wondering where she'd got to. Julian's eyebrows raised high upon seeing her enter the dining-hall with Patrick.

They explained how they'd gone down to the shops to buy the new ping-pong ball. Patrick whistled cheerfully and bounced it on the table a few times. Elizabeth watched, admiringly.

Later, when they went to feed the ponies, Julian joked about Patrick.

'Poor Elizabeth. That's what comes of being a monitor. Bad luck!'

Elizabeth would normally have got the point at once and giggled. But today she looked at Julian in surprise.

'Bad luck? What do you mean exactly, Julian?'

'Having to partner Patrick down to the village shop,

of course,' he replied, patiently. 'No wonder you looked cross when you got back for tea. Was he a pain, as usual?'

'No, of course not. Patrick's not a pain!'

Julian looked at her in surprise.

'Oh, I know he is sometimes,' Elizabeth added hastily. She drew a deep breath. She must be careful. But she must also come to Patrick's defence. 'Your cousin's quite decent really. He's got hidden depths, you know.'

'Hidden depths?' Julian laughed out loud. 'So well hidden you'd never find them in a million years. Have you gone potty, Elizabeth? Or is this a bad attack of the goody-goody-monitor-itis disease?'

'Of course it isn't, Julian,' retorted Elizabeth, indignantly.

'I think I prefer you when you're being the Naughtiest Girl,' he grinned.

Drat Patrick, thought Elizabeth, not letting her tell anybody about his brave deed! She was longing to tell Julian but her lips had been sealed.

Patrick was pretending it was because he wanted nobody to find out that he'd been breaking a school rule. But Elizabeth was not convinced about that.

The real reason, she believed, was that, as with any true hero, Patrick was determined that his heroism should go unsung. And, although it made her cross, it also made her admire him all the more for it.

She decided she would try to express her admiration secretly. Somehow she'd find a way to be especially nice to him!

CHAPTER FOUR

# AN UNEXPECTED DISCOVERY

WITH THE whole school assembled in the big hall, Thomas and Emma announced the new award. They left it to the very end of Friday's Meeting. Every pupil listened attentively, from the junior children sitting cross-legged on the floor at the front, to the seniors on benches at the back. No boys and girls were allowed to miss the weekly 'parliament'. The joint headmistresses, with Mr Johns, the senior master, sat at the very back of the hall. They were there as observers. They never took part in the Meetings unless, for very difficult matters, their advice was needed.

Elizabeth and Joan sat in chairs on the platform with the other monitors, just behind the head boy and girl. Thomas and Emma sat at a special table, from where they conducted the Meeting.

There had been all the usual business to get through. Money was collected up from pupils who'd received some this week, then given out again to every member of the school in the form of the two pounds weekly allowance. At Whyteleafe School, all money had to be fairly shared. Then 'Special Requests' for extra money were listened to. They were discussed and then either granted or refused. There were no complaints or grumbles to be heard this week but there were several sports announcements. Elizabeth was proud to hear her name read out as a member of the table-tennis team for tomorrow's match against Hickling Green.

Jake's name was again missing from the hockey team list. From her vantage point on the platform, Elizabeth had watched him arrive for the Meeting. His limp, if anything, seemed more pronounced than ever. His ankle was still supported by a thick crepe bandage.

'We are all sorry that Jake will not be able to play for us at Hickling Green tomorrow,' announced Thomas, 'and we take this opportunity to wish him well and hope that his injury is better in time for our next hockey fixture, which will be against Milford Grange.'

Then Emma took over.

'Finally, we have some exciting news to tell you,' she said.

Elizabeth and Joan glanced at each other. At last! They had been waiting eagerly for the moment when the William and Rita Award would be announced. It had been a strain having to keep it secret since the MM. Now the whole school would hear about it. How would it be received? Had the monitors been correct when they'd all voted for it, so sure that their classmates would approve?

They need not have worried. The news was greeted with cheers and applause. It was very well received indeed! Soon a buzz of chatter ran up and down the rows.

A new honour, to be called the William and Rita Award!

To be given not for being brainy or good at games or anything like that but for Outstanding Conduct, such as bravery or unselfishness . . . or exceptional kindness. It would be handed out each half-term. What a fantastic idea!

'What are you so quiet for, Patrick?' asked their classmate, Arabella Buckley. 'Don't you like the idea?'

'Just thinking, that's all,' muttered Patrick. He had been listening attentively to the announcement. He appeared to be scowling.

'I think it's an excellent idea,' continued Arabella, primly. She was already trying to work out how she might get to win the new honour. 'The brainy people get paid too much attention around here.'

'What do you think, Julian?' asked Arabella's friend, Rosemary. 'I like the way it's called after William and Rita, don't you?'

# AN UNEXPECTED DISCOVERY

'It's a good idea,' conceded Julian. 'And, yes, it's a good name, too. I'm sure they'd approve!'

Julian glanced up towards the platform, at Elizabeth's glowing face. So this was what the secret had been the other day? He was pleased to be privy to it at last. It was difficult, in some ways, the Naughtiest Girl being a monitor.

As the noise level in the hall grew, Thomas had to bring the Meeting to order. He banged the gavel sharply on the small table.

'Silence! We're pleased you all like the idea! But if you've any questions or suggestions to make, please address them to the whole Meeting and not just to each other!'

Arabella was the first to put her hand up. She rose to her feet.

'Please, Thomas, Emma says we're allowed to put forward names for the award. But when should we do it exactly?'

'At any time, Arabella. At any time you see someone in your own form behaving in a way that deserves a nomination. The school office has a supply of special forms, called citation forms. You simply collect a form, fill in the person's name and your reason for naming them, then hand it to your monitor.'

'What happens to the forms then?' asked Arabella, eagerly.

'Any monitor who has been given a citation form will read it out, at the next Monitors' Meeting. Each one will be heard out in the privacy of that meeting. The best will go on a shortlist. Just before half-term, Emma and I will go through the shortlist with Miss Belle and Miss Best. They will help us to decide who has won the first William and Rita Award. But the Award will be presented once every term. It will, we hope, become a regular feature of school life and something that all can strive for.'

'Thank you, Thomas,' nodded Arabella. She sat down, her dainty face a little pinker than usual.

There were a few more questions. After that, the Meeting was declared closed.

Patrick waited for Elizabeth as she came out of the hall and pulled her to one side. He seemed agitated.

'I couldn't bear it, Elizabeth. You do understand, don't you? You do promise?'

'Of course I promise, Patrick.'

She patted his arm soothingly and smiled. She was feeling in a very good mood. How well the announcement had gone. The whole school approved of it! Thomas and Emma were absolutely right; courage and kindness and unselfishness were the most important qualities in the world. It was right that they should be recognized.

'You are much too modest, Patrick,' she said. 'But

your secret is safe with me. I can't help wishing you would change your mind, though! You were so brave!'

At that moment, Julian came out of the hall, looking for Elizabeth. He was confronted by the sight of her with Patrick. The pair of them were whispering together, smiling and looking at each other in a silly way.

'Come on, Elizabeth,' he said sharply. 'Let's go and have tea.'

'Just coming, Julian!'

As they made their way to the dining-hall together, a feeling of exasperation swept over Julian.

'You seem to be getting very thick with my horrible cousin,' he commented.

'Oh, please don't be silly, Julian,' replied Elizabeth.

She was thinking hard. The glimmering of an idea was forming in her mind. She had thought of a way in which she could recognize Patrick's modesty and courage with a small noble deed of her own. It was no more than he deserved and it would be a gesture that she would find deeply satisfying.

Unfortunately, it was going to annoy Julian even more.

'Drat! I've got a horrid headache,' announced Elizabeth the next day. 'I don't think I'm going to be well enough to play in my match today!'

Julian stared at his friend in surprise.

It was Saturday dinner-time. Elizabeth had been laughing and talking cheerfully during the meal and had eaten heartily. The boys and girls had been out blackberrying during the week. From the bags full of succulent fruit brought to the school kitchens, Cook had concocted a whole shelf-full of summer puddings. They had been served today, with a choice of cream or custard. Elizabeth had eaten three helpings. Delicious!

'You must have eaten too much,' observed Julian.

'Oh, poor Elizabeth,' said Joan anxiously. 'But you mustn't miss the match! The coach leaves in twenty minutes . . . You'd better go and see Matron for some aspirin straight away!'

Further along the table, Patrick's ears had pricked up.

'It's no good, Joan!' Elizabeth ran her hand across her brow for dramatic effect. 'I just know I won't be able to play my best today. Patrick will have to play in my place. He's first reserve and he is very good, you know.'

For a moment, Patrick had felt upset that Elizabeth was feeling unwell. But now, unable to help himself, a look of incredulous joy crossed his face. The Naughtiest Girl felt very pleased with herself as she noted his expression.

'Oh, Elizabeth, I'll be glad to take your place if you're

not feeling up to it. Shall we go and see Emma right away and talk to her about it?'

'Yes, Patrick. Let's!'

They rushed off to see Emma, who was just leaving the seniors' table. It was almost time to go and get ready. As team captain, she agreed at once that Patrick should take Elizabeth's place. A jolting coach journey to Hickling Green School would make the headache much worse for Elizabeth, she reasoned.

As Patrick and Elizabeth walked back to their own table, Julian strained his ears to hear what was being said. Elizabeth was gazing at Patrick with that silly expression on her face again. Patrick was talking to her as though they were very dear friends.

'Oh, Elizabeth, I've been waiting for this chance for so long. I won't let you down, I promise. I'll play the best table tennis of my life.'

'I know you will, Patrick.'

'And I'll do it specially for you, Elizabeth! I'm going to win my match today, as a present for you.'

'Thank you, Patrick.'

'I don't think I've got time to finish my pudding. I'd better dash straight off and get changed and find my lucky table-tennis bat.'

He rushed away, brimming over with excitement. Elizabeth slipped back into her seat between Julian and

Joan, a satisfied little smile on her face.

'Poor Elizabeth,' repeated Joan, who was just getting up from the table. 'What a shame. Promise me you'll have a quiet lie-down this afternoon.'

'We'll want to go and wave the coach off first, won't we, Joan?' replied Elizabeth, eagerly. 'We can wave to them and wish them good luck!'

Secretly, the Naughtiest Girl wanted to see Patrick's face again as he climbed on to the coach in his smart tracksuit. That happy look on his face made it all so worthwhile.

'I can't, Elizabeth,' Joan apologized. 'I've promised to go on an outing with Susan this afternoon. Look, she's waiting for me now.'

Sure enough, Joan's friend Susan, who had gone up into the third form this term, was signalling to her. Miss Thomas was taking a group to the indoor swimming pool in the town and Susan was a very keen swimmer. Thinking that Elizabeth would be away at her match, Joan had arranged to go too.

As she hurried off, Elizabeth turned to Julian.

He was bent over his pudding, a puzzled gleam in his green eyes. He was a very clever, bright boy. He was not easily tricked. He was convinced that Elizabeth was play-acting and did not have a headache at all. She was trying to give Patrick a chance in the table-tennis team, that was all!

He was used to never knowing what went on inside her head. At other times, it was one of the things he liked best about her! But not today. Why was Elizabeth being so nice to his worthless cousin? It didn't make sense.

And Julian found it intensely irritating.

'You'll come with me to see Patrick off on the coach, won't you, Julian?' smiled Elizabeth. 'And it's a lovely afternoon. We could go out on the ponies, after that. We could have a good long outing.'

'Certainly not,' said Julian. 'Why should I want to see Patrick off on the coach? As for going for a ride, I thought you had a headache.'

'Well, yes, but . . .' Elizabeth thought quickly. 'I'm sure the fresh air will do it good!'

'I'm sorry, Elizabeth. I've fixed up to go riding with Harry and Robert. As you're not well enough to play in your match, I suggest you go and have a good lie-down, as Joan suggested.'

'Yes, of course,' sighed Elizabeth.

Soon after that she left the dining-hall and went outside into the school grounds, for a walk. She wanted to collect her thoughts. Julian was annoyed with her! He couldn't understand why she was being so friendly towards Patrick. If only she could explain to him what a fine person Patrick really was and that he *deserved* some reward. But she couldn't. She'd promised!

The coach was waiting on the back drive.

Shortly before it was due to leave, she went across there and hid in the shrubbery. She could see all the boys and girls climbing aboard, the hockey team as well. They were all laughing and talking together. Patrick was already in his seat, on the far side of the coach, so she couldn't see his expression, after all. Unable to wave the coach off with her friends, she knew she would feel a bit silly doing it on her own. So she decided to watch it leave, from here, without being seen.

The warm glow that she'd felt a few minutes earlier had faded. As she watched the last passengers climb aboard and the coach doors shut, she felt very wistful. They were all off to Hickling Green without her. She was going to miss all the excitement! And what was she going to do with herself? The afternoon stretched ahead, bleak and empty . . .

As the coach moved away and trundled off down the drive, a figure standing behind it was suddenly revealed. He was waving, rather forlornly.

It was Jake, seeing the coach off.

But as soon as the vehicle disappeared, Jake's arm dropped to his side and he did an extraordinary thing.

Never dreaming that Elizabeth was watching him

286

from her hiding place, Jake shook his fist at the sky then ran furiously down the drive after the coach and took a flying kick at some loose gravel, to relieve his feelings. He then ran off down a side path and disappeared from view.

'He was running!' realized Elizabeth. 'He didn't have a limp at all! He must have been pretending all this time. There's nothing wrong with his ankle whatsoever!'

It was a very surprising discovery.

## CHAPTER FIVE

# ELIZABETH GIVES JAKE AWAY

ELIZABETH FOLLOWED in Jake's tracks.

'He's limping again, now that people can see him!' she realized, as she reached the other end of the path where it emerged from the bushes. Here, some junior boys and girls were playing on the back lawn.

Jake limped slowly past them, heading for the school buildings. For a moment she wondered if she could have just dreamt it. But only for a moment.

'No. I definitely saw what I saw. So why is Jake play-acting like this?' thought Elizabeth, hot-temperedly. 'It's so mean of him! How can he bear to let our form down in this way, as well as the hockey team and the whole of Whyteleafe School!'

She very nearly dashed after him, there and then. But, even with her temper up, she did not quite dare to confront him. Besides, he was surrounded by some junior boys now. Jake was one of their heroes.

What should she do?

'Julian will know the best thing to do!' Elizabeth

decided. 'I'll ask his advice. I'd better run all the way, if I want to catch him before he goes off!'

She raced across the grounds to the school stables. But the boys had just left.

'They went that way, Elizabeth,' the stableman told her, pointing up the bridle path.

'Thanks!' gasped Elizabeth.

She veered off through the trees. She could hear voices some distance ahead and the clip-clop of the ponies' hooves. Then, through a gap, she glimpsed them turning off at right angles, where the path divided. They were riding in single file, Robert, then Harry, Julian bringing up the rear. She scrambled over a bank and through tangled undergrowth, to cut off a corner. It brought her within hailing distance. She cupped her hands to her mouth.

'JULIAN!' she shouted, with all her might.

Startled, Julian reined in his pony. He wheeled the animal round and spotted Elizabeth, frantically waving her arms. He told Harry and Robert to wait for him.

He trotted back to meet her.

'Whatever's wrong, Elizabeth?'

Gulping to get her breath back, she told Julian what she had just discovered. She was bristling with indignation. He listened carefully.

Then, to her surprise, he gave a dry laugh.

'So that's two of you trying to get out of playing in school matches, is it?' he commented. 'You're a fine one to be cross, Elizabeth. How's the headache, by the way?'

Elizabeth fell silent.

Julian spoke more gently then.

'I think you must have imagined it about Jake, you know.'

'I did not, Julian. I certainly did not! I was hoping to hear your ideas – about the best thing to do.'

'Well, I know that *you* have a reason for getting out of *your* match, Elizabeth. Even if it is a totally potty one! So *Jake* may have a reason, too. You will have to go and speak to him and ask him to explain. After all . . .'

Down the bridle path, Harry and Robert were signalling impatiently. They were cross to have been held up like this. Julian wheeled his pony round. He was suddenly feeling rather cross himself.

'. . . *You* are the monitor, Elizabeth, not me. Good luck!'

Julian rode off then, without a backward glance. He was annoyed to have been reminded like this of Elizabeth making sacrifices on behalf of his worthless cousin, Patrick. Just when he had managed to put it out of his mind!

Elizabeth walked slowly back to school, feeling very subdued.

Her temper had evaporated now. Julian's words had rather shamed her. He had guessed that she had made it up about the headache. He had also guessed the reason why! She longed to explain to him about Patrick's brave deed but she was not allowed to. And, of course, Julian was right. She was a fine one to feel indignant about Jake!

But she also knew that Julian's advice was correct. As Jake's monitor, she should go and speak to him and give him a chance to explain the reason for his strange behaviour. She should then persuade Jake to go and own up to the teachers. However, Elizabeth remembered the last time that she had spoken to the big boy as his monitor. How grumpy he had been with her – and with good reason, with so much to hide.

How much grumpier he would be if she dared to confront him now! And he would probably think that she had been spying on him. He would be furious!

All that afternoon, Elizabeth tried to screw up courage to go and speak to the older boy. But her courage failed her. She decided that perhaps she would speak to Joan about it, at teatime. If Joan agreed, they would go and see Jake together, this evening.

It was only when Joan did not turn up at teatime that Elizabeth remembered that the swimming group had been excused tea today. They were having tea in town.

## ELIZABETH GIVES JAKE AWAY

Julian turned up late, glowing from his ride, and did not even bother to ask Elizabeth if she had spoken to Jake yet. Elizabeth was relieved about that.

After that, she did her piano practice and then decided to go and wait for the return of the school coach. She longed to know how the table-tennis team had got on at Hickling Green. What fun Patrick would have been having today, so much more fun than her. She'd never known such a dreary time. How she would have loved to play in the match!

The first person off the coach was Mr Warlow.

'Hello, Elizabeth. Feeling better? You'll be pleased to know that we won the table tennis. Patrick played very well.'

Elizabeth felt some relief at those words. She had done the school no harm then, by not playing in the match! But – she had never seen the sports master look so careworn.

'Is there anything wrong, Mr Warlow?' she asked.

'I'm afraid the hockey match was a disaster. We were beaten 6–0. We had our chances to score but we didn't take them. We needed our star shooter and that's a fact. It would have made such a difference if Jake had played. That wretched ankle of his. I have never known a simple sprain take so long to get better!'

The young sports master looked so unhappy,

Elizabeth longed to cheer him up! She smiled impetuously and, before she could stop them, the words flew out of her mouth, unbidden.

'It's better now, Mr Warlow! It's just got better!'

'Elizabeth, is this true?' asked the teacher, looking excited. 'Have you spoken to Jake, then?'

Elizabeth gulped. What had she said? What had she *done*?

There was no going back now.

'I – I haven't actually spoken to him. But I saw him outside and the ankle's suddenly looking . . . well, really fine. I'm sure it's going to be all right for the match against Milford Grange, Mr Warlow! I'm sure if you get Jake to have a check-up . . .'

'I'll drive him to the doctor myself!' exclaimed Mr Warlow, in delight. 'I'll go and find him straight away! If we hurry, we'll just make surgery before it closes.'

He strode briskly away.

'This is very good news, Elizabeth!' he called back over his shoulder. 'Thank you so much for telling me! What a good monitor you are!'

'Hello, Elizabeth! What's this about good news? I've got some good news myself!'

Patrick had appeared at her side. Some members of the Whyteleafe first hockey team were beginning to trudge past, heads bowed, eyes downcast. But Patrick was beaming with pride.

'I won both my games, Elizabeth!' he was saying. 'I told you I would, didn't I?'

Elizabeth was watching Mr Warlow, as he disappeared into the school building. He was determined to find Jake at once. He wanted to take him to the doctor's! What a shock the big boy was going to get. Elizabeth could not help feeling a little trembly. She had let her tongue run away with her.

With an effort, she turned her attention to Patrick.

'Congratulations!' she said, looking pale. 'I'm so pleased for you. Was it a good outing then?'

'A marvellous outing! We had the most splendid tea!' Patrick was looking elated. 'But you haven't heard the half of it, Elizabeth! Donald didn't play at all well today. If it hadn't been for me, we'd have lost. My last game decided it. From something Emma said to me, I think I'm going to be chosen instead of Donald next time.'

They started to walk over to the school together.

'Oh, Patrick, I'm so glad I gave you your chance!' Elizabeth blurted out. 'It's no more than you deserve.'

'Gave me my chance?' asked Patrick, looking puzzled.

Elizabeth took a deep breath. She had been stung by

Julian's words earlier. It would make her feel better if Patrick, at least, knew the truth . . .

'I didn't really have a headache,' she confessed. 'I was just desperate to make sure that you got some reward at least for your brave deed.'

'Elizabeth!' exclaimed Patrick. He looked horrified. 'You shouldn't have done that.'

'I had to,' she replied. 'You are such a fine person, Patrick. I don't know how I'm going to hold my tongue at the next MM, I really don't . . . you do deserve the William and Rita Award, you really do!'

'No!' The boy paled. 'You promised!'

'It's all right, it's all right,' she said soothingly. Seeing how upset he was, she slipped her arm through his as they walked towards the school steps together. 'Only joking, Patrick! I am sure a lot of fine deeds will be coming up at the MMs. I expect Thomas and Emma will have far too many to choose from when the time comes! I must say I'm looking forward to hearing some of them.'

Patrick nodded, visibly relieved. He liked having Elizabeth on his arm like this. Somebody was coming down the steps, and would be passing right by them in a moment . . .

'Hello, Julian!' he said cheerfully. 'I won my games today! Nice evening, isn't it?'

'Is it?' asked Julian, curtly. 'Joan's back, Elizabeth. She was looking for you.'

And he passed on his way.

Elizabeth took her leave of Patrick almost immediately.

She found Joan resting on the bed upstairs.

'Oh, Elizabeth, I have had such a wonderful time! But I am quite exhausted now!'

Gentle Joan had never shone at sports. But today she had made an exciting discovery. It seemed that Miss Thomas believed that she had the talents of a born swimmer. The teacher was hoping to get up a Whyteleafe swimming team some time. She had told Joan that, with the right training, she could well be a member of it.

'Miss Thomas is going to give Susan and me and some others regular fitness training in the gym,' Joan explained. 'Oh, Elizabeth, I never thought I'd ever be good at sports but I really think I might enjoy swimming.'

'Joan, this is the most thrilling news!' exclaimed Elizabeth, pleased to see her friend so happy.

For once Joan was too full of her own news to question her friend about the headache, or how she'd spent the afternoon. That came as a relief to Elizabeth.

She was beginning to feel very ashamed that instead of having the courage to go and speak to Jake, she had ended up blurting out his secret to a teacher. She could not bring herself to confess what she had done, even to her best friend.

But what would happen now?

CHAPTER SIX

# A HORRID MESSAGE APPEARS

ON SUNDAY morning, Jake was seen running up and down the hockey pitch with Mr Warlow, practising his stick work. The teacher wanted to see his star player back on top form as quickly as possible. He would be needed for the Milford Grange match, needed very badly!

Several second form boys turned out to watch him. Martin, Kenneth, Harry and John McTavish were all fans of his. He was such a marvellous player for a boy of his age; Kenneth was already a friend of his in the second form. The others had admired him even when they were only in the first form.

It was great news, the boys all agreed, that the sprained ankle had now made a complete recovery. Mr Warlow had got the doctor to check it over last night. There had been no sign of bruise or swelling there. He was pronounced fit to play hockey again.

'What a shame it wasn't in time to play against Hickling Green yesterday!' observed Harry.

'But he'll be able to play against Milford Grange!' smiled Martin. 'It's a home match so we'll all be able to watch!'

'We'll thrash them!' said John jubilantly. 'Jake will see to that.'

They were all very pleased.

'Did you speak to Jake then, Elizabeth?' asked Julian, with interest, at one point during the day.

'Not exactly,' she mumbled, in embarrassment, and hurried off.

For the only person who was not pleased was Jake.

Secretly, he was very upset. He did not want to play hockey against Milford Grange. He did not want to play hockey at all. When he passed Elizabeth in the dining-hall at breakfast-time, he had given her such a fierce look. Mr Warlow might think that Elizabeth was a good monitor, to have spotted that Jake's ankle had suddenly made a recovery, but Jake did not share that opinion! He was very taken aback by it all and became convinced that Elizabeth must have been spying on him, in secret. How long had she been doing so? he wondered.

She had also got him into trouble. For the doctor had informed Mr Warlow that from all appearances any injury to the ankle must have repaired itself some time ago. The teacher was baffled that Jake had made out the injury to be far worse than it really was. He had accused him of laziness and of letting down the school.

Jake was such a big, silent, powerful character. The fierce look he had given Elizabeth had made her flinch! She spent the rest of the day avoiding him. She was very puzzled by his strange behaviour. At the same time she was truly ashamed that his secret had come out in the way that it had. She wanted to find some way of showing him that she was sorry.

By the evening, when she felt hopeful that Jake would have cooled down somewhat, she took her chance. He was standing drinking cocoa in the second form common room, surrounded by the gang of boys who admired him.

'Have my chocolate biscuit, Jake,' she said, walking up to him. 'It will build you up for the match against Milford Grange! May I come and cheer you on, please?'

'Don't bother,' replied Jake curtly, ignoring the plate. 'I can manage without you.'

Elizabeth had a hot temper. It immediately flared up.

'How rude!' she gasped, gazing up at the boy as he towered above her. 'You're not to talk to a monitor like that!'

That immediately inflamed Jake.

'I'm tired of girl monitors,' he stated. 'Little girl monitors would do a lot better to mind their own business.'

'Hear, hear!' agreed Martin. He had no idea what Jake was talking about but he could see that the big boy was very angry.

Elizabeth's own anger easily matched Jake's.

She wanted to blurt out that it was not just her business but everybody else's if a person pretended they had something wrong with them when they hadn't and deliberately let a school team down! But then, to her horror, she remembered that she'd just done the same thing herself. Even if, by good fortune, Patrick had won his games and prevented the table-tennis team from being defeated.

She bit back her words, turned on her heel and marched out of the common room.

She slammed the door loudly behind her.

'What's up between you and her, Jake?' asked his friend Kenneth.

'She told tales, that's all,' replied Jake, looking morose. 'She exceeded her authority. She shouldn't poke her nose in my private business. I'm fed up with bossy girl monitors thinking they know what's best for us boys.'

'Joan doesn't do that,' Harry pointed out, fairly.

'No,' agreed Martin. 'And she's been one for ages. Elizabeth's new, which makes it worse.'

'I expect it's gone right to her curly head,' sighed Jake, wearily.

He clammed up then. He became his usual strong, silent self and refused to answer any more questions.

But after he'd left the common room, the other boys were all agog.

They liked the Naughtiest Girl. But they all knew how she'd got her nickname! And there was no doubt that she could still be headstrong and impulsive and do crazy things sometimes. They admired Jake and they trusted him. If he was angry with Elizabeth then she must have seriously overstepped the mark in some way.

'She wanted to wear a monitor's armband, didn't she, Harry?' remembered Martin. 'And Julian teased her and said it would make her look like a member of the secret police!'

'And it sounds as though she's been behaving like one!' commented John McTavish. 'What a nerve, telling tales on someone like Jake. Thinking she knows what's best for him.'

'I wonder what it was all about?' pondered Harry.

The news of the quarrel spread around the boys' dormitories that night, and grew in the telling. The joke about the armband, and the secret police, was also passed around.

Julian felt rather badly when he heard his joke being repeated. He was going to say something in Elizabeth's defence but then Patrick stepped in.

'Elizabeth is a very good sort!' he declared. 'Shut up, all of you.'

So Julian shrugged his shoulders and said nothing.

Elizabeth slept badly that night. There were tears of frustration in her eyes. She so much wanted to be a successful monitor but things were starting to go wrong.

At breakfast-time, on Monday morning, she could tell that some of the boys had started to turn against her.

'Where's your armband, Elizabeth?' Martin teased her. 'We won't know to do what we're told if you don't wear an armband.'

Arabella tittered loudly.

'It's not that funny, Arabella,' said Julian, airily. 'It's rather an old joke by now. Can't you think of a new one, Martin?'

Elizabeth was glad to escape from the dining-hall.

She went up to Room 14 to clean her shoes and brush her hair and get ready for lessons. Joan, Kathleen and Jenny, who had all been sitting at the other table today, drifted in. Elizabeth enjoyed chatting about other things with her room-mates and began to feel a bit better.

Drat boys! she thought. It was fun just being with girls sometimes! She began to look forward to her first lesson, which was French, with Mam'zelle.

'Let's get down to the form room nice and early,' suggested Joan.

'Yes!' nodded Elizabeth. 'My desk needs a bit of a tidy-up.'

The form room was empty when they arrived. The two friends had adjoining desks. Elizabeth boisterously flung up her desk lid.

'Oh!'

She quickly closed it again, her cheeks pale.

'What was that?' asked Joan quickly. 'What was that piece of paper taped to the inside of your desk lid?'

'It – it seems to be some kind of horrid message,' said Elizabeth.

Gently, Joan opened the desk lid again.

Together, the two friends gazed in silence at the anonymous message, carefully written in block capitals.

WHY HAS THE SECOND FORM GOT

## A HORRID MESSAGE APPEARS

TWO GIRL MONITORS? NOT FAIR!
GIVE DANIEL HIS CHANCE BACK,
ELIZABETH. GIVE THE BOYS A
MONITOR OF THEIR OWN!

At that moment Mr Leslie, their form-master, came into the classroom to put some things away. Joan carefully removed the message, folded it and placed it in her pocket. They would have to discuss it later.

## CHAPTER SEVEN

# THINGS GO FROM BAD TO WORSE

'WHAT'S ALL this about, Elizabeth?' asked Joan, at morning break. 'Have you any idea who could have written it?'

'I believe I know exactly who has written it!' replied Elizabeth.

The two friends were sitting on the school steps in the pale October sunshine. Joan had taken the piece of paper from her pocket and unfolded it. Why had somebody turned against Elizabeth? It was all very upsetting.

'Who?' asked Joan, in surprise.

'Jake, of course!' Elizabeth blurted out. 'How mean of him not to sign it. What an underhand thing to do!'

'*Jake?*' asked Joan. She liked the gentle giant of a boy and felt she knew him quite well. He had joined the second form even earlier than she had. 'Why ever should Jake be feeling cross with you, Elizabeth? Especially as I'm sure he must be in a very good mood at the moment with his poor ankle better.'

'That's just it, Joan! He's not in a good mood at all

about his ankle! He should be, but he isn't. And he's simply furious with me!'

Joan's eyes widened. She spoke gently.

'What's been going on, Elizabeth? What have you been keeping from me?'

Shamefaced, Elizabeth told Joan everything that had happened concerning Jake the previous day. It was a relief to do so, at last.

But Joan, as Elizabeth feared she would be, was very disapproving.

'It was very wrong of you to speak to Mr Warlow before you had spoken to Jake himself, Elizabeth!' she scolded. 'You know that's not the way we do things at Whyteleafe. Jake must have had some very private reason of his own for wanting to get out of hockey, something that he was determined to keep secret. As his monitor, you should have asked him to talk it through with you and then tried to persuade him to go and own up to Mr Warlow. No wonder he is cross with you!'

'I was too scared to,' Elizabeth confessed. 'I was sure Jake didn't respect me as a monitor and the note proves I was right. He thinks the other monitor should be a boy! And because I've upset Jake, some more of the boys are turning against me! What should I do, Joan? Do you think I should resign?'

'Of course not, Elizabeth!' her friend replied, firmly.

309

She folded the note up and replaced it in her pocket. 'You can't give in to this sort of thing. It's not always easy being a monitor and we all make mistakes. Just try to tread carefully for a while, Elizabeth. Everybody likes you very much and wanted you to be a monitor this term. I'm sure this will all blow over in a few days.'

'Oh, do you really think so, Joan?'

Elizabeth felt very cheered.

But her cheerfulness did not last long.

Far from blowing over, the trouble with the boys got worse.

Elizabeth was still being teased. And the feeling that it was unfair not to have a boy monitor seemed to be spreading. Jake continued to be unfriendly towards her and Elizabeth strongly suspected that, as well as writing the note, he was encouraging the other boys in some kind of campaign to get rid of her. Had she made a powerful enemy?

In Martin's dormitory, they were starting to have pillow fights at night. These were forbidden, of course, but apparently great fun!

Martin openly bragged that, as girls were not allowed to enter the boys' quarters, they could do what they liked as they only had girl monitors in the second form. No monitors could come and stop their fun!

Julian gave Elizabeth a friendly word of warning.

'I shouldn't report them, if I were you, Elizabeth,' he said. 'Not if you know what's good for you!'

Elizabeth had never actually admitted to Julian that she'd given Jake's secret away because she and Julian were far less close than usual. She was sad but there was nothing she could do about it, without explaining to him the story of Patrick's bravery. However, on the Jake front, Julian had very quickly worked things out for himself. Like Elizabeth, he was mystified as to why the big boy had pretended about the injury in the first place.

'Don't worry, Julian,' she sighed. 'I know I'm in enough trouble already. I haven't the slightest intention of reporting them.'

She would love to have had a proper chat with him about everything. But he was already strolling away, whistling.

Patrick was a real nuisance! she thought.

She thought so again, the following day.

The next Monitors' Meeting was due. In Elizabeth's class, only one written nomination had been handed in. Quivering with importance, Rosemary had handed the special form over to Joan. But Joan was not able to attend this week's MM. Miss Thomas had arranged the first fitness session for the would-be swimming team. It would clash directly with the MM but it was the teacher's only free time. Joan dare not miss her very first workout.

'I'm afraid that you are going to have to read this out at the MM, Elizabeth,' she said later, with a wry smile, passing across Rosemary's form. 'What a lovely job for you!'

'Oh, no!' groaned Elizabeth, reading what was written there. 'This is going to be so embarrassing. Must I really? Ugh!'

They both laughed.

Nevertheless, after lessons that day, Elizabeth set off eagerly for the MM. This was going to be very interesting. What kind of citations would the other monitors be reading out, from their classmates? Surely they'd be more exciting than Rosemary's? She certainly hoped so!

She arrived on time this week and collected her mug of tea. There were chocolate digestive biscuits again. Good!

'It's all right, Elizabeth, there are plenty. You may take two!' smiled Emma.

She settled down on the floor, next to Peter, letting Donald have the place on the bench. It was quite comfortable on the floor this week as Thomas had managed to find some cushions.

'Hello, Peter,' she said to the young first form

monitor. 'Have you been given any citations yet for the William and Rita Award?'

Peter shook his head. He seemed to have something else on his mind.

'Not yet, Elizabeth. I keep asking for them, though.'

Soon all the monitors had crammed into the cosy study. Elizabeth was disappointed to see that not many had brought citations with them. She gave Joan's apologies. Then various minor school matters were discussed. Peter put his hand up.

'Please, Thomas and Emma, can you all give me some advice? Some of the boys in my class were squirting water pistols indoors. They wouldn't stop when I asked, so I confiscated them. When d'you think I should give them back?'

They all discussed Peter's problem.

'There we are, then! We're all agreed,' Thomas concluded. 'You can keep them for a week. A week seems quite a long time when you're in the first form! Then, as long as they promise only to play with them out of doors in future, you can hand them back!'

At last it was time for the citations to be read out.

'You first, Elizabeth,' said Emma. 'I can see you've got one in your hand.'

'It's only just the one so far, I'm afraid,' apologized Elizabeth. 'It's been submitted by Rosemary Wing.'

She tried her best to hide her embarrassment as she read out loud the second form's only citation.

*Yesterday, my hamster looked very droopy and I was worried about him. Then Arabella Buckley performed a very unselfish act. Arabella is very fond of chocolate herself but she sacrificed all the chocolate she had left for the whole week and fed it to Hammy, so as to cheer him up. I would therefore like to nominate Arabella Buckley for the William and Rita Award.*

Some of the monitors snorted and sniggered.

'I expect poor Hammy was sick on the spot!' whispered Donald.

Elizabeth's cheeks burned. She felt so ashamed of her classmates. It was obvious that Arabella had put Rosemary up to this! Surely, between them, they could at least have invented something better? She'd tried her best to read it nicely and put the correct expression in her voice. But it had still sounded completely silly.

'Thank you, Elizabeth,' said Emma, sympathetically. 'That was very nicely read.'

'And those of you who are giggling, I'm ashamed of you,' added Thomas. 'All citations are to be listened to in silence, please. I think we are all agreed that this one's not suitable for the shortlist, so let us pass on.'

Elizabeth at once felt better. Now that the second form citation had been dealt with, she could settle down and look forward to hearing the other forms' contributions.

But there were, indeed, only a few. And although they were all much more genuine than Rosemary's effort, they were not very inspiring.

After hearing out the last one, read by Eric, the head boy and girl shook their heads.

'I don't think anything we have heard today is quite suitable for the shortlist, do you?' asked Emma, ruefully. 'The William and Rita Award must be given for an act of real courage or unselfishness, not everyday acts of kindness, pleasing though it is to hear about them.'

'We seem to have got off to a slow start, I'm afraid,' agreed Thomas. 'Luckily there's plenty of time yet. We must look forward to something really splendid coming in over the next couple of weeks.'

But Elizabeth could tell that they were both very disappointed.

It was so frustrating! How she longed to tell them that a member of the second form had performed an act of real courage.

As she left the MM, she decided that she must go and find Patrick at once. He had just finished a game of table tennis with Daniel.

'Listen, Patrick, I've been thinking,' she said, as she took him outside. There was a pleading note in her voice. 'You know, about your brave deed. I know you don't want it talked about and I know you must be worried that you broke a school rule that day, being down in the village on your own. But supposing, when I go to the next MM, I just talk about this certain boy, without giving his name away? Supposing I just talk about this certain boy being worried about breaking this strict rule and see if they think that matters . . . ? And then . . .'

'Elizabeth! Stop being so tiresome!' exclaimed Patrick, impatiently. 'I am not in the least bit worried about being punished for breaking a school rule. That has nothing to do with it really!'

'But . . .'

'I just don't want to be held up as some kind of hero, Elizabeth!' He stared at her, looking baffled and angry. 'Why are you bringing all this up again?'

'I'm sorry, Patrick. I just wondered if perhaps – well, all us monitors want the first William and Rita Award to be something really special! Can't you see that? And I thought, if it was just the school rule you were worried about . . .'

'Well, it's not!' Patrick almost shouted the words. 'Please forget the whole thing. You promised.'

'I – I'll try.'

'Drop it, Elizabeth! Please don't mention this again!'

# THINGS GO FROM BAD TO WORSE

Elizabeth walked away after that.

She was still filled with admiration for Patrick. How could she not be? But it was very annoying of him, all the same. The William and Rita Award was such a lovely idea. But supposing nobody came forward with anything worthwhile by half-term? Thomas and Emma would not be able to make the award, after all. What a bad start that would be.

Nothing seemed to be going right at the moment.

In fact things went from bad to worse.

When she went along to collect some homework from her desk, after tea, there was another anonymous message stuck inside the lid. Once again, it was written in block capitals:

SOME OF US ARE FED UP. THERE
ARE PILLOW FIGHTS NOW -
KEEPING US AWAKE AT NIGHT.
THE SECOND FORM NEEDS A BOY
MONITOR TO KEEP ORDER. WHY NOT
RESIGN PLEASE, ELIZABETH?

Paling slightly, she hurried outside to find Joan.

## CHAPTER EIGHT

# THE NAUGHTIEST GIRL VERSUS THE BOYS

'MY SO-CALLED secret enemy has struck again, Joan!' she said crossly, showing Joan the message. 'Not all that secret, in fact. I'm quite convinced that it's Jake who's writing these notes. I know I'm a coward, Joan, but shall we go and see him together and tell him to stop it? He might take some notice of you.'

'We can't do that, Elizabeth,' replied Joan, biting her lip as she read the note carefully. 'We can't be sure it's Jake. Is this really Jake's sort of thing? And we certainly can't walk up to him and accuse him without any proof!'

'I suppose not,' sighed Elizabeth. She read the note through carefully, once again. 'To be fair, it must be very annoying for Jake if these pillow fights are keeping him awake.'

'If it is Jake,' Joan reminded her, gently.

'Well, Jake or whoever it is. Anybody who doesn't specially enjoy pillow fights,' said Elizabeth. She was looking thoughtful. 'As I *am* a monitor, I should be thinking what to do.'

'I shouldn't worry, Elizabeth!' said Joan hastily, noting the light in her eye. 'We can't take any notice of anonymous messages. If anyone comes forward with a proper complaint about losing a lot of sleep, then that would be serious and you'd have to report it to the teachers.'

'What, tell tales?' asked Elizabeth, aghast, remembering Julian's advice to her. 'But that would make my position even worse, Joan.'

'This would be quite different, Elizabeth. You couldn't possibly deal with a whole crowd of boys on your own. But, of course, someone would have to make a formal complaint first, not just write a silly note like this. And I don't suppose anybody will.'

Elizabeth did not follow Joan's logic. In any case, she was hardly listening.

She'd suddenly remembered young Peter's water pistols and an excited gleam came into her eye. She knew exactly how to handle this problem! She certainly didn't want anybody making a formal complaint to either Joan or herself and then having to go to the teachers. She didn't agree with Joan at all about that. The boys would never forgive them.

She must act quickly, before there was any danger of it happening.

Later, a cheerful sparkle in her eye, Elizabeth slipped off to talk to some of the other girls. They were good sports, all of them.

Then she went to find Peter.

'I'm not going to involve Joan in this,' she thought. 'But I'll jolly well show those boys who's the monitor around here!'

Even as Elizabeth was borrowing the water pistols from Peter, an even younger boy was seeking out Joan, for the junior class did not have a monitor of its own. The small boy was in pyjamas and dressing-gown but was not looking forward to going to bed. For two nights running he'd been woken up by bumpings and crashings in the second form dormitory and had been unable to get to sleep again. His bed was right against the dividing wall. There were dark rings under his eyes.

'Go straight to bed now, Rupert,' Joan told him, after hearing him out. 'I'll see this is sorted out. I'll see to it myself, I promise.'

'And I won't involve Elizabeth,' she thought. It's true what she says. 'She is in enough trouble already.'

After that, Joan decided, she would go to bed herself. The fitness training in the gym had been very enjoyable but had left her tired out and aching in every muscle.

* * *

'Sssh, Kathleen! Sssh, Jenny!' whispered Elizabeth. 'We mustn't wake Joan!'

'No danger of that, Elizabeth. She's dead to the world!' Kathleen whispered back.

'Miss Thomas really puts them through it, I gather!' commented Jenny.

'Such luck!' giggled Kathleen.

'Sssh!' repeated Elizabeth.

It was after Lights Out, and the three girls had slipped out of bed and were putting on their dressing-gowns and slippers. They had waited until they were sure that Joan was in a very deep sleep. On no account, Elizabeth explained, did she want to involve Joan in her plan.

'I shall take full responsibility for this,' she had told her room-mates earlier. 'I don't want to have to report those boys to the teachers and I don't want Joan to either. They think it's so clever having pillow fights but we'll soon cool them down!'

Belinda and Tessa were waiting for them in the corridor.

'Got the water pistols, Elizabeth?' whispered Belinda, eagerly.

'I've hidden them in the bathroom!' the Naughtiest Girl whispered back.

The five girls tiptoed along the corridor to the big bathroom. They were all trying hard not to giggle. This was going to be such an adventure! Elizabeth took the five water pistols out from their hiding place in the big linen box.

She handed her friends one each.

'Right,' she said. 'Now let's load them. As full as full can be.'

With Elizabeth their commander-in-chief leading the way, the girls crept along the dimly lit corridors until they reached the boys' quarters. Their pistols were at the ready, loaded with water up to the hilt.

'Martin's dormitory,' she whispered crisply. 'Number 17. Just at the bottom of these stairs. Come on, now. Party – advance!'

'I think I can hear them now,' whispered Kathleen excitedly, as they crept down the short flight of stairs. 'Voices!'

The door was ajar. There seemed to be torches flashing around inside. It was after Lights Out but there were figures moving about and some whispering going on. The nightly pillow fight must be just about to commence!

Eyes sparkling with anticipation, Elizabeth waved her water pistol above her head in a signal to the other four.

'Ready, steady – CHARGE!' she hissed.

With their monitor at their head, the girls hurled themselves down the last few stairs and burst into Room 17.

'FIRE!' cried Elizabeth and they squeezed the triggers, spraying fine jets of water at the figures that moved in the dark.

'Break it up, boys!'

'Cool down!'

'Pillow fights not allowed!'

As they shouted their war cries, the girls were laughing with glee.

'Bulls-eye!' cried Elizabeth, as she squirted her best jet of water towards the back of somebody's neck.

'Got you!' she added triumphantly. 'Now perhaps *that* will cool you down just a little bit . . .'

At that very moment the figure turned, receiving it full in the face.

'ELIZABETH ALLEN!' roared the person, shining his torch on her. 'What on earth do you think you are doing?'

Elizabeth and her friends recoiled in dismay. It was a man's voice. They knew it well. Elizabeth shone her own torch, while behind her somebody switched on a light.

Elizabeth found herself face to face with Mr Leslie,

their form-master. He had three senior boys with him, including Thomas, the head boy. These were the only figures who'd been moving around! They were holding torches. All of them had water dripping down their shirts. Martin and co., from all appearances, were asleep in bed. Only now were tousled heads raising themselves from various pillows.

'Hey!'

'What's going on?'

'Who's put that light on?'

– came the innocent-sounding cries.

Elizabeth stared at her teacher in horror.

'I'm t-t-terribly sorry, sir,' she stammered.

Mr Leslie looked very cross.

'And so you should be, Elizabeth. We were told there might be some horseplay tonight but we expected to find *boys* misbehaving not girls. Please return to your own quarters this instant, all of you.'

The five girls dived out of the door, in relief. They couldn't wait to escape! From the stairs, they heard Thomas's voice.

'It's all right, boys. Sorry you've been disturbed. You can go back to sleep now.'

The girls returned to their quarters in silence. What a disaster, thought Jenny and co. Somehow the boys had got wind of Elizabeth's plan and neatly turned the tables. When the girl monitor and her troops had turned up to put a stop to the boys' pillow fights, they'd run straight into their teacher and his inspection party, with the second form boys pretending to be fast asleep!

The boys had won. The girls were going to get into trouble and Elizabeth, as ringleader, would get into the biggest trouble of all!

But all Elizabeth could think about, as she tried to get back to sleep that night, was her enemy. *Somebody* had reported her plan to Mr Leslie. And she was sure she knew who. What a mean thing to do!

But the next morning, she got a shock.

'Of course it wasn't Jake!' exclaimed Joan, in horror, as she listened to Elizabeth's tale of woe. 'Oh, Elizabeth, what a dreadful mix-up. What a dreadful thing to happen! It was me!'

'You, Joan?' squealed Elizabeth, in surprise.

Her loud squeal brought Jenny and Kathleen running over.

In distress, Joan explained to her room-mates about little Rupert.

'The child was desperate about it. He turned to me for help, as a monitor. It left me with no choice but to go and report to Mr Leslie that Room 17 was being noisy at nights, though I didn't say anything about the pillow fights. I'm sorry I didn't tell you, Elizabeth. I didn't want to involve you.'

'I'm sorry I didn't tell you about *my* plan,' said Elizabeth, very shamefaced. 'Oh, what a muddle!'

'Thank goodness it wasn't one of the boys, anyway,' said Kathleen, with a sigh of relief.

'Yes, that makes us feel a bit better about it,' agreed Elizabeth. She frowned. 'But, Joan, how did Martin and co. know to be well-behaved last night? That's what I can't understand.'

Joan thought about it carefully.

'John McTavish walked past last night, when Rupert was talking to me in the corridor. I didn't think he had heard anything. But obviously he must have done.'

'Ah!' said Elizabeth.

So that, too, was explained.

When Mr Leslie came into class to take the register that morning, the boys owned up about the pillow fights. That, at least, came as a great relief to Elizabeth, Joan and co. They were a nice crowd really.

'Humph, yes, well I'm not stupid, Martin,' said Mr Leslie. 'I did realize that something must have been going on. That the fault would not be all on one side. As your high jinks have been depriving some of the other boys of their sleep, Thomas is going to raise the matter at this week's Meeting.'

'Is he going to raise the matter of Elizabeth, as well?' asked Jake, with interest. 'Our *monitor*.'

Some of the boys laughed.

Elizabeth flushed deeply at Jake's intervention.

'I understand that Elizabeth will be dealt with at the next Monitors' Meeting,' replied Mr Leslie, curtly. 'Now, will everybody please get their pencils and paper ready. Miss Ranger will be here very shortly and today's the day you have your spelling tests.'

After that Julian made some sympathetic 'hen clucking' noises to try to cheer Elizabeth up. He had heard all about the episode in Room 17 and had found it highly diverting. Would the Naughtiest Girl even last till half-term as a monitor? he wondered.

But Elizabeth was not amused. She concentrated hard on the weekly spelling test. After that, for the rest of the English lesson, she kept her head bent over her work. She felt a sense of despair. She had so much wanted to be a successful and popular monitor this term, one who enjoyed the respect of the whole form, like Joan. But she could see that Jake was not going to allow that to happen.

Of course, the water pistols had not been such a good idea. She had been silly and hot-headed and she could not blame Jake for that. But it was getting those horrid notes that had stirred her up and made her behave foolishly. Now some of the boys were laughing at her.

She smouldered as she thought of the notes and she came to a decision.

'I have decided to tackle Jake about those mean notes,' she whispered to Joan, toward the end of the lesson. 'I know you don't want to, so I've decided to speak to him on my own. I shall tell him what I think of him!'

Joan just looked helpless and shook her head.

At that moment Miss Ranger called the two monitors out.

'Elizabeth and Joan, would you please give everybody their spellings back? I have marked them now.'

As the two friends shared out the bundle between them, the English teacher spoke pleasantly to the class.

'Elizabeth and Joan will bring your spellings round. Julian has come top today with 20 out of 20. Jake, you would have had full marks, but once again you forgot your silent Gs. You always forget them! You spelt both SIGN and RESIGN without the G! When you think of SIGN, think of SIGNATURE and that will help you remember. And when you spell RESIGN, think of RESIGNATION. It's a shame you have such a blank spot about this, or you would have come equal top . . .'

'Yes, Miss Ranger.'

As the English teacher chatted on, Elizabeth was staring at Jake's spellings which were on top of the batch in her hand. Twenty words were written down. Eighteen had red ticks by them and two had been marked with a red cross.

'. . . I'm afraid, Jake,' the teacher was saying, with a humorous smile, 'that SIGN and RESIGN become two completely different words when you leave the Gs out. RESIN is something produced from sap. And SIN is something you commit when you forget your silent Gs!'

Everyone laughed.

But Elizabeth's scalp prickled as she gazed at Jake's spellings; at that word RESIN, with its cross beside it. Briefly, she shut her eyes, then opened them again.

'And I've made a mistake, too,' she realised. 'Jake didn't write those notes. He couldn't have done.'

For on yesterday's message, she was quite sure the word RESIGN had been spelt correctly.

CHAPTER NINE

# ELIZABETH LEARNS JAKE'S SECRET

'HOW CLEVER of you to remember, Elizabeth,' said Joan, when they discussed it together at dinner-time. 'I'd never have thought of it. Thank goodness you remembered the wording of this message and worked out that it couldn't be Jake. Only just in time. You were planning to rush off and accuse him!'

'You're the really wise one, Joan,' said Elizabeth, humbly. 'You warned me I was being hot-headed! I was too stubborn to listen.'

They were both staring at the second anonymous message, which she had collected from upstairs. WHY NOT RESIGN PLEASE, ELIZABETH? it ended and it was all spelt correctly. The message was written *before* today's spelling test. If Jake had looked up the spelling to write the message, he would hardly have forgotten it for an important test.

'Jake's always struggled with English,' mused Joan. 'That's why he's still in the second form. I couldn't quite imagine him putting pen to paper to write messages.

330

Jake's style is just to say things straight out!'

'Yes,' nodded Elizabeth. She looked rueful. 'And he's certainly done that as far as I'm concerned. But it was wrong of me to leap to conclusions.'

It was a warm day. The girls were sitting beneath the weeping ash tree, in the school grounds. All the leaves had turned colour in the past week. They were starting to float down now, carpeting the grass around them. Elizabeth caught a fluttering leaf in her hands and examined it. She was thinking hard. She so loved it here at Whyteleafe School but it was horrid having an enemy. Who DID write those messages?

'If Jake isn't the enemy then I want to know who is, Joan!' she said, angrily.

The two girls discussed the mystery all dinner hour. They badly wanted to solve it. They went through possible suspects, as real detectives would.

'We can be sure it's a boy, and we can be sure he's in the second form,' said Joan, softly. 'So that narrows it down.'

'Not very much though,' replied Elizabeth, ruefully. 'The first thing is to think of the motive. It's got to be somebody who hates the idea of there being two girl monitors, who thinks it's unfair. Somebody other than Jake.'

'What about Daniel?' suggested Joan, tentatively.

'Oh, surely not Daniel!' exclaimed Elizabeth, in dismay. He was a gentle, sensitive boy. 'I like Daniel! And I'm sure he likes me! Except . . .'

She broke off, remembering the wistful expression on Daniel's face last week, when she'd come from an MM. Oh, they do sound fun! he'd said. Under his gentle exterior, could Daniel secretly be regretting that he'd stood down after his few days as a monitor, to give Elizabeth her place back?

'I don't want to think it's Daniel, Joan!' she stated. 'Let's think of somebody else. In books, it's always the last person you suspect . . .' she laughed. 'Say, Julian, for instance . . .'

Even as Elizabeth spoke her friend's name out loud, her laughter faded on her lips and her heart gave a jolt.

'Julian!' she whispered. 'Is it possible? He has been quite cutting lately about my being a monitor!'

'Oh, that's just his usual teasing, Elizabeth! The reason he's so cool is because you're being nice to Patrick. You know how those two cousins hate each other!'

'But you don't understand, Joan. He thinks I'm being nice to Patrick only because I am a monitor!'

*Is this a bad attack of the goody-goody-monitor-itis disease?* he'd asked her.

'I see,' said Joan. Then she looked at her friend in

surprise. What did Elizabeth mean by 'only'? What other reason could she have for being specially nice to Patrick? 'Perhaps you've been overdoing it, Elizabeth. I do believe Julian's a little jealous.'

Elizabeth rapidly changed the subject. It was more than she could bear to think of Julian being her enemy; far worse, even, than it being Daniel.

'We're being silly, Joan,' she declared. 'It couldn't possibly be Julian! Or Daniel, come to that. Let's think of some other people.'

After a while, the two girls came to the most obvious conclusion. The message writer was probably one of the gang of boys who admired Jake. Martin, or Kenneth, or John McTavish . . .

'They're probably all in it together,' decided Joan.

But Elizabeth didn't find that any comfort, either.

In the distance, the bell went for afternoon lessons. As the two girls got to their feet and walked slowly back to school, Elizabeth looked thoughtful.

'Perhaps it doesn't matter who's writing the messages, Joan,' she sighed. 'The fact is, I've made a mess of being a monitor. I shouldn't have told tales on Jake. And I shouldn't have allowed myself to get wound up and tried to stop the boys' pillow fights in the way I did. I'm no use as a monitor, if half the boys in the class don't respect me. Perhaps I'd *better* do as the note suggests. Offer to resign.'

'You can't do that, Elizabeth,' said Joan, giving her a sidelong glance. 'You can't give in to anonymous messages.'

'I'm in disgrace, anyway,' the Naughtiest Girl pointed out. 'Don't forget that Thomas is going to deal with me at the next MM! That's what Mr Leslie said. I may have no choice in the matter. I may be asked to resign, anyway!'

It was a horrid thought.

'We will just have to see about that, Elizabeth,' replied Joan kindly. 'Won't we?'

In spite of her own troubles, Elizabeth began to feel very worried over the next few days about a member of her class.

She had a growing sense of there being something seriously wrong with Jake.

Nobody else noticed much but Elizabeth found herself keeping a watchful eye on him. She was sure it was connected with the forthcoming hockey match against Milford Grange. She believed he might be dreading it with a sickening fear.

At first she thought it was her imagination, her own guilty conscience at work. But as each day passed, and the match drew inexorably nearer, she was sure that the big boy was becoming more and more desperate.

'Why don't you want to talk about the big match, Jake?' she heard his friend Kenneth ask him, peevishly. 'Why aren't you bothering to practise?'

'My hockey stick will have to do the talking,' Jake had snapped in reply. 'When it needs to!'

He seemed to be avoiding the other boys and they tactfully left him alone.

'He seems a bit tense about the match,' Martin commented. 'I suppose it's because he hasn't played since last season.'

'Jake? Tense about a hockey match?' scoffed John. 'It's school work getting him down, I expect!'

On Friday evening, at the school Meeting, Elizabeth watched Jake from her vantage point on the platform. She thought how glum he looked, wrapped in his own thoughts. He seemed to take no interest at all when the head boy and girl dealt with the matter of the pillow fights in Room 17.

'As the culprits have owned up, we've decided to let them off lightly,' announced Thomas, while Emma wrote it all down in the school's Big Book. 'They must sleep without pillows for a whole week. That will help them to remember that it is thoughtless to keep other boys awake at nights! After next week, their pillows will be returned to them.'

Even as Elizabeth sat there wondering what her own punishment was going to be, at next week's MM, she noticed that Jake had suddenly gone very pale.

'Finally, we hope you will all turn out and cheer the school hockey team tomorrow morning,' Thomas was saying. 'Milford Grange will be here at eleven o'clock and they are bringing two coachloads of supporters. I am sure you will all be very pleased to know that Jake is fully fit again and is now back in the Whyteleafe team. We are sure he plans to shoot plenty of goals for us tomorrow! Right, everyone. You are dismissed.'

There was laughter and cheers and the sound of benches scraping back. The Meeting was over! The boys and girls were all looking forward to the weekend.

Watching closely, Elizabeth saw Jake rise to his feet and sway slightly. She thought for a moment that he was going to faint. Then he hurried from the hall.

'Jake is terrified of tomorrow's match!' she realized. 'I'm positive now. The very thought of it seems to be making him ill. And it's all my fault! I'm the person who's put him in this position. I think I may have done a dreadful thing!'

Elizabeth hurried down off the platform. Her heart was beating fast. She could not begin to understand what was wrong with Jake, nor why he had been going to such extraordinary lengths to get out of playing hockey for Whyteleafe. But she was racked with guilt to see his suffering.

'I've got to catch up with him and tell him how sorry I am!' she decided. 'I don't care how rude he is to me, I've got to tell him I'm sorry and ask him to forgive me. Oh, what is wrong with him? I do wish there were some way I could make him feel better!'

She raced outside on to the lawn, just in time to see Jake disappearing in the direction of the school gardens. She hurried in pursuit.

When she got there, she saw him sitting quite alone on the wooden bench by the big greenhouse.

The gardens were silent and very still, with no breath of wind today. The rows of runner beans stood like withered green wigwams, their crop near its end. A blackbird rustled in the nearby yew hedge.

Elizabeth's warm heart ached with pity to see the big boy sitting on the bench, doubled up as though in pain. She tiptoed towards him. He was making little moaning sounds.

'Jake!' she whispered.

He raised his head. His eyes looked red.

'Elizabeth!' he gasped in surprise. 'What are you doing here? Please go away. I have such terrible stomach cramps. I can't bear anyone to see me like this, least of all a girl. Please go away – and don't tell anybody

you've seen me in such a state!'

'I will NOT go away, Jake!' Elizabeth came and sat beside him and placed an arm round his big shoulders. 'I have come to ask your forgiveness. I know I have done something terrible, giving you away. And now you are scared to play in the match tomorrow. *I* can't bear it to see how scared you are.'

'You've guessed?' asked Jake, in alarm.

He buried his face in his hands. Elizabeth patted his heaving back, trying to soothe him.

'I can't bear it that a girl should see me like this,' he moaned.

Elizabeth continued to pat his back, gently.

'Please tell me what's wrong, Jake,' she begged. 'I promise on my honour that I'll keep your secret. But I'm so worried about you. I will cry *myself* if you don't tell me what's wrong!'

'I am so very, very scared, Elizabeth,' the boy blurted out. 'I am so frightened that the same thing could happen again.'

'What, Jake?' she prompted him gently, almost in tears herself.

He raised his head and gazed at her. He saw the anguished expression on her face and knew that, in this moment, she was living through his anguish with him. What a fine girl she was, he realized. He suddenly felt sure that he could trust her.

'A month ago, Elizabeth, I nearly blinded somebody,' he stated. 'The person I admire most in all the world. My coach, Henry Hill. Since my father died, he has been like a dad to me! He used to play hockey for England and he's coached me since I was a little boy. But I nearly blinded him. It was touch and go! He's only just come out of hospital.'

'What a terrible thing to happen!' gasped Elizabeth. 'Jake, please tell me the whole story. It will make you feel a little better to talk about it, even if it's only to me.'

At last Jake's strange behaviour began to make sense as he explained that, on the last day of the summer holidays, he'd played in a match for his home town hockey club. The club's non-playing captain was Henry Hill, a former England international, the man whom Jake so loved and admired. He had coached Jake for years, convinced that the boy would himself play for his country one day. His own playing days were over but because the team was one short that day, Henry had stepped in at short notice to fill the gap.

It had been a dramatic and closely-fought contest but then had come disaster. A hard-struck ball by Jake had flown off at an angle and the ball had caught Henry in the eye with great force. An ambulance had been called and he'd been rushed to hospital. Only an emergency operation had saved the sight in his left eye.

'It was the most terrible day of my life,' Jake confessed. 'I will never be able to forget it. Henry's cries of pain . . . the ambulance wailing . . . then waiting all afternoon for some news from the hospital . . . I still have bad dreams about it. I really *did* hurt my ankle that day. It was just a slight sprain and my mother bandaged it up for me. Then, when I got back to school, it gave me an idea. I desperately wanted to give myself time! To try to get over what had happened . . .'

'And you didn't want to explain things to Mr Warlow, then?' ventured Elizabeth.

'No! He would have told me to put this behind me! He would have tried to rush me. And now, I *have* been rushed and the terrible thing is that I *can't* put this behind me, Elizabeth. I will never put it behind me! It is cowardly of me but I have completely lost my nerve. It could happen again, at any time! It could be something worse next time. Please don't tell anybody about this, Elizabeth. You are the only person who need ever know what a coward I am. I will have to find some new excuse but . . .'

He buried his face in his hands again.

'I can't play in tomorrow's match. I just can't.'

Elizabeth touched his arm.

'You *must*, Jake,' she whispered. 'You really must,

341

you know. There's somebody you haven't been thinking about in all this.'

He looked at her in surprise.

'Who?'

'Henry, of course. You say he has coached you all this time and believes you will play for your country one day. The accident was a terrible thing but a younger person would have been able to react more quickly and dodge that flying ball. Henry shouldn't have been playing! But now, having given him one kind of pain, you are planning to make it much worse. You have been his life's work and now you are going to destroy all his dreams for you.'

Jake fell silent.

'I hadn't looked at it like that,' he said, at last.

Elizabeth remembered the time that she had fallen badly from her pony. Her governess had forced her instantly to remount. *The longer you leave it, Elizabeth, the more frightened you will be* she had told the little girl.

'You must play tomorrow, Jake,' she pleaded. 'For Henry's sake you must try to overcome your fears as quickly as possible and get back to playing a hard match once again. Please promise that you will try to overcome your terror.'

'I can't promise, Elizabeth,' Jake said, in despair. 'I am so very, very scared about it. Let me just sit here on my own for a while and think things over.'

'Yes, Jake.' Elizabeth rose to her feet. 'And your secret is safe with me. But will you at least promise me something else?'

'What's that, Elizabeth?'

'Ask if you can use the school telephone this evening! Telephone your coach, for he would be pleased to hear from you. And ask his opinion of what he thinks you should do.'

Leaving Jake deep in thought, she tiptoed away.

And the following morning Jake did, indeed, turn out for the match against Milford Grange. His jaw was clenched and his face pale as he ran out on to the pitch with the rest of the Whyteleafe first eleven.

Two people cheered him even louder than the rest. One of them was Elizabeth. The other was a man on the opposite side of the field who had just arrived with his wife. He had a large dressing over one eye, held securely in place by special bandages.

'That's my boy, Jake!' he called out loudly, raising both fists high.

After last night's telephone call, Henry Hill had asked his wife to drive him the thirty miles from their home town, so that he could watch Jake's match.

Jake made a nervous, even tentative, start but as the pace hotted up he began to get into his stride. He ran here, there and everywhere, tackling fiercely, soon caught up in the excitement of the hard-fought game. By the end of the match Whyteleafe had won 6–4 and Jake had scored five of the six goals!

As he walked off the pitch, Henry Hill came striding across to shake his hand.

'That was marvellous, Jake.' His face was shining and so was Jake's. 'I'm very proud of you, my boy. Keep it up. What a tonic for a poor sick invalid!'

'I've got to drag Henry away, Jake,' apologized Mrs Hill, tugging at her husband's arm. 'We're due at the hospital. The bandages come off today. Isn't that good news? I'm hoping the dear man has seen sense at last. I've told him to face the fact that his glory days are behind him. I hope that's going to be his last game!'

'It is. It is. But Jake's got all his glory days ahead of him. I'm so proud of you, my boy!' the man repeated, as he pumped Jake's hand and slapped him on the back. 'Good luck! See you at half-term!'

Jake watched his coach walk away. He was overcome with emotion.

Some of his classmates came racing over then and tried to close in on him. Martin, Kenneth, John . . . they were all very excited.

'Was that your famous coach, Jake?'

'Was that Henry Hill?'

But Jake strode away from them.

'Where's Elizabeth?' he demanded. 'Where's our famous monitor? That's who I want to see right now.'

To everybody's surprise, when he found Elizabeth he lifted her clean off the ground and swung her up on to his shoulders.

'Thank you, Elizabeth! You're the best monitor in the school! If anybody says any different, tell them to come and see me!'

They second form boys all looked at one another in amazement.

'What's Elizabeth done, then?' asked Kenneth.

'Given me my nerve back, that's what she's done!' Jake informed them. He was not ashamed to admit it to anyone now. 'I'll tell you the whole story later!'

Julian and Joan were surprised to see Jake parading round the hockey pitch with Elizabeth perched up high on his shoulders. He wanted her to share in his glory. She was laughing and waving to everybody. Some of the boys were cheering her!

'What's the Naughtiest Girl been up to now?' wondered Julian.

The story of how Elizabeth had helped Jake soon spread around the school. There were no more anonymous messages after that.

But the Monitors' Meeting still lay ahead.

## CHAPTER TEN

# A MYSTERY STILL UNSOLVED

'IT WAS a reckless thing to do, Elizabeth. You had no business charging into the boys' quarters at night and encouraging some of your friends to join you! You must have known you were breaking a strict school rule,' said Thomas. 'That is hardly a sensible way for a monitor to deal with others who are breaking rules. By breaking one herself!'

The next MM was taking place. Silent and ashamed, Elizabeth sat next to Joan on the bench in the cosy little study. The moment of reckoning had come at last, the moment she had been dreading.

'You will never live down your Naughtiest Girl nickname if you do things like this, Elizabeth,' Emma pointed out. 'Because you are a monitor, we have spared you the shame of discussing this at the weekly Meeting. But it cannot go unpunished.'

'We understand that you were provoked,' went on Thomas, as the rest of the monitors listened with interest. 'Joan has told us that you were being teased and receiving anonymous messages from boys who appeared to think it unfair that your class has two girl monitors. They should have thought of that before, when they held the election! So Emma and I have decided on quite a modest punishment. You and your four friends must all go to bed one hour earlier for the next seven days. Do the other monitors think that sounds fair?'

There were murmurs of agreement from everyone. They all liked the Naughtiest Girl. She did crazy things sometimes but she had a very warm heart. They had all heard the story about Jake by now.

How marvellous that Joan had been and spoken up for her, thought Elizabeth. She felt herself going weak at the knees. She had got off lightly! What a relief! And what a relief it would be to give the good news to Jenny, Kathleen, Belinda and Tessa. She had felt guilty about leading them into trouble. She was sure they would not mind having to go to bed early for a few nights, any more than she did.

But just as her heart began to lighten, Emma spoke again.

'However, this whole situation has raised an important issue. Tom and I have had a long talk about it and we've talked it over with Joan, too. There are a lot of boys in Form 2. We feel that perhaps a mistake was made in appointing two girl monitors. What do you think, Elizabeth?'

'I – I—'

Elizabeth's spirits plunged. So she was going to be asked to resign, after all!

'If the form had had a boy monitor in office, some problems might have been avoided,' Thomas observed. 'For example, Jake is a big boy who prides himself on his physical strength. It was extremely difficult for him to confess to a girl how very frightened he felt. He might have found it easier to talk to another boy. It's just possible. And a boy monitor would certainly have ensured that the pillow-fighting craze was nipped in the bud.'

'Yes,' agreed Elizabeth. She steeled herself. 'If you want me to stand down then, I will quite understand . . .'

'Oh, Elizabeth, of course not!' exclaimed Joan. 'Not you – me!'

'Yes, cheer up, Elizabeth!' smiled Emma. 'Joan has already offered us her resignation. She feels that she has had a very long stint as monitor, whereas you have only just started. Even more important, she is finding that being a monitor is starting to clash with her swimming commitments. She has assured me that she will be perfectly happy to make way for a boy and she believes this is necessary.'

'Joan!' whispered Elizabeth, in surprise. 'Is this

true? And is it true that you are going to be quite happy about it?'

'Perfectly true!' replied her friend. 'And perfectly happy!'

After further discussion it was agreed that Joan would stand down as monitor at the end of the next school Meeting. And after that, the second form boys could elect a monitor from amongst their number in time for the last Meeting before half-term.

Towards the end of the MM, the head boy and girl asked anxiously if any more citations had been handed in for the William and Rita Award.

There were three this week.

They all agreed that one of them was outstanding and should go on the shortlist. Elizabeth was very pleased about that. For it was one that Elizabeth herself had written out on the special form. Joan had read it beautifully.

'Won't it be lovely if our citation wins the award, Joan?' she said, as they walked into tea together. 'What an honour for the second form!'

'What's that?' asked Patrick in alarm, for he was just behind them.

'Don't worry, Patrick!' Elizabeth turned round and smiled at him. 'You shouldn't eavesdrop. But you can relax now. Something else has come up, so you're quite safe!'

'Whatever was that about?' asked Joan, looking puzzled as she watched Patrick stroll on past them, whistling softly.

'Oh, nothing, Joan,' Elizabeth replied quickly.

She smiled to herself. Dear Patrick. He could sleep easily in his bed at nights. Perhaps one day she would be able to persuade him to be nominated, in time for a future award. But there was no hurry now.

She was so pleased that she was going to be able to continue as a monitor. Joan really did not want to be one any more. But she was going to miss her. It had been so wonderful having a best friend as the other monitor, somebody to talk over the MMs with, to their heart's content. Who would the new monitor be? she wondered. Who would the boys elect? She would find out soon enough. She hoped it would be somebody she liked.

The one small irritation was the matter of those anonymous messages. The person who'd written them had in part got his way! Although he'd not succeeded in getting rid of Elizabeth as a monitor, there *was* going to be a boy monitor, which would no doubt please him. It was annoying to think of her enemy being pleased.

Who had written the notes? Would she ever find out?

It was a mystery still unsolved.

CHAPTER ELEVEN

# JULIAN SPRINGS A HUGE SURPRISE

TRUTH WILL always out and the truth about the enemy came out in an amazing way. It was the last person that Elizabeth suspected. It came out at the next Meeting.

All the usual weekly business had been conducted. And then Emma announced that Joan would be resigning as a monitor.

'There are a lot of boys in the second form this year. It has been decided by all concerned that it would be better to have one boy and one girl monitor. We shall be asking the second form boys to elect their representative at next week's Meeting, ready for the second half of term. In the meantime could we all give Joan a round of applause, please, for her long and distinguished service to the second form.'

There was prolonged applause for Joan. Some of the boys and girls cheered and stamped their feet, as well. Sitting proudly next to her on the platform, Elizabeth glanced at her friend affectionately. How she was going to miss the great adventure of their being monitors together! But Joan had set her heart on getting strong and fit enough to be a member of Miss Thomas's swimming team and her time was going to be rationed now.

As the applause died away, the children all started chattering. They thought that the Meeting was over. But Thomas rapped the table sharply with the little gavel.

'Silence, please. There is one more matter to attend to. I'll let Emma do the talking.'

The head girl stood up.

'Somewhere in this hall, there is a boy who broke a school rule and went to the village on his own, two or three weeks ago,' she stated. 'It was very wrong of him for the rule is a very strict one. But just this once he will not be punished. I can see you are all wondering why,' she added, for a great hush had fallen over the hall. 'Well, I can tell you why. A woman has been to see us today. She brought this with her.'

Lying on the table, next to the school Book, was a large cardboard box. Emma took something out of the box. With a dramatic flourish she held it up for the whole school to see.

It was a giant box of chocolates.

All the children gasped with excitement. What was coming next? Elizabeth stiffened. She stared down into the hall to the second form benches. Patrick was sitting there, a slow pallor creeping up his cheeks.

'With no thought of danger to himself, this boy rushed into the road and saved the woman's child from being run over. The child was walking straight into the path of an oncoming car and would no doubt have been injured – or worse – without this boy's intervention. However he hurried away without waiting to be thanked.'

Emma paused for breath.

'After that, the woman saw the boy on a more recent occasion. The child recognized him at once. On this occasion the mother managed quickly to thank him but once again he hurried off. She feels he deserves some proper reward and she has asked that he be presented with this box of chocolates in front of the whole school. So, Thomas and I would now like our shy hero to stand up and make himself known. Who is he, please?'

The pupils were enthralled. They started whispering and nudging one another, gazing all round the hall. Who would stand up?

Elizabeth was staring at Patrick in deep fascination. What was going to happen now? In spite of all his efforts to keep his heroism a secret, it was going to be impossible for him to hide it now!

Patrick seemed to be frozen to the bench. His eyes were darting this way and that. Once or twice he craned his neck to look round at the benches behind him.

'He's still trying to keep it secret, even now!' thought Elizabeth. 'He's looking round, like everybody else. Pretending that he's waiting to see who's going to stand up.'

Emma stood there, holding the chocolates. The seconds ticked by. And Patrick still sat there, gazing all round. Two or three places along on the bench, Julian scratched his head and looked puzzled. Other children were talking in low voices. It was beginning to get embarrassing.

'Would the boy please stand up?' repeated Emma, colouring a little.

Still no one did so. Then Thomas lost patience.

He banged the gavel hard on the table.

'Would the boy in question stand up at once, please?' he said. 'That's an order.'

Elizabeth managed to catch Patrick's eye. And then – slowly, very slowly, Patrick rose to his feet, his face drained of colour. But then Elizabeth gave a little gasp. For something very strange was happening. At exactly the same moment, Julian was slowly rising, too! Languidly, his hands in his pockets.

Both boys were standing up together!

'Was this child a girl and did she have red hair, by any chance?' enquired Julian.

'Yes, she was a girl. And her mother certainly has red hair,' replied Thomas. 'Why, do you know something about it? Please take your hands out of your pockets, Julian.'

With Patrick now standing frozen in horror, a little further along the same bench, Julian took his hands out of his pockets and grinned.

'I think it must have been me, then. I'm afraid I'd forgotten all about it. What perplexed me was Emma saying the boy was seen in the village a second time. You see I haven't been down again since the other week when that kid ran in the road! But now, I realize –' he turned and smiled at Patrick with a scornful gleam in his eye '– that she could have confused me with somebody else.'

Patrick looked as though he wished the ground would swallow him up.

Slowly, he subsided back down on to the bench.

Elizabeth gazed from one cousin to the other, in shock. She was reminded how alike they looked, with their matted black hair and brilliant green eyes! How easy it would have been for the child to make her mistake!

It was not Patrick who'd performed the brave deed at all. It was Julian! And now Julian was strolling up to the platform and being presented with the chocolates! And the whole school was clapping and cheering him!

While, down below, Patrick sat miserably hunched on the bench.

And when all the excitement had died down, Thomas held his hand up for silence one last time. He asked Patrick to get to his feet.

'Don't ever try to do that again,' he told him, shaming him in front of the whole school. 'Of all the kinds of stealing there are, to try to steal another person's glory is the most despicable.'

The head boy was angry enough. But Elizabeth's own anger put even his in the shade. She could hardly wait to vent her feelings.

'You complete and absolute worm!' she told Patrick afterwards, dragging him outside on to the terrace. 'No wonder you didn't want me to name you for the William and Rita Award! If I'd done that, the person who had really performed the brave deed would soon have had something to say about it, wouldn't they? How could you bear to let me think you were a hero all this time? You have made an absolute fool of me. I hate you!'

'Please don't hate me, Elizabeth,' begged Patrick. 'You never gave me the chance to explain that the little girl had made a mistake. You really didn't! I had no idea who'd really saved her. I hadn't a clue. But it was just so thrilling to have you looking up to me and liking me for a change! I would have explained straight away but you never gave me the chance, Elizabeth! And after that I thought, what harm could it possibly do anyone else, the child making a silly mistake and you thinking it was me?'

Elizabeth's anger began to subside as she saw how distressed the boy was. She also realized that he was telling the truth. She'd given him almost no chance at all to explain there'd been a mistake! She'd made such a fuss of him at the time. It must have been awkward for him.

'It all seemed so simple at first,' Patrick confessed. 'It was so nice that you liked me. And the woman seemed really pleased to have someone to thank! I thought nothing more would come of it. But then it was dreadful when this business of the Award came up and you wanted to put my name forward! I longed to make a clean breast of things but when you told me that you'd given up your place in the table-tennis team, I was finished! That was the worst thing of all, Elizabeth. After that, I became desperate that the truth should never, ever come out. I even wrote those silly notes—'

'YOU wrote the notes, Patrick?' gasped Elizabeth. 'YOU were the enemy? I thought of everyone else but I never thought of you!'

'I'm not an enemy, Elizabeth. But I knew that as long as you kept on going to those MMs of yours, sooner or later you'd have blurted something out about my so-called brave deed. I know what you're like! So I was hoping, with some of the boys making trouble for you anyway, that you might get fed up with being a monitor.'

'I see.'

Elizabeth frowned. She didn't know whether to be angry or amused. For she was relieved to discover that she did not have a real enemy.

'Patrick, I think you are pathetic!' she added.

'Well, I really *did* think it was unfair having two girl monitors,' Patrick objected. 'I've always said that.'

Elizabeth thought back over all the time she'd known Patrick.

It was true! He had often said it. In fact he didn't really approve of the school having girls in it, at all!

How silly of her not to have remembered that.

'Well, there's going to be a boy monitor anyway,' she pointed out.

'Yes,' replied Patrick smugly. 'Thomas and Emma seem to agree with me on that.'

Elizabeth turned on her heel. Julian had appeared on the terrace, looking for her. She called back to Patrick, over her shoulder.

'I only hope it's not you, Patrick!'

Julian grinned.

'Hello, Elizabeth. Been giving my cousin a telling-off about something? Here, have a chocolate. They're delicious.'

It was the last Meeting before half-term. A gleaming little silver trophy stood on the head boy and girl's table. The very first William and Rita Award was about to be announced.

'We ended up with four citations on the shortlist,' Thomas was telling the assembled school, 'of which two were quite outstanding. Miss Belle and Miss Best and Emma and I had a very difficult job deciding between them. One was for Julian Holland, signed by several boys in his class. For his brave action in saving the little girl from being run over. The other was for Jake Johnson, signed by Elizabeth Allen, for his courage in overcoming a personal crisis.'

While the whole school hung on to his words, Thomas paused for maximum effect.

'Which one were we to choose? Which boy had shown the greater courage? As we talked it over, we came to realize that Julian's fearless deed had come as second nature to him. It was truly fearless for he had felt no fear. He saw the child in danger and instantly took action. We are very proud of him for that. But his brave deed meant so little to him that he had some difficulty in remembering it afterwards.

'Jake, on the other hand, and I know he does not mind us telling you this now, felt absolute terror at the thought of playing hockey again after inflicting a grave injury on someone he loved and admired. Yet somehow he faced that fear and fought it and in the end, he overcame it.

'Fearlessness and courage are not the same thing. A high form of courage is to know real fear – and then to overcome it. The school therefore takes great pride in giving the very first William and Rita Award to – Jake Johnson.'

The school clapped and cheered as the gentle giant of a boy shambled up on the platform and took the little silver trophy from Emma's outstretched hand. He clutched it proudly and shot Elizabeth an embarrassed smile. She was sitting behind Emma on the platform, clapping so hard that her palms stung.

As the Meeting broke up, she turned to the boy sitting next to her.

'A lot of the boys wanted you to have the Award, Julian, but I think the Beauty and the Beast and Thomas and Emma have all made the right decision, don't you?'

'Most definitely,' agreed Julian.

'And at least the boys elected you as monitor!' she said, with a happy sigh.

It was nice to have Julian sitting next to her on the platform.

She would still have a friend as her fellow monitor, after all. A truly marvellous friend. Poor Patrick! But what fun it was going to be from now on, she and Julian being monitors together!

'Yes, I'm a monitor,' replied Julian, with a cheerful grin. 'I still can't believe it and as a matter of fact, Elizabeth, I don't know how I'm going to manage it. But for your sake, I suppose I'd better try.'

'You suppose right, Julian,' she laughed.